♦

Hardcover Edition
ISBN: 9798483661689

To Jane, with love.

Publisher's Note: To provide important context, it is recommended that this edited version of this incredible historical record be read concurrently with its well-researched footnotes.

Diary of Agent
355

Mystery Lady of Washington's
Culper Spy Ring

Franklin Alfred
Kirby Edwards

When the British cracked down on spies in the American Revolution, Abraham Woodhull of the Culper Spy Ring wrote a secret message to spymaster Colonel Benjamin Tallmadge of the Continental Army on August 15, 1779, saying he recruited a "355," code for "lady" spy: "I think by the assistance of a 355 of my acquaintance [I] shall be able to outwit them all." The true identity of "Agent 355" is the last remaining mystery of the American War of Independence. That much is history. What follows is fiction. Although, one suspects something like this must have happened in the chaos of the American Revolution.

Foreword by
Franklin Alfred Kirby Edwards

I attended an Ivy League university and as a freshman roomed with John Walker Spivey at Straus Hall, built in 1926 in memory of a victim of the Titanic disaster, and a dorm still alive with tantalizing tales of such disparate luminaries as Beat Generation author of *Naked Lunch*, William S. Burroughs, and billionaire and perpetual kid-faced Mark Zuckerberg of Facebook.[1]

Spivey made multimillions in junk bonds on Wall Street and promptly retired to the unfettered amazement of finance colleagues convinced he would be thoroughly bored doing nothing. Rather than "doing nothing," Spivey bought a sizable farm in Setauket, or Brookhaven, New York in the fall of 2014, and began to completely restore the old farmhouse dating back to the eighteenth century.[2]

In the summer of 2015 I received his call.

"Franklin," Spivey said from the farm, all excited, "you've got to see this dingy manuscript." We've been friends a long time and he knew of my love of old books and papers, especially anything from Colonial America. "I'm sure it's old – Setauket's historic."

Of course I knew Setauket played a role in the American War of Independence – you don't get four degrees in history

---

[1] Harvard University, Cambridge, Massachusetts, established in 1636.

[2] John Spivey was a young investment banker who learned the junk bond market at a distance by observing one of the wizards of Wall Street, the man who invented the "junk bond" market, Michael R. Milken. While in his later years Mr. Milken has been known for philanthropy and his good works in cancer prevention, in April 1990 he agreed to plead guilty to charges of securities fraud and pay fines of $600 million. Junk bonds are securities issued by generally troubled corporations at high interest because of the high risk of owning them. Spivey told me privately in the early 2000s that using techniques pioneered by Mr. Milken he made more money in five years than Milken paid in fines. It should be noted that the "junk bond" market is a legal part of the United States securities business. Spivey's farm is half mile from the famous Brewster House in East Setauket, in the town of Brookhaven, New York. The Brewster House at 18 Runs Road is the tenth oldest home in New York, built in 1665, and is on the National Register of Historic Places. It was home to six generations of the Brewster Family, and during the American War of Independence, Joseph Brewster, cousin of Caleb Brewster, operated an ale house and store. His regular clientele included redcoat soldiers, and the tavern was the perfect place for patriot Caleb to pick up information on British troop movements.

without knowing such minutia. "Is there a name and title on the manuscript?" I asked, desirous to drill down quickly to the nitty-gritty. Colonial recipes on how to make spice cake would hardly excite my scholarly interests.

"Yes," said Spivey. "But it is not a name per se."

Dumbfounded, I think I said, "Huh?"

"It's more of a number."

With a sigh and a plea, I invited clarification.

He read me the "name" on the first page of the document, and no fooling, I nearly dropped my cell phone. "Watch how you handle it," I instructed him in the next breath. "In fact, don't touch the paper at all. If it's who I am sure it is, the paper's two hundred years old."

I was on the red-eye to New York that very night. After driving in from LaGuardia Airport, he told me the next morning at his farm that he had found the stack of one hundred and ten pages in a wooden box, which was wrapped in scratchy cloth and bound with twine in a tiny crawl space between the second story and the attic of his house. "It seems like someone hid it purposefully," he speculated.

"I've no doubt of it," I told him, positively.

"Agent 355?" said Spivey. "Sounds like someone back in history is pulling our leg."

"Not at all, my friend," I responded. "You have stumbled upon one of the last remaining secrets of the American Revolution." I watched his blue eyes poke open wide, and then explained. "Agent 355 we are sure was female, and a member of the masterfully successful Culper Spy Ring, which by the way, operated out of Setauket."

"I've seen signs and historical markers in town but paid no attention," Spivey said. "Imagine, quiet, little Setauket?"

"Uh-huh, a hotbed of Revolutionary James Bonds."

"Any significance to the number 3-5-5?"

Leave it to a Wall Street mathematics genius to divine the numbers angle.

"Absolutely, there is," I said. "The Culper Ring used a secret code system to communicate. It substituted numbers for words and letters. Number 355 stood for the word 'Lady.' Basically she was known as 'Agent Lady', if you will."

"And her true identity has never been uncovered?"

"There is speculation that Anna Smith Strong was Agent 355, ever since existence of the Culper Spy Ring was first discovered by a scholar in the 1930s," I said.[3] "The other idea is Agent 355 is another woman who probably lived in Setauket around 1778-1783, when the ring was active. The third theory is, and you've just blown a hole through it, is that Agent 355 never existed. That it was all a mistake when an error was made in a coded message sent by the ring to General George Washington, in which it was believed an 'Agent 355' was mentioned."

"Who is Anna Smith Strong; related to the Strongs Neck area?"[4] His question came in a Wall Street guru growl. "If this is by her, it would be well to know who she is."

---

[3] Popular historian Alexander Rose whose book, *Washington's Spies: The Story of America's First Spy Ring* is about the Culper spies, contends without proof in his well-researched book that he knows the identity of Agent 355. "She was Anna Strong, Woodhull's neighbor," he writes. Well, Dr. Rose, who earned a doctorate at Cambridge University, since we're making statements of fact without supporting evidence, other than our own speculations, I will counter with, "No she wasn't." The writers of the hit TV drama *TURN: Washington's Spies* – the basis for which is Rose's book – make Agent 355 a former slave owned by Anna Strong who later works as a domestic in the home of British spy chief, Major John André, and funnels intelligence to the Culper Ring. In 1948 historian Morton Pennypacker, then Long Island's antiquarian who is credited with first discovering Robert Townsend as a member of the Culper Spy Ring, gave a talk to a group of Brooklyn residents, working to find permanent burials for rebels who died on the British prison ship *Jersey*, said he discovered that Agent 355 was really the mother of a baby boy fathered by bachelor Townsend and who was arrested by the British and incarcerated on the ship, where she died after having Townsend's baby. The problem with Mr. Pennypacker's assertion is while he provides evidence that Townsend bought the child gifts such as toys after he was removed from the prison ship, Pennypacker provides no hard evidence that the mother of the child was Agent 355. It might show Townsend and this woman he calls "Mrs. Townsend" were lovers, but it doesn't prove Agent 355's identity. Pennypacker's account was reported in the May 30, 1948 *Brooklyn Eagle* under the headline, "Girl Who Spied for Washington Died on Wallabout Prison Ship," with two subheads, "Revelation Made By Authority on Colonial Heroes" and "Say Child Was Born to Her in Hulk of Vessel." Wallabout Bay is where the ship was moored. The newspaper story reports that before his death, the boy who was given the name Robert Townsend, Jr., worked hard to find proper burials for prisoners, including his mother, who perished in terrible conditions on the ship, which held 1,100 at a time. Historians have gone a few rounds over whether females were ever sent to the vile British prison ships, with some saying they were not, and others who say British archives of 14,000 prisoners show names of "several" women. The Culper Ring was revealed to the public in 1930 after Pennypacker examined letters written by Robert Townsend Sr. in his family home and compared the handwriting with letters to George Washington written by spy "Samuel Culper Jr.," which was Townsend's code name. Similar handwriting in the two sets of documents revealed for the first time that Townsend was Samuel Culper Jr. It is not a surprise that those involved never talked about spying after the British lost the war. Actions taken by the ring obviously led to deaths of British soldiers and American Loyalists, not something members of the spy group wanted their names linked to, in fear of retribution. It is amazing Townsend's spy role stayed secret for 150 years. Can anyone imagining this happening today, what with leaks from government officials?

"If you watch television you know she is one of the most important women in the War of Independence. Don't you watch TV?"

"CNBC mornings," he said. "I can't dismiss Wall Street completely. But, afterwards, TV's off."

"A popular TV drama called 'TURN' on AMC Networks was about the American War of Independence and focused on the Culper Spy Ring in Setauket. Anna Strong was a character on the TV show."

"TV character? You said she was a real person?"

"A very resourceful one," I assured him.

"How about Agent 355 – she in the show?"

Now Spivey was playing with me, something people of vast wealth like to do with financial underlings.

"John, they didn't know who in the blazes Agent 355 was, for Christ's sake." My anger flared, and I quickly apologized. (I might need a loan of money one day.)

My friend didn't relent his little game playing. "They could have written her into the script as 'Agent 355,' couldn't they? Like Maxwell Smart and Agent 99."

I breathed in and out a couple of times to lower my blood pressure. "Some viewers thought Agent 355 was a young female slave in the show named, 'Abigail'; I don't know," I said. I sighed openly.

"You always were too serious, Franklin," he said, verbally poking me again. "Even your name's too consequential – Franklin Alfred Kirby Edwards. Sounds like a Wall Street brokerage house."

"Now you're attacking my Mum," I said, although with a smile of good spirits and no ill-will.

Not showing a hint of contrition he returned a smile. I let him have his little fun, and looked hard at the handwriting of the manuscript. It was typical cursive and eighteenth century. I almost opined that it's this kind of penmanship

---

[4] Strongs Neck is on the north shore of Long Island and part of the town of Brookhaven. It was the home of William Smith, grandfather of Anna Smith Strong, who married Selah Strong, for which Strongs Neck is named. It was at Strongs Neck that Anna Strong hung out wash to signal that messages from the Culper Ring were ready for transport to General Washington. The Strong Family still owns the site of the original Smith home and many Smith ancestors are buried there.

that's lost today, but withheld it as irrelevant. "All right, I give in," Spivey said, waiting for me to lift my eyes from examining the extremely dry papers. "What's this television drama about?"

"It's based on fact and real people of the Revolution, such as turncoat Benedict Arnold and obviously George Washington. But largely the show had a lot of fiction tossed in to liven it and maintain viewer interest."

"They had to hype the American Revolution?"

I admit I laughed hard at his insight.

Then Spivey said: "But Culper's Spy Ring was not fiction." It was put in the vein of a statement rather than a question.

At this point I gave my friend background on spying in the American Revolution and detailed the Culper Spy Ring, its membership and how it used a secret code and invisible ink, Spivey listened with both ears piqued in interest until I finished: Spying was commonplace in the American Revolution. In 1775 the British moved against Concord after Loyalist spies said munitions were stored there. In turn, Patriots thwarted the effort when Colonial spies disclosed the British plans. The Culper Spy Ring was the first group of organized spies not part of the military. Prior spying was the purview of military men, such as Nathan Hale, soldiers who dressed as civilians and secretly reconnoitered enemy installations. The Culper Ring was civilians, save two members – Lieutenant Caleb Brewster, transporter of messages, and Colonel Benjamin Tallmadge, the ring's spymaster. In fall of 1778 Washington named Tallmadge chief of military intelligence and tasked him with organizing a spy network for New York, headquarters of the British. New to the spy game, Tallmadge sought help from friends in his hometown of Setauket. They became the most successful network of informants in the Revolution. His Setauket friends were Anna Strong, Caleb Brewster, Austin Roe and Abraham Woodhull. Added to this network was Robert Townsend, a journalist and New York coffee shop owner who presented himself to the British as a Loyalist. As a journalist Townsend collected information on the British military at social events. Other members were our mysterious Agent 355, and two other females, Robert Townsend's sister Sally Townsend and Abraham Woodhull's sister, Mary Underhill. Occasional informants were Captain Nathan Woodhull, Abraham's uncle who was a Loyalist but slipped his nephew information; Joshua Davis, who filled in for transporter Brewster; Nathaniel Ruggles, a medical doctor; George Smith, a former whaler and buddy of Brewster; Joseph Lawrence, a Long Island resident; William Robinson, a shopkeeper; a man who is only identified by his code name, "John Cork"; Amos Underhill, husband of Abraham Woodhull's sister, Mary; Jonah Hawkins, an early messenger for the ring who was fired because Robert Townsend thought he was a wimp; and the brothers Nathaniel and Philip Roe. In addition, tangential Culper Ring members were Hercules Mulligan and his black slave Cato, who, although recruited to spy by Alexander Hamilton, time and again funneled information to Townsend.[5] Mulligan owned a clothing store near Townsend's business. Also a spy ring member, although treated shabbily by writers of the AMC TV drama, was Tory newspaper publisher James Riverton. His loyalist Riverton's Gazette lambasted the rebels at every turn, which kept the British from discovering his real motives, and cleverly encouraged loyalist officials and military sources to tell him secrets. Operating for five years the Culper Ring was named after the code name "Samuel Culper Sr." used by chief agent Abraham Woodhull. During its existence none of its key agents were ever discovered, although Abraham Woodhull came under suspicion and Anna Strong's husband, Selah, was imprisoned for being an "insurrectionist" and suspected of spying.

---

[5] Mulligan's slave, Cato, was probably named after the play written by Joseph Addison in 1712, *Cato, a Tragedy*, based on the life of Marcus Porcius Cato Uticensis, who stood up to the tyranny of Julius Caesar. The play was a hit in the Colonies and an inspiration to many of the Founding Fathers. A quote attributed to Nathan Hale on the gallows came from the play. "I only regret that I have but one life to lose for my country" are words, Hale, according to historian Alexander Rose, did not utter, and are similar to this line in Act IV of *Cato*: "What a pity it is that we can die but once to serve our country." George Washington was a great admirer of Addison's fine play, and I can imagine his pleasure in accepting the information about an English plot to murder him from a slave of the same name.

Today spies use modern technology such as long-range listening devices and cameras on space satellites. Basic spycraft, however, hasn't changed over the centuries. Keen observation and keeping ears close to the ground are now and were a must in the American Revolution. Implementing secret writing, codes, secret rendezvouses and dead-drops for messages were as much a staple of the Culper Spy Ring as they are to today's Central Intelligence Agency.

Cleverly the Culper Ring used a code system similar to one developed two hundred and fifty years prior by a priest. To communicate they used a numbering system with 763 numbers. Each number designated a word. For instance, say Abraham Woodhull had travelled to New York and spied British warships in the harbor. His message to Tallmadge would read: k.ni.219.72.592.in.727.473. Translating the letters and numbers using the Culper Ring's code "dictionary," the message is: "Five 74-gun British ships in New York port." In other words, k means "5"; ni means "74"; 219 means "gun"; 72 means "British"; 592 means "ship"; the word *in* is spelled out; 727 means "New York"; and 473 means "port." Simple yet just sophisticated enough.[6] The spy group used invisible ink developed by James Jay, a physician and elder brother of New York's John Jay, a close Washington confidant. The British also used invisible ink at the time.[7]

---

[6] Of course the Culper Ring wasn't the only ones using secret codes in the war. Here is a brief sample of a code used by Benedict Arnold in a letter to British spymaster John André on July 12, 1780: "I 293.9.7 to C_t. B. 103.8.2. the 7th 152 9.17. that , a F___ 112.9.17. and 22.8.29 were 105.9.50 to / 4 9.71 in 62.8.20 with , 163.8.19 A 22.8.19 at with 230.8.13. 263.8.17 I gave Mr. S---y a 164.8.16 / 147.8.261 to be 209.9.216 in C----a and have from 163.8.17 to .163.8.17 .58.8.27 to him." Decoded he is providing the British with key information about American and French troop movements he learned from Washington, and it contains a promise to provide more "crucial information" once he became commander of West Point. These rudimentary substitution ciphers, however, were child's play compared to polyalphabetic encryption codes of the enigma electro-mechanical rotor cipher machines of the Germans and Japanese in World War II. The enigma machine was invented by a German engineer to protect military and diplomatic correspondence after World War I.

[7] His spies used disappearing ink Washington called "Sympathetic Stain" and "white ink." The liquid developed in England by James Jay, 1732-1815. made messages reappear. It was used on blank white paper. It wasn't until 1808 that information about the invisible ink came out in House of Representatives records after James Jay sought payment from Congress for his chemical process. His petition to Congress called for "settlement of a claim against the United States, for moneys advanced, and services rendered, of an important and secret nature, during the Revolutionary War

To gather information Setauket business owner and spy Austin Roe travelled fifty miles to New York to get supplies, going through British lines. In Robert Townsend's New York coffee shop he used the name "John Bolton," alias for Colonel Tallmadge, and gathered messages from Townsend for delivery to Woodhull back in Setauket. Roe hid the secret materials among supplies he bought for his business in New York.

An unassuming cabbage farmer, Woodhull's specialty was spying on the British Royal Navy on Long Island and, on trips he saw as more dangerous, on troop movements in New York City. His information would be sent to Washington through Caleb Brewster, who operated whaleboats in the Sound. Anna Strong would signal Brewster to pick up Woodhull's coded messages for Washington. Brewster sailed to Fairfield, Connecticut across the Sound and delivered the material to Colonel Tallmadge, who presented it for the eyes of Washington only at his New Jersey headquarters.

"Sounds exciting," said Spivey, once I finished this professorial lecture.

"Not really, it created a lot of anxiety on the part of the spies, but in practice," I said didactically, "spying is a solitary and boring business." (Editor's note: Once I read the *Diary of Agent 355* in its entirety, I vowed never again to call spying, "boring.")

"What do you propose we do about this manuscript?" Spivey asked, pointedly.

I told him we required three things: authorship, authenticity and provenance.

"Like when I purchase fine art," he said.

"The same, precisely."

---

with Great Britain." The House voted to stall the claim indefinitely and was dumb enough to mention it in its proceedings as being for a "secret mode of correspondence (that) was very useful in the Revolutionary War, and no doubt might be again." But the Americans weren't the only combatants to use invisible ink in secret messages. As early as May of 1775, Benjamin Thompson, a British spy acquainted with a member of the provincial Congress in Massachusetts used invisible ink to alert the British to a resolution by the Continental Congress to raise a 30,000-soldier army, which signaled the seriousness of the war aims of the Colonies. Thompson who was on British General Thomas Gage's staff was a Loyalist also reported secretly on movements of the "Rebel Army."

I spent two days going through Suffolk County land records. Records of ownership of Spivey's farm didn't exist for the period 1735 to 1780, and officials in Setauket had no explanation why. After that date I found a record showing a "Miss Colmer" owned the property in 1783, but in further sleuthing the records noted she was an invalid much of her lifetime. In checking the Anna Smith Strong being Agent 355 angle, I found no evidence that Anna or her husband, Selah Strong, 1737-1815, ever owned the farm Spivey purchased from a widow whose husband had been an attorney in Manhattan for an international bank.

Disappointed at my fruitless labors, I was ready to abandon the hunt.

However, on the last day I was approached by a young girl who worked in the land records office who had heard I was researching the Strong Family. "You might want to check out this document," she said, a courteous smile brightening her face.

I began to peruse the document while she held it. I read the name of "James Woodhull" on the record, which said he owned the property and "all appurtenances" at the address of Spivey's farm in 1784.

"I was looking for Strong, Anna or Selah, not a Woodhull," I said, politely, lightly dismissing her.

"This is of the Strong Family," she said. "Keturah was Anna Strong's daughter, born around 1761, and she was married to James Woodhull. This was their farm in 1784."

I didn't require more smacking about the head to make sense of it, and I thanked her for her propitious help. I returned to John Spivey's homestead, enlivened.

"Keturah Strong Woodhull lived in this house," I told him, "and in 1778, when the Culper Spy Ring was formed, she would have been 17 years old. A young age for a spy, yet, she cannot be ruled out as Agent 355."

"I'll be frank with you, Franklin. I don't see it in a familial sense," Spivey opined. "Her mother knew the perils of spying. I strongly doubt she'd risk having her precious daughter's neck put in a British noose. This wasn't long after

Nathan Hale was hanged for spying. I don't believe Mrs. Strong would use her daughter like that. I just don't."

"If she knew," I said, weakly.

Spivey rolled his eyes in disgust.

"All right," I said, "we're back to the possibility – and still a valid one – that Anna Strong was Agent 355. That she wrote this diary and hid it in her daughter's house, or that her daughter, Keturah, secreted it in that wooden box in the crawl space two centuries ago. Do we agree on this point?"

Spivey said yes, with a flash of his bushy, pepper-colored eyebrows.

I knew of course that the Culper Spy Ring was first discovered by a historian comparing Robert Townsend's known handwriting with similar handwriting found in letters from the Culper Ring among President Washington's personal papers. The manuscript in question was written in the stylish longhand of the era, with flourishes of style and grace. But because an exemplar of Anna Strong's cursive is nonextant, a comparison was impossible. The 1784 land record carried only the signature of Keturah's husband, James Woodhull, which wasn't helpful.

Curiously, the "First Part, 1774-1778" of the "diary" is dated as being written in 1809. The "Second Part, 1779-1781" was written a year later. Anna Strong died in 1812, and this fact will probably contribute to opinions that this "diary" is hers. It is easy to assume that she wanted to get her story told before she died. In addition, statements in the manuscript itself are certain to incite a sloppy history scholar to rush to judgment of Agent 355 and Anna Strong being one in the same. Here is an example: "As close as peas in a pod is Anna Strong and me, and at times indistinguishable when observing us from the distance of her clothesline and the Long Island seawater beyond. This means it be only a bug's ear of difference in us." Is this Anna dropping hints to her authorship? The manuscript has many other mentions of Anna Strong as well. All right I fully accept these women who probably lived in the same tiny burg were friends. But I could not wrap my brain around the concept that Anna had written the manuscript. Before reading it, by the way, I wasn't even convinced it had been written by a woman.[8]

In Vegas I play the odds and I knew that while sixty percent of New England men were literate in 1776, the percentage of literate women was far less, in the thirties. Therefore, playing probability, the manuscript was written by a male. When Thomas Paine's "Common Sense" was published in 1776 it sold over one hundred thousand copies, a breathtaking amount for Colonial times. Today, by comparison, the biggest best-selling books don't reach a number remotely approaching sales of "Common Sense" in 1776, when factoring in population differences. Yet, as counter-argument, facts cannot be overlooked. Back then reading and writing were taught as separate subjects, meaning that even if Colonials could read, it did not guarantee that they could also write. This is shown by examining Colonial documents, upon which so many Revolutionary Americans affixed them with a "mark" or X. Tossed into this unhappy mix is the fact that educating females wasn't high on a Colonial family's priority list.

Still at John Spivey's farm, and not having yet read the "diary," I was more skeptical than ever that Anna Strong had authored the document. Of course she might have simply dictated her story to her daughter, Keturah, who wrote it down for her. I summarily cast out this naive notion once I returned with the manuscript to my ranch in New Mexico, and read it. Let's play a game as explanation. Your teenaged daughter convinces you to tell your life's story. In relating your memoir you confess that you had many adulteries and sexual affairs while her father was locked for years on a prison ship.

No, it ain't happening.

A mother isn't going to do that.

Oh, a bitch on TV's "The Real Housewives of (Pick Your City)" might tantalize her impressionable teen with her

---

[8] I was summarily disabused of this notion once I read the *Diary of Agent 355*. This spy was involved in so much whoring and bed-chamber intrigue that I was absolutely certain the manuscript was written by a female, a woman richly schooled in the world's first oldest profession, and well, also in the world's second oldest profession, spying.

extramarital sexual acrobatics, but not a well-bred woman like Anna Smith Strong. Not in the eighteenth century! Thereby, Anna Strong categorically did not relate this story to her daughter Keturah to write down for her.

In fact, this story is so bawdy, I doubt with much conviction that Anna Strong was Agent 355. (In reading it I lost count of the number of men promiscuous Agent 355 bedded to elicit pillow talk or to save her own life. I began calling her "Mata Hari of the American Revolution.")[9]

Additionally, in the annuals of the American War of Independence it is difficult to find a woman comparable in the warrior deeds of Agent 355. The single example who comes closest is Nancy Ann Morgan Hart, 1735-1830, a rabid patriot who made it her mission to rid Georgia of redcoats, loyalists and anybody else who disagreed with her, and, like Agent 355, at the point of a musket. It is certain Agent 355 and Nancy Hart were not the same person, in that Agent 355 was a good-looking female who attracted men like a Queen Bee attracts drones. While Nancy Hart was a freelance spy for the Georgia Militia, well. . . . In a brief description of Nancy Hart, Clay Ouzts, history professor at the University of North Georgia, wrote in 2005: "Aunt Nancy, as she was often called, was a tall, gangly woman who towered six feet in height. Like the frontier she inhabited, she was rough-hewn and rawboned, with red hair and a smallpox-scarred face. She was also cross-eyed. One early account pointed out that Hart had 'no share of beauty' – a fact she herself would have readily acknowledged, had she ever enjoyed an opportunity of looking into a mirror."[10]

---

[9] Mata Hari was a Dutch exotic dancer who spied for Germany in World War I and was caught and executed by firing squad in France. Her name was Margaretha Zelle, 1876-1917, and her stage name was Mata Hari. She had relationships with high-ranking military officers, politicians, and others in influential positions in many countries. Liaisons with powerful men frequently took her across international borders.

[10] The illiterate Nancy Hart was a sharpshooter with a round-ball musket, despite being cross-eyed. She also served as a freelance spy by disguising herself as a man and walking to British troop positions, later reporting on numbers and equipment. Professor Clay Ouzts of Northern Georgia University provides this apocryphal story of one of her famous "escapades" against the British. "A group of six (some accounts say five) Tories came to her cabin and demanded information concerning the location of a certain Whig leader. Only minutes earlier, the Whig, hotly pursued by the Tories, had stopped by the Hart cabin and enlisted Hart's aid as he made his escape. Hart

As "diary" author, I should note, I also ruled out known female spies of the era who had worked for the "wrong" side. For example, Ann Bates was a Philadelphia schoolteacher and double-agent who spied mostly for the British as a card-carrying member of General Henry Clinton's secret network. Another was the infamous "Miss Jenny" who spied for German mercenary Baron Ottendorf, himself a turncoat who abandoned the patriots for the redcoats. "Miss Jenny" spied on French troops allied with the Continental Army in 1781, but was caught.[11]

So, you ask in frustration who was Agent 355?

---

insisted that no one had passed through her neck of the woods for days. Convinced that she was lying, one of the Tories shot and killed Hart's prized gobbler. After ordering her to cook the turkey, the Tories entered the cabin, stacked their weapons in the corner, and demanded something to drink. Hart obliged them by opening her jugs of wine. Once the Tories began to feel the intoxicating effects of the wine, Hart sent her daughter, Sukey, to the spring for a bucket of water. Hart secretly instructed her to blow a conch shell, which was kept on a nearby stump, to alert the neighbors that Tories were in the cabin. As Hart served her unwanted guests, she frequently passed between them and their stacked weapons. Inconspicuously, she began to pass the loaded muskets, one by one, through a chink in the cabin wall to Sukey, who had by this time slipped around to the rear of the building. When the Tories noticed what she was doing and sprang to their feet, Hart threatened to shoot the first man who moved a foot. Ignoring her warning, one Tory lunged forward, and Hart pulled the trigger, killing the man. Seizing another weapon, she urged her daughter to run for help. Hart shot a second Tory who made a move toward the stacked weapons and held off the remaining loyalists until her husband and several others arrived. (Husband) Benjamin Hart wanted to shoot the Tories, but Hart wanted them to hang. Consequently the remaining Tories were hanged from a nearby tree. In 1912 workmen grading a railroad near the site of the old Hart cabin unearthed a neat row of six skeletons that lay under nearly three feet of earth and were estimated to have been buried for at least a century. This discovery seemed to validate the most oft-told story of the Hart legend."

[11] Stories of the two female spies for Britain are interesting. Philadelphia schoolteacher Ann Bates was a Loyalist who spied for both the patriots and the British but mostly for the cause of the Crown. She joined General Clinton's spy network in 1778. Bates was particularly adept at identifying Continental Army equipment such as artillery pieces and rifles. She disguised herself as a woman selling goods and pretty much would have her way in American encampments. She would count every man in the regiment and every cannon being hauled, and, when she sold all of her goods she reported to Sir Henry Clinton's spy boss, Major Duncan Drummond. Selling good like combs and thread she called herself "Mrs. Barnes." On a mission to Washington's camp in White Plains, New York she counted 199 cannons and 23,000 Continental soldiers. The female British spy "Miss Jenny" worked for Baron Ottendorf, a German mercenary who joined the British in 1777 after he was booted from the American ranks by General Washington himself. Miss Jenny infiltrated the French army. In 1781 General Clinton learned that Washington's army and Comte de Rochambeau's French troops planned to attack New York City by crossing the Hudson River. Once they crossed the river Miss Jenny moved into the ranks and even though she was detained and taken to Washington as a suspected spy, she was released and reported to Baron Ottendorf that the enemy armies were ready to move on New York. The attack, however, never came. Washington instead moved his troops on French ships to Yorktown, Virginia and attacked General Cornwallis, who surrendered and effectively ended the war. By listening to spies such as "Miss Jenny," General Clinton retained his army in New York, aiding the rebels in Yorktown.

I'd like to say her name was Tabitha Baldwin, Mary Fletcher or Virginia Redman, and indeed, it was all three. But that tells us nothing because these names were used by Agent 355 over the life of her spying career, and each is false, an alias. Cagily, craftily and carefully she limits her "diary" to details of her spying activities only. She makes no mention of her private life (other than to reveal she fell in love with Alexander Hamilton at Yale). This means questions of what she did between dangerous spy missions, where she lived and who she lived with, who she was related to, whether she was married or single or whether she had a job other than spying cannot be answered and only guessed at by reading between the lines of her "diary." She does make vague references of being in Setauket and New York when not spying, but that's it.

So, in my investigation, I was forced to take a different tack. In researching Anna's family history – daughter of Colonel William Smith whose grandfather was on the New York Supreme Court – I surmised Anna was an educated female. Along this line, I reasoned that the girlfriends Anna Strong picked to "hang out with" weren't babbling idiots, but like her, articulate, educated and interesting. As I read *Diary of Agent 355*, I came to the opinion that the author was not only educated, she was highly intelligent, albeit unpolished, especially in her writing skills. In earnest I began researching women of Anna's age who were known to be well-bred and educated in Setauket.

Based on reading the "diary," I made assumptions about this mystery woman. She was white, unmarried and in her mid-twenties, with pretty features in body and face, as she was sexually alluring to men; she could be well-spoken and mannered as she was invited to receptions with the finest of Colonial families. Although I must offer this caveat: she had what might be called a "potty mouth" in her use of slang words of the era. But she was also charming and witty as men found her conversation enticing and interesting, including generals. Finally, and importantly, she was worldly in the ways of the boudoir as she was a favorite liaison of officers and any man who could see out of both eyes.

Interestingly the "diary" never once provided a scintilla of "personal information" such as eye and hair color or height and weight, telling features which could be used to identify her. This perhaps is not surprising, as she was a clever, clandestine spy who shielded her true identity meticulously, after all.

I came up with a dozen names, all residents of Setauket in the Revolutionary period, of which none might be her, but it was worth the old college try.

1. Candace Dunn.
2. Amity Thorne.
3. Patience Goetz.
4. Emeline Lynch.
5. Catherine Atheling.
6. Virginia Downs.
7. Hester Cameron.
8. Cornelia Willet.
9. Mary Titus.
10. Rebekah Ferry.
11. Henrietta Mattock.
12. Elizabeth Allen.

I began to conduct personal interviews with relatives on Long Island, knowing that kinfolk, especially those many generations removed, often talk proudly of their "great-greats," and if you maneuver them into the right mood, might whisper untoward family rumors as well.

My first session was a complete washout as Catherine Atheling, a stunner in a painting I was allowed to see, had been born deaf.

Agent 355 wasn't Catherine.

The second interview went better, and I learned Emeline Lynch had been married three times, even though she had married at the "shocking age of 34 for the first time," and family gossip had it that she had gotten into a "slapping fight" on a street corner with an out-of-town Loyalist who was loudly talking up King George. I figured Emeline was a candidate, giving the wear-and-tear on her womanhood in the war, and her rabid rebel politics. But when I saw an old painting of her, I winced – not on the outside but inside – because she had the face and wide body of my mailman.

It wasn't Emeline.

But I had learned a good lesson. People of Setauket take their family lineage very seriously, along with their deep American roots and rich early American history. (I have come to realize the U.S. has no history but that of the Colonies.)

For the third interview I was invited to have tea at the home of a relative of Agent 355 prospect, Amity Thorne, who lived in the Port Jefferson area of Brookhaven. Sipping his tea, the gentleman in his sixties got me excited right away in saying that his "sixth-great-grandmother (Amity) Thorne was at the Battle of Setauket in 1777."

Now I was getting somewhere. But, out of a sense of caution, I asked whether he had any pictures of Great-Grandma Thorne.

"All destroyed in a fire in the 1920s."

I moaned.

He went on to tell me what I already knew.

"A contingent of the Continental Army led by Brigadier General Samuel Holden Parsons conducted a raid on a small force of British regulars led by Lieutenant Colonel Richard Hewlett in August of that year. Loyalist spies warned Hewlett in advance and he fortified the Presbyterian Church with earthworks and headstones from the cemetery for defense. When Colonel Hewlett refused to surrender, fighting began but quickly ended. There was little damage, and Parsons retreated to Connecticut."

Then he looked at me quizzically.

"You're looking for spies on Washington's side?"

I said yes.

"Great Grandmother Thorne was a Loyalist."

"However," I said. "It was part of the craft for spies to slip enemies tidbits of information to ingratiate themselves to enemy leaders. This, in hopes of scoring significant information from them in the future. In the larger scope of the war, the Battle of Setauket was a minor skirmish."

"Perhaps," said the old man, unconvinced, and shaking his head. He then argued for a half hour about his grandmother being a "dyed-in-the-wool Loyalist who never spied for Radicals."

Nevertheless, based on what I had so far, I put Amity Thorne at the top of my list. Though I had no direct proof she was Agent 355.

"Do you have anything with her handwriting?"

"All lost in the fire," he said.

What rotten luck, I thought.

"What are you going to say about my grandma in your book?" the man said, abruptly, staring at me, eagle-like.

The query caught me off guard, and I asked for a second cup of tea to stall.

When he left the room for the drink I thought about what I had read in the *Diary of Agent 355*. Sex, intrigue, betrayal, scandal, death. It's all there in black and white to be read. Or not. His words "my grandma" weighed heavily on me.

The old man returned and poured green tea gently into my cup. By the time I sipped the last drop I had decided to halt my enquiries into the identity of "Lady" spy, Agent 355. "She doesn't fit the profile," I said of his ancestor, a half-lie. "If I mention her, it will be that she was a Loyalist who was present at the Battle of Setauket."

The man smiled and shook my hand, and I thanked him for inviting me into his lovely home. Call me old fashion, trite, unedgy, out-of-step with today's tell-all "Dr. Phil" culture, and even a literary coward. I wasn't about to drag some reputable family's sixth-great-grandma's name through the muck of being a spying whore for George Washington.

For readers disappointed that I did not uncover the diary's author's identity, I understand. But, honestly I likely would not have discovered her identity anyhow. Historians have failed trying since 1930. So I must be satisfied in knowing that this "diary," which was lost to history for two centuries has been rescued from obscurity by my good friend John Spivey. Lacking the author's name makes the "diary" no less readable. Because what's important is what is written and not who wrote it. That, I assume, is one reason why Agent 355 decided to write it, but stayed anonymous.

In truth, it really isn't a "diary" as her own title suggests. As a genuine and successful spy, Agent 355 was well cognizant of the hanging of spies Nathan Hale in December 1776, and Britain's John André four years later. She would never have kept a day-to-day log of her spy activities. Found out, it would have been the fast-track to the gallows for this daring female, especially once they learned the number of bodies left in her wake.

Instead of being a "daily diary," it is a memoir, and a carefully crafted one after the fact.

The penultimate question I want to explore is why the identity of Agent 355 has remained unknown all these centuries, when Abraham Woodhull's, Robert Townsend's, Anna Strong's and the names of the other Culper spies have been outed, though not until the twentieth century. This is a bold statement, yet I wholeheartedly subscribe to it. The other Culper spies, all except Anna Strong, her childhood friend, feared her.

Agent 355 was cunny, cool and ruthless and had specialized training they knew of but never wanted to see in action up-front, close and personal. She was a killer of men, amorously and otherwise, as you will learn. Her compatriots stepped lightly to never cross her, and milquetoast Abraham Woodhull, chief spy of the ring, stepped gently to avoid any slipups that might expose her real name and rouse her ire against him. More so than for the rest of his band of spies, Woodhull took extra precautions to protect her identity from disclosure – for his own safety's safe. Put yourself in his shoes. You have the Colonial female equivalent of James Bond working for you. How are you going to treat her?

Carefully, very carefully.

How about the document's authenticity?

I know since Clifford Irving's fake autobiography of Howard Hughes in the 1970s people are naturally skeptical of manuscripts purporting to be of the "long lost" variety.[12]

---

[12] Novelist Clifford Irving's fake "autobiography" of reclusive billionaire Howard Hughes was to be published in 1972, but when Hughes held a telephone news conference and called the book a hoax,

And to be sure the question of this diary's historical authenticity is one I intensely grappled with as a scholar of historical records. Was it a forgery? With two famous forgeries in mind – the "diaries" of Adolf Hitler "discovered" in 1981, and the "diary" of Jack the Ripper "discovered" in 1992 – I subjected the *Diary of Agent 355* to a rigorous test, which to my knowledge wasn't performed on either of those forged "historical documents."

I had the handwritten diary digitized, which is to say, typed on a computer by two professional stenographers, both ex-court reporters. I then applied a program invented by a friend of mine in Silicon Valley, which analyzes the "etymology" of words in a document. Etymology is the study of a word's origin in English and other languages and reveals how meanings change over centuries, and indicates when a particular word was first used. For example, say she had written the word "feminist" – and she certainly was a feminist for her day. The etymology program shows the word feminist wasn't used in English until 1892, eighty years after the diary's authorship. Had I found "feminist" in the diary I would have judged it a fake. Let's take the noun "micturition," which she used in the diary. It means a "very bad need to urinate." This word passes the etymology test because it is from the Latin *"micturitum"* and was used by English speakers in the 1700s. I performed the etymology examination many times on the diary. It proved beyond a reasonable doubt that every word used by Agent 355 to write it was in use in the eighteenth century or before. This lack of "modern terminology" tends to show its historical authenticity. In addition, I had a handwriting expert examine the diary's original penmanship. This expert attested it was "typical of mid-to-lower class eighteenth-century cursive."

---

it was not published by McGraw-Hill, which held its rights. Irving claimed he had interviewed Hughes at secret locations around the world for the book. The author served a prison term for the fraud and in 1981 wrote *The Hoax*, the story of how he researched and wrote the fake autobiography. The fake Hitler Diaries, a set of 50 journals, emerged in 1981 and was purchased by the German magazine, "Stern," which wrote a story two years later about them. The diaries portrayed a kinder and gentler Adolf Hitler. The diaries were soon denounced by World War II historians and found to be fakes. "The Diary of Jack the Ripper" was "discovered by a scrap metal dealer in 1992, but after a forensic analysis of the work showed it was written in prose not of the Victorian era (it was considered very 1990s), the diary was called a fake.

Obviously the diary's paper and ink couldn't be carbon-dated. However, the manuscript is written on paper with a distinctive watermark, a dove, which according to archival records was in popular use in the eighteenth century.[13]

All these efforts on my part are not conclusive of its authenticity. However, as empirical evidence, I am sure lawyers would say it is more inculpable than exculpable.

Some notes on the text.

Agent 355's prose style isn't as articulate, artful and lyrical as say an elite of the era like Alexander Hamilton, Thomas Jefferson or even a Benjamin Tallmadge. In fact, understandably, the writing is often clumsy. It is the writing of a "mid-to-lower-class" person in the Thirteen Colonies, as my handwriting expert put it. But the writing is engaging and can be infectious once readers immerse themselves in its cadence, phrasing and word use. Remember this is a Colonial woman who while able to read and write lacks the polish of a skillful wordsmith schooled in English. At times her slang is terribly irksome, though from an editor's point of view, not only is it often colorful it is indicative of the language spoken by people of her class in the 1770s.

As a serious student of Colonial Americana, the editor finds her prose, as the French say, *un jardin.*

The reader must also keep in mind this is not a full history of the Revolutionary War. She writes only of her spying without providing the fuller context of the war, such as battles being fought hither and yon or who is winning or losing. Her focus is on her own survival! This is where the editor's footnotes that provide elaboration, context or clarification come in handy. It is the publisher's opinion that these notes be read concurrently with Agent 355's original prose. Of course this is subject to each reader's discretion.

The editor has corrected most misspellings. Although Agent 355's overbearing habit of using apostrophe d ('d) for past tense words – "kill'd" for "killed" for example – has

---

[13] Scientists tell me carbon-dating is effective only on materials many thousands and millions year old. At most, the paper upon which the diary is written is just over 200 years old. Additionally, an analysis of the ink used by Agent 355 was inconclusive and unhelpful in establishing when the diary was written.

been unedited to maintain the Revolutionary-era diary's character. She also uses the pronoun "me" instead of the determiner "my" and this usage has been unedited as well. Another literary idiosyncrasy of hers is writing "ye" for "you" and "yer" for "your," but as a patient reader I soon learned to accept it. In addition, where an ampersand (&) appears in the text, which was common usage in the 1700s, the editor has changed "&" to "and." When Colonial-era slang is used, the editor has elaborated where appropriate in footnotes. However, to minimize footnotes the editor has inserted a modern word inside [brackets] next to the slang in the text to explain its meaning. Such definitions of Colonial slang are often crucial. For example, when a Colonial said, *"He is clear,"* they were actually saying, *"He is very drunk."*

Moreover, it is important for the reader to know that the original prose has been scrupulously adhered to, even when minor or wholesale changes in syntax were obviously required for clarity. In a few instances the editor has inserted a [bracketed] word in the narrative to avoid reader confusion. Still for the sake of historical integrity, such editing has been kept to a minimum.

Finally, when word circulated last year that John Spivey had found "an important historical record" in his farmhouse, he got offers from collectors to purchase it. One collector (a fan of AMC's TURN) said he would pay $150,000 sight-unseen for it, thinking likely that Spivey was just an ignorant farmer. Spivey told me he laughed at the guy. "He had no idea of my net worth," Spivey told me. "My wife spends more than $150,000 shopping on vacation."

My very rich friend has given his permission for publication of *Diary of Agent 355*, which follows in its entirety.

Franklin Alfred Kirby Edwards,
October, 2017

DIARY

First Part, 1774-1778
Written Down
December 31st to March 4th, 1809

There is to be readers which ask me why I reveal in this public document secrets of spy'g and of private matters of womanhood know'd and done by me in the Great War of Rebellion against King George III. This unambiguous explanation is in order. First, it is to be know'd: on God's word I never dreamt of writing this diary of me war experience. But something happen'd which change'd me way of thinking on this subject in 1808, which is last year. It is this. On a clear, warm spring day which progress'd like all other yawners in Setauket, I meet me old friend Lieutenant Colonel Benjamin Tallmadge at the Caroline Church. This is the church, which amidst the rebellion, Loyalists board'd windows and in what many call rapacious sacrilege rip'd up headstones from sacred burials and pile'd same as a redoubt to fight off Patriot raiders led by General Parsons in 1777. General Parsons gallantly retreat'd with wounded to show for his heroic effort, and today, in 1809, he is honor'd with colorful flowers put at Patriots' Rock, from where rebels fought Loyalists in the church.

I mention'd meeting Colonel Tallmadge at this church. After expect'd cordial pleasantries – me asks how he is and how is his wife – thus Colonel Tallmadge says to me: "As we speak candidly, I contemplate writing a memoir of the war. I've been ask'd for it by me own family and obliged."

It is the first I ever know'd of a "memoir" by Tallmadge, and it is me purpose to be positive on it, yet I be unsure, too.

"I know'd you write a convince'g letter of love, dear Benjamin," I says, with coquetry and a pretty smile, remember'g his false "love" missive to Anna Strong to fool British General Sir Henry Clinton of Washington moving on New York. "Yet a telltale work of literature; no, all is not to be told be ye for public reading and discourse, certainly, is it?"

He takes me meaning immediately. Tallmadge is witty from days as a member of Yale College with his friend Nathan Hale, after which they both took to school mastering before mustering in the Continental Army. "To a degree, yea, yet to which is not ascertained by me," he answers, his voice in the usual this-is-the-facts-of-it tone I hear'd in 1778, 1779, 1780, and 1781, a time I be most active in spy'g for Tallmadge; thou shan't be misled, reader, to think Colonel Tallmadge is me only benefactor. In all truth me beginning in this treacherous spy endeavor begins in 1775 in Philadelphia under the tutelage of me friend, Alexander Hamilton.[14]

In a memoir from man-proper Tallmadge I do not expect a quill of nastiness, but not one dipped in the ink of pure truth, either. To what degree of exposure and truth, I immediately asks me self? So I says to Tallmadge in candid fashion: "Meseems [it seems to me] a ponderous road, and you should think on it long prior to take'g up yer ink cup and quill to write this telltale memoir."

Tallmadge see'd how me face is set serious.

"Say yer piece, then," he invites me.

"Secret things like spy'g be secret for a purpose," I says, and I see'd his wife look'g at me from near the road, and I know'd she is think'g what is this old wench say'g to me good husband? "There is much haranguing of our merchantmen by the Royal Navy at French ports in the King's war on Napoleon, and impressing of American able seamen is happening and is a sore wound. I hear of clamoring in Congress of revenge on the Crown, like calls for a war

---

[14] It was known that Hamilton, 1755-1804, recruited Mulligan and his slave Cato into spaying for the Continental Army, but this mention is the f rst that the Founding Father and the nation's first Secretary of the Treasury also recruited the woman spy known as Agent 355.

declaration," I says as forthrightly as can be uttered by an earthly being. "I do not now predict another fight with the King's army is nigh, nor in practice, winnable."[15] The Colonel winces at me remark, seeing how he makes his proud name winning our Great War against his former countrymen and King, and, Tallmadge know'd if he is call'd again he will win again; although we is less spry these days than when the call is made by the Declaration in 1776. I goes on in vociferation: "Is it wise to tell of secrets of a last war when a new war simmers in the stew pot?" Tallmadge admires these words I can tell by watch'g his face, and I says: "Or is it the wiser road to keep yer secrets secret and yer head attached?"

He is think'g on these words with a dire expression.

I goes on, looking out at his wife: "In town I hear'd of setting up a committee of safety – with many who is quiet and loyal to the Crown in membership; we know'd they spy for the King's interest at ports and encampments."

Wise Tallmadge need hear no more.

"Yer console is amongst those I value."

He tips his hat and walks away to join his lovely wife, Mary Floyd, daughter of Major General William Floyd, a

[15] Agent 355 is obviously talking to Colonel Tallmadge about tensions with Britain which led to the War of 1812, which lasted until 1815. This war accomplished little for each side but caused much American consternation when in August 1814 British troops burned the "Federal City" of Washington's public buildings, including the "President's Palace" (later the White House), where, after President James Madison's wife, Dolley, saved a few items from destruction, British commanders ate a meal prepared for the President and his Cabinet and then lit the place on fire. On the good side, the war led to Francis Scott Key writing a poem as he watched the British bombard Fort McHenry, which later when being put to music became the U.S. national anthem in 1931, "The Star Spangled Banner." Historians still argue over who won the War of 1812. As Agent 355 mentioned in her diary the impressment of Americans by the British Royal Navy, a major reason the war was fought, continued after the peace treaty was signed.

[16] Agent 355 did not live to see publication of Colonel Tallmadge's memoir in 1858. The *Memoir of Col. Benjamin Tallmadge* does not reveal information about Agent 355 or other Culper Spy Ring members. It mentions Caleb Brewster but not in connection with spying. The book has a preface written by his son, Frederick A. Tallmadge, a lawyer and New York state senator, which states: "The following Memoir of Colonel Benjamin Tallmadge was prepared by himself, at the request of his children, and for their gratification. It is confined, principally to those incidents of the Revolutionary War with which he was more immediately connected, and therefore becomes the more interesting to his descendants and family friends. For their convenience, and for the additional purpose of contributing to the authenticity of our Revolutionary History, I determined to publish this Memoir; and. as it terminates with the close of the Revolutionary struggle, have added a brief sketch of his subsequent life."

signer of the Declaration. She wait'd for our private discourse to cease. She is know'g of me previous "endeavors with men" in the Great War, and it is not outrageous to think she strenuously will seek all details of our discussion in the privacy of their domicile to-night. Even at this age, I cast a much alluring countenance to men of like experience. I never know'd if Colonel Tallmadge acted on me advice as he often did in the war. I never see'd publication of his memoir on the late fight to know if he discussed me spy'g in a public book.[16] I suspect if he mention'd the Culper Spy Ring, the masculine names of Washington's spies will triumph over these feminine personages involve'd. Such women as Anna Smith Strong, Sally Townsend, Mary Woodhull and me self warrant nary a footnote. Women should git honors just like men do when they operate in the same dangers as men in the domains of war. Certainly it is to be so when they operate outside the chores of a homestead, and do spy'g work for a cause against the King of England, as did these women. This is the opinion I come to believe with all of my human heart after much reading and contemplation. This is not revolutionary thinking, of women as equal of men. By 1765 women spread influence in the Colonies, being bold and seeking equal treatment by men, with the fight over the evil Stamp Act bringing women to debate with menfolk at street posts and public halls. I remember personages of the Culper Ring mentioning Mrs. John Adams herself writing a letter in 1776 to her husband, who circulate'd the Declaration to sever ties with England's King. She sends in the letter the admonition to "remember the ladies and be more generous and favorable to them than yer ancestors" in laws of the new commonwealth. Thusly, during the Great War I loved Abigail Smith Adams. By this date I read political essays by Judith Sargent Murray in *The Gleaner*:

"Amid the blaze of this auspicious day;
"When science points the broad refulgent way;
"Her iron scepter prejudice resigns;
"And sov'reign reason all resplendent shines."

Likewise I enjoy'd poems of Anne Dudley Bradstreet, wherein the family is the moral spirit of communities, and I hear'd among the talk of women at the Presbyterian Church of Lydia Chapin Taft, who cast a vote at a meeting in the town of Uxbridge, Massachusetts in 1756; and today, I be concern'd of plight of females in our Republic.[17]

◆ ◆ ◆

I cannot write another word in this diary without this preamble. Necessary, first to clear the record for posterity for me friend Anna Strong. Second is a cathartical need, a confession, to cleanse me Heavenly soul of a dastardly secret, which is a anguish of mind and a heart-ache to me all me life.

As close as peas in a pod is Anna Strong and me, and at times indistinguishable when observing us from the distance of her clothesline and the Long Island seawater beyond. This means it be only a bug's ear of difference in us. I tell you this for her because of girlish remarks about her from Robert Townsend's sister, Sally Townsend, and by Mary Underhill, sister of Abraham Woodhull. After the Great War Anna tells me one day the two women chide her in private discourse for hang'g a "black petticoat" on her hillside clothesline to alert Caleb Brewster of Abraham Woodhull's dispatches for General George Washington.

---

[17] "The Gleaner" was a magazine in the late-1700s and essayist Judith Sargent Murray was a feminist two hundred years before Betty Friedan, 1921-2006, wrote *The Feminine Mystique* in 1963 and journalist Gloria Steinem sparked the modern feminist movement in the 1960s. Murray's pieces had titles such as "Future Prospects of Women in this Enlightened Age" (1798), "Observations on Female Abilities" and "On the Equality of the Sexes." She was part of America's new sense of itself and Murray argued that women were as much "Republican citizens" as men. Wrote Murray in 1798: "I take leave to congratulate my fair country-women, on the happy revolution which the few past years has made in their favor; that in these infant republics, where, within my remembrance, the use of the needle was the principal attainment which was thought necessary for a woman, the lovely proficient is now permitted to appropriate a moiety of her time to studies of a more elevated and elevating nature. Female academies are everywhere establishing, and right pleasant is the appellation to my ear." Anne Dudley Bradstreet, 1612-1672, was the first English poet to be published in the Colonies. She once wrote: "Authority without wisdom is like a heavy axe without an edge, fitter to bruise than polish." Lydia Chapin Taft, 1712-1778, was a feminist by accident. She was the first woman in America to vote at a town hall meeting in Massachusetts. She was married to Josiah Taft who became a wealthy farmer in Uxbridge and a captain in the French and Indian War. When Josiah Taft died in 1756, just before the town was to vote on continued financial support for the French and Indian War. The only male left in the Taft home at the time was a minor, and due to Lydia Taft's wealth and the impact of the vote on her estate, the town allowed her to cast her dead husband's vote. In the American Women's Suffrage Movement Lydia Taft became an instant icon in the fight in the early twentieth century to allow females to vote, which led to ratification of the 19th Amendment to the federal Constitution.

"A black petticoat for sin," Anna tells me by way of private complaint on a visit with her on me sojourn to Setauket from New York city, and this gossip displease'd her.[18] To oblige me friend, let us dispense with this black petticoat business. It is verily a small concern. Yet if three decades after the Great War with scoundrels Clinton, Cornwallis, Howe, Burgoyne and Gage and the rest of the Redcoat Army and all the Loyalist rascals who lick'd boots of same, and me friend Anna Strong still hear'd private merrymaking over this petticoat, then it is necessary to speak up of it. Alas! She never own'd a black garment such as this petticoat, and, now today it is the intention to strike it from ever growing into the fabric of Setauket lore.

We know'd the clothesline trick is true.

Yea, Anna put up the signal on the line for Brewster's eyes.

True.

But Anna is a proper woman and hanging a black petticoat on the clothesline to signal Caleb Brewster to pick up spying is rubbish. This petticoat nonsense is concocted by Archibald Cunningham, late of Boston, who is banish'd from New York in 1778 for Tory leanings. I understand his cunny scheme to discredit Anna Strong and her family, husband Selah mainly, with rumors: picturing this good woman as a non-Puritan evildoer wearing a black petticoat and flying it on the line like the Devil's pennant.

It won't fly, Sir!

Hanging from her clothesline on Strongs Neck and see'd from Brewster's whaleboat is a cape which is the color of a dark stone from a river she wear'd on cold days in Setauket. I know'd this. We buy'd capes together on a call to the city. Me cape is a lighter gray than hers is. Anna tells me she laughs thinking back. Only if the British Redcoats, and specially Major John Graves Simcoe who live'd in Robert Townsend's house in Oyster Bay with his Queen's Rangers, and her

---

[18] This is one of the few times in the diary that Agent 355 hints that she does not live in Setauket, but has travelled "from the city" to see Anna Strong who lived there all of her life. I am guessing, but it is a guess based on carefully reading her diary, that she lived mostly in the city of New York, first settled in 1624.

Setauket Loyalist neighbors be as astute as they give theirselves credit for, they may of seen through it. She says to me one day: "I wash'd the cape more times than ever necessary in ten winters in Setauket."

I, in good humor, says back: "Ye pull'd the cape over those eyes, ye did!"

We be old women, and laugh'd like giggling girls on it.

◆◆◆

The second item in this preamble is not funny or good-spirited, nor can I ever laugh at it; and today I cry think'g of it afresh. Of every burden entomb'd in me heart in this long life, even me kill'g many British and Loyalists, none is of greater weight or more painful inside me breast than this be.

I ignited the Great New York Fire of 1776.

This is a confession. Woe. What a great sin. Here it is which happened.

In September 1776, coveting the advantages of New York harbor, British troops under command of General William Howe chase'd General Washington's weak Continental Army, which occupied New York Island, from town. After this there is hushed talk about making "a harsh winter for the King's Men." Patriots who come under harassment by Loyalists once Howe takes control all know'd what this meant: burn down this city!

I be still under the care of Mister Alexander Hamilton and return'd from me training by Robert Rogers and his Northern Indian troops. I hear'd from me friend in the Army, Benjamin Tallmadge, who says General Nathanael Greene, the one who drives General Cornwallis out of the Carolinas, advises His Excellency Washington to burn New York so British Army cannot obtain comfortable billets in the cold and snows of winter.[19] In turn, according to our information,

---

[19] Agent 355 gets ahead of herself in the diary by mentioning Robert Rogers of Rogers's Rangers fame, whom taught her what would pass today for "guerrilla warfare." Apparently Alexander Hamilton was introduced to Rogers in Philadelphia 1766 when Rogers and his wife were on their way to Upper Michigan where King George III has appointed Rogers governor. The King had tasked Rogers with looking for the "Northwest Passage. Rogers was a fierce Indian fighters who implored measures of tomahawks, bows and arrows and other Indian weaponry and at some point trained Agent 355, at Hamilton's behest and payment, in there deadly use. She talks about this experience, some of which she calls "harrowing" in a later section of this diary.

Washington seeks advice from the Continental Congress which disproves of arson of New York dwellings. So, nay, to fire by Washington.

One night at Roe's Tavern in Setauket, Caleb Brewster strikes up a conversation with owner Austin Roe, who becomes Culper Spy Ring member in 1778, and Caleb tells Roe this Congress is being cowards on this argument over burning New York. Tobacco is a source of money in 1776, and I hear'd helps pay costs of this war. On my journeys in New York I buy tobacco for Austin Roe's business, and after one delivery, he tells me of his friends in the Sons of Liberty who talk of burning down New York to deny it to the "bloody" British.

From that propitious session, I takes action on me own.

Me and a Patriot who I must shield his name because same can be discovered by his date of demise, dress in vagabond's clothing and gaudy adornments and make our ways all the fifty miles from Setauket to the West Side on the southern end of New York Island. The intent of ours is to set fire to the harbor and wharf district so British ships be hindered and denied mooring.

I carry a New York-made glass decanter of whale oil under me gray cape, and me compatriot keeps a flint and steel striker in his trousers to light the flame. I possess a light dragoon pistol, a gift from Mister Rogers who tells me no man can survive a shot from its large ball at close range. The pistol has no sights and is nine inches long. It is easy to hide on a sling under me cape.[20]

When we gits to a downtrodden area where our threadbare accoutrements blend with the poor souls who walk about in the district, we know'd we is above suspicion and is with a free hand for this intend'd mischief. We be on the way to the wharf at the Fighting Cocks Tavern near the

---

[20] About nine inches, this was the smallest pistol known in the Revolutionary War. Some pistols were as long as 16 inches, making them difficult to conceal. The relatively small handgun Agent 355 carried was only accurate at very close range, with its unrifled barrel. It is not known whether the gift from Rogers was a pistol made for officers or for enlisted men. The officer's handgun was far more ornate.

docks at Whitehall Slip when three Bloody Backs [British soldiers] approach us.

They be a smiling and talking, likely about finding women at a "disorderly house" in this shabby, poor district. Still me partner is overcome by panic and he implores me to rid me self of the whale oil evidence. He whispers excitedly and convinces me we can use wood kindling in its place, and, says he, rightly: "What normal person carries whale oil under a full shawl covering?"

Like I says, he is right, I thinks.

He starts stuttering his words and heaving like he cannot breathe. He motions to me he wants to run. I know'd his unnerve is about to call the jackals on us, unintended but surely so. At the side of the tavern I see'd a narrow opening and, as the soldiers approach a hundred paces distance, I remove the decanter of whale oil and pitch it by its fancy neck topsy-turvy into the dark alleyway beside Fighting Cocks Tavern.

Crack! I hear'd it break.

In moments the Redcoats pass by, barely with a notice of us, much to our relief.

Me friend whispers his apology for loss of nerve, and I comfort same by patting his back like a puppy dog.

Whoosh!

The next thing I see'd is a tall finger of flame reach up from the side of the Fighting Cocks. I looks through the narrow opening and see the building next to the tavern horribly ablaze, and, realize only now that I toss'd the oil on discard'd ashy embers of coal from the public house's kitchen.

"There!" came a scream, which turns me head violently towards it. The three Redcoats run at us, muskets in front.

I crouch and climb through the narrow opening, pulling me cape in behind me with a jerk, and I do not know if I be entering Dante's Inferno or what. Fire climbs like a glowing mountaineer up what looks like a storehouse, and I do not tarry for the heat is great. I make me way by it and to a petty alleyway, which is darken'd from loss of sun.

"Halt!" I hear'd call behind me. One of the Redcoats is wriggling his self through the tiny hole, and I hear'd him cursing about tearing his pretty regimentals [uniform].

Down fifty feet I comes to a dead end.

Naught! I is trap'd like a beaver for its fur.

I steps in a shallow alcove, the last doorway in the place behind Fighting Cocks Tavern. I uplift the French pistol from its sling. I keep it tight in both hands as Robert Rogers teaches me, and I waits in the darkness of this tiny space. The Redcoat's steps hit hard on the cobblestones of the alleyway and I hear'd same over the crackling intensity of the fire burning behind me. The sound increases as he gits closer and closer to me hiding place. Then I notice every several steps the sound of footfalls stops, and I guess he is halting at each doorway alcove, checking for me in it. Me heart pounds rapid in me breast. I be never telling Rogers this! He teaches a mind thinks slyly when ye slay yer fear. The thought quiets me. The footsteps be close, and I raise the pistol to what I figure is his eye-level. Then his musket reels out of the darkness and points into me alcove. I sees his startle's eyes which stare in fright at the barrel of me short gun.

I pulls the trigger – boom!

The thunder of the shot and the rancid smell of the powder fills me senses, deafens and nauseates me at once, and I choke.

His mouth cannot scream as the hot ball rips through his face and out the back of his head. He falls instantly dead on his back on the stones of the alleyway, and his legs git bent in ways unnatural under his body. Stepping from the smoky alcove I examine a moment, knowing his poor mother cannot recognize her boy at his funerary wake. I runs back up the alleyway and see'd the fire above me jump from building to roof-top, and it be pushed by a brisk southwesterly wind. At the narrow hole I pull me self through it and see people all a hurry-scurry on the street, and yelling in terror. These same souls carry belongings and shout for God to save them. Full of dread these people do not notice me wiggling like a little polliwog through the narrow opening, fire feeling hot on me arse. I re-sling the pistol under the cape, and blend into the chaos which I wrought by accident and chance.

Sadly I learn much later me friend be shot in the back by his two Redcoats in chase, and when I hear'd this, I rejoice at killing the third King's lackey in the alleyway as his revenge. But, lo, these not be the only deaths this night. The fire rages all night and I stays in the city searching for me co-patriot, and I hear'd the Sons of Liberty is accused by Loyalists of starting this conflagration. In their vengeance, Loyalists throw'd some Sons of Liberty into the flames and kill'd same.

O, lament. The original intent is damage the port so British ships be curtail'd. We never dreamt to burn buildings and dwellings and send thousands of New York inhabitants, certainly not Whigs, and even not Loyalist dogs into the cold of winter, which I know'd all these years after is what happen'd. Today this burnt land in the city of New York is a sty of whores, gamblers and disease called "Holy Ground" because it touches Trinity Church, which is sacrilegious itself, and if ye want to curse me and say it is all me fault it is true.

Say it!

It is a violent city now, I warn ye; I not see'd the last of.

Ye may not know'd this but Washington his self secretly praise'd the arsonist. His acclamation never makes me think I acted right in burning the city, and I never muster'd guts to admit what happened to anybody. Not a day goes by without me thinking of the people I sent into the cold streets with me ill-advised foray into Revolutionary politics. I takes this action without counsel, which I learn't never to do again. This is me confession, though, do not leap like at the Feast of the Assumption and say I be a papist. Truly, once I be gone from this earthly world and, if, I be deter'd from Heaven's gate, I know the reason why without ever asking it.[21]

---

[21] Her account of deaths of members of the Sons of Liberty confirms information in the chapter, "The Great Fire of 1776 in NYC," in the book about New York published in 1909, *Cradle Days of New York, 1609-1825*, by Hugh Macatamney. Pushed by high winds and low humidity the fire spread quickly north and west, destroying the densely packed area of homes and businesses. Begun on September 20, the blaze burned all night into September 21, crossing Broadway and destroying everything to the Hudson River, when a change in wind direction slowed it. Even in 1809, thirty-three years after the fire, which destroyed 500 buildings in the lower part of the Island of

1774

I be affectionate with Alexander Hamilton when he be a member of King's College in May 1774, when he be 19, the first time I see'd this boy. His high forehead is topped with medium-length sandy blond hair and his flourishing blue eyes, which, when he gazes at me that first time, peer inside me own maiden's heart. I remember watching Hamilton at the Liberty Pole at King's where speeches be yowled, and I admire'd his powers of oration, though for me taste, I thinks his voice octaves high for a man. He is quick to anger and is of a surliness at times, which as many know'd wrought tragedy in 1804.[22] But, mostly he is kind to me. Like the time

---

Manhattan and burned at least a quarter of the city of 30,000 people, some sections of the fire still had not been rebuilt and wouldn't be for another two decades. The British detained as many as two hundred people and questioned them about the blaze, but no arrest was made. Agent 355's account of how she inadvertently ignited the fire coincides somewhat with a statement in historian Alexander Rose's *Washington's Spies: The Story of America's First Spy Ring*, published in 2007, which says new evidence shows that the 1775 fire was accidently started by the wives of British soldiers cooking in a fireplace in a storehouse next to the Fighting Cocks. The wives placed pine boards in the fireplace, he asserts, which later caught the floor of the storehouse on fire after they left. The fire created hundreds of homeless who lived in tents on streets. It also led to marshal law by the occupying British after looting broke out. As for public safety, the fire was responsible for banning wooden frame doors, blamed for the fast spread of the blaze. Hugh Gain, in his Universal Register for the Year 1787, wrote that "New York is about a mile and a half in length and half a mile broad, containing before the fire . . . 4,200 houses and 30,000 inhabitants." People who were taken to the provost guard for examination and remained there for three days were released by proving loyalty to the King. However, Hugh Macatamney writes that, "Mr. White, a decent citizen and house carpenter, rather too violent a Loyalist, and had addicted himself to liquor, was on the night of the fire hanged on a tavern signpost, at the corner of Cherry and Roosevelt streets." It is revealing that Agent 355 calls her telling of burning New York a "confession" and states, "do not leap like at the Feast of the Assumption and say I be a papist." Is she purposely steering the reader away from thinking she is Roman Catholic, even while mentioning a Catholic holy day, Feast of the Assumption celebrated August 15, and probably not an event every Protestant has close in mind. Remember she is keen on keeping her identity secret, and if researchers thought she were Roman Catholic they might peruse Catholic Church and cemetery records on Long Island.

[22] Hamilton's temper had gotten him into several duels before, and there is little doubt Agent 355 refers to the duel between Hamilton and then-Vice President of the United States Aaron Burr on July 11, 1804, in which Hamilton lost his life. The gunplay was culmination of a decade-long political dispute between Burr and Hamilton which began in 1791 when Burr defeated Hamilton's father-in-law Philip Schuyler for the U.S. Senate. In the early morning duel in New Jersey Hamilton apparently fired his pistol first unintentionally and the ball hit over Burr's head. Burr then fired hitting Hamilton in the abdomen, which damaged his liver and he collapsed. He died the following day. Although dueling had been outlawed in New Jersey, Burr never faced legal punishment. Curiously the same pistols were also used in an 1801 duel in which Hamilton's son, Philip, died.

he invites me to a social at the estates of his King's College roommate, Robert Troup, in New Jersey, and there we experience enjoyable events and kindle a friendship in which he says I may be his lady-love. It is his youth which talks of it, but he says he likes talking to me. He shares his sad early life, of the fact his mother and father is unwed at his birth and of being abandon'd by his father after his mother dies, and of being orphan'd. He tells me he is rescued from abject poverty by a cousin and later by the family which gives a better life and education at King's. Politics burns inside Alexander and he talks much of tyranny of the British Crown and rights of Congress to oppose it. He shows me letters he writes called "The Monitor" for a New York pamphleteer, publishing same without his name, which as I remember it, is the first time I realize Hamilton's proclivity for secretiveness. I see'd he is proud of his self for what he writes down.

Our relationship of being more friend than lover goes on for months and I is present whence he leaves King's College to enlist in the militia and later rises to rank of Captain and becomes a confidante of George Washington his self in the Great War. In 1779, Hamilton meets Elizabeth Schuyler, a wealthy general's daughter whence he be encamped at Morristown, New Jersey. Her family be owning much land and I thinks he likes this state of affairs. They marry late the next year, and it be suspicion by me but I thinks Miss Elizabeth falls for his blues eyes, too. There is a prurient side to Alexander and we be coupled in intimacy during our relationship, so, it be without surprise ten years ago I read in New York papers of his sex scandal because I know'd me self how easily he is carnally excitable.[23]

---

[23] Take a look at all men printed on U.S. paper currency produced since the 1920s, and two, Alexander Hamilton on the ten dollar bill and Andrew Jackson on the twenty standout as the handsomest. Of them, Hamilton wins the "good-looking dude" prize, with his flowing hair, bedroom eyes and manly nose. Therefore, is it any shock to learn at age 34 he is involved in a sex scandal? Here is the scoop from a pamphlet he wrote defending himself from allegations of money speculation. "Sometime in the summer of 1791 a woman called at my house in the city of Philadelphia and asked to speak with me in private. I attended her into a room apart from the family. With a seeming air of affliction she informed that she was a daughter of a Mr. Lewis, sister to a Mr. G. Livingston of the State of New-York, and wife to a Mr. Reynolds whose father was in the Commissary Department during the war with Great Britain, that her husband, who for a long time

Once the Great War ignites, in fact it is in May 1775 before smoke clears from Lexington and Concord, Alexander Hamilton contacts me in New York for a favor, a life-changing entreaty. He says he is to form a small band of informants who can tell movements of British soldiers and ships in Philadelphia, and report it to his self only. He says it requires the talents of a woman who is trustworthy and sharp of mind.

Hamilton calls me by me real name and says, "It is ye."

I says I be flattered to think he thinks of me this way after our amorous relationship ends in friendship, and I says,

---

had treated her very cruelly, had lately left her, to live with another woman, and in so destitute a condition, that though desirous of returning to her friends she had not the means – that knowing I was a citizen of New-York, she had taken the liberty to apply to my humanity for assistance. I replied, that her situation was a very interesting one – that I was disposed to afford her assistance to convey her to her friends, but this at the moment not being convenient to me. I must request the place of her residence, to which I should bring or send a small supply of money. She told me the street and the number of the house where she lodged. In the evening I put a bank-bill in my pocket and went to the house. I inquired for Mrs. Reynolds and was shown upstairs [and] she . . . conducted me into a bed room. I took the bill out of my pocket and gave it to her. Some conversation ensued from which it was quick y apparent that other than pecuniary consolation would be acceptable. After this, I had frequent meetings with her, most of them at my own house; Mrs. Hamilton with her children being absent on a visit to her father." During their fling she told Hamilton that her husband wanted her back, and she confessed that her husband was involved in currency speculation with the help of a Treasury worker. "I sent for Reynolds who came to me accordingly. In the course of our interview, he confessed that he had obtained a list of claims from a person in my department which he had made use of in his speculations. I invited him, by the expectation of my friendship and good offices, to disclose the person. After some affectation of scruple, he pretended to yield, and ascribed the infidelity to" . . . a former department employee. James Reynolds then hit Hamilton up for a cushy government job, which Hamilton refused. It was then that Reynolds began blackmailing Hamilton by hinting that he would make the sexual affair public. Hamilton paid Reynolds an initial $1,000 for having sex his wife (either a duel or cash was acceptable to restore honor) and two more payments of $100. The young woman must have been a pretty hot tomato because even during this time, Hamilton wrote: "The intercourse with Mrs. Reynolds . . . continued; and, though various reflections, (in which a further knowledge of Reynolds' character and the suspicion of some concert between the husband and wife bore a part) induced me to wish a cessation of it; yet their conduct, made it extremely difficult to disentangle myself." *Her* conduct? Anyhow, James Reynolds was later arrested for currency speculation, and pointed a finger at Hamilton as a co-conspirator. Confronted by the allegations Hamilton denied it and the political brouhaha died down. But in 1797, two years after he left Treasury, the money manipulation allegations leaked out, and Hamilton wrote the public account of the sexual affair to defend himself. In other words I wasn't speculating in currency with the man I was having sex with his wife. (Got to give Hamilton credit, he took a much more honest approach than President Bill Clinton, who denied having sex "with that woman" when confronted with the Monica Lewinsky sex scandal in 1998.) Hamilton was a giant in banking but penniless in street smarts for not figuring the obvious from the beginning: the Reynolds couple lured him into a sex-extortion trap. Hamilton's wife, Elizabeth, ultimately forgave him for the dalliance.

"In many ways I be weak and naive and unskilled. How can I do this?"

Hamilton says he know'd this, and is why he arrange'd for me secret training in "Indian ways" by a great Indian fighter who thinks he is helping brew "a nest of Loyalist informants."

"Ways of savages," I say, surprised by what he informs me.

"How to walk silently, how to survive in cold," he says. Then he adds, and I suppose this is what he is getting at: "What you can learn of what Robert Rogers plans in New York is important."

I never hear'd of Robert Rogers a fore.[24]

Hamilton says Rogers is a famous frontier Indian fighter in the war with the French, and earns a wide name as a skilled raider and tracker. He says he is a great teacher of warriors. "Hurting for money and returning to America, for which, his motives is unknown," Hamilton tells me. "He is arrested by the Committee of Safety for spy'g, and I convince Rogers he is needed by the King to train Loyal spies and will be paid well for his service. Rogers is a mercenary. Watch him, he drinks spirits to excess."

Methinks to say, "Go to Hades, Mister Hamilton." Nay! This be a good friend who presently climbs ranks in the Army, and I feel inside me this desire to help his cause, and America's. I cannot say no.

Today I wish I hadst.

---

[24] Born to Irish parents in Massachusetts, think of Major Robert Rogers, 1727-1795, as "the Davy Crockett of Colonial times." I like to refer to him as America's first Green Beret – a warrior who uses guerrilla tactics but without the modern "rules of engagement." After all, Rogers while commanding Rogers Rangers in the French and Indian War, was accused of killing woman and children when he burned an enemy town in 1759. Rogers learned to fight in the ways of the Indians and was expert with such weapons as the tomahawk and in tactics of lightning fast raids on encampments, and in close-combat behind enemy lines. In his early years Rogers was successful financially and purchased land in Massachusetts, New York and New Hampshire, and later married. However, in 1778 his wife divorced him. His reputation as a frontiersman was widely known in America and England but unfortunately he was never able to translate his fame into cash, and lived hand-to-mouth much of his life. Historians contend money woes led to an addiction to alcohol, which plagued him in the latter part of his life. Early in his life Rogers got involved with counterfeiter but he was never tried. In the Revolutionary War he was in the Colonies and not trusted by George Washington, who ordered Rogers's arrest. Rogers fled and pledged alliance to the Crown and formed the formidable Queen's Rangers to fight the Patriots.

1775

I be blindfold'd for the journey by horse to Robert Rogers's secret camp in Indian land somewhere north of the Pennsylvania Colony. I hear'd immediately Rogers is git'g much pay for me training because the men say he never trains females for fighting. I hear'd among the talk Rogers trains guards for Congress members and even for General Washington and me friend Hamilton, and, Rogers takes in mercenary fighters who kill for payments from any person who is wealthy, and any side in this war.

At first I admire Rogers who has eyes which look like they will pop from his face any moment and a nose large for his head. A broganier [Irish accent] if there be doubt about his lineage. He is wont to wear rough, stout shoes until he trades same for moccasins when he fights Indians. Rogers treats me like a proper woman at first, and he impresses me with his intelligence, telling me of a theater play he writes about Chief Ponteach and his rebellion at Fort Detroit, which he says is performed on London's stage.[25] His papers of

---

[25] Major Robert Rogers's play published ir 1766 is titled, "Ponteach," which is spelled in modern times (and by the General Motors Corporation), "Pontiac." The full title is "Ponteach or the Savages of America: A Tragedy." The play is known for its sympathetic portrayal of Indians. A telling part of the play is when English trader, M'Dole, bargains for furs:

"Enter a number of Indians with packs of fur.

"First Indian: So, what you trade with Indians here to-day?

"M'Dole: Yes, if my Goods will suit, and we agree.

"Second Indian: 'Tis Rum we want, we're tired, hot, and thirsty.

"Third Indian: You, Mr. Englishman, have you got Rum?

"M'Dole: Jack, bring a Bottle, pour them each a Gill. You know which "Cask contains the Rum.

"First Indian: It's good strong Rum, I feel it very soon.

"M'Dole: Give me a Glass. Here's Honesty in Trade. We English always drink before we deal.

"Second Indian: Good Way enough; it makes one sharp and cunning.

Indian fighting be published in England, he says to me, and King George likes his work and names him a governor in Indian country.[26] When he drinks spirits he gits boisterous and one time talks of being ruined financially and landing in debtor's prison in New York. But he says he escapes.

"'Tis not a prison built to keep Major Robert Rogers pen'd," he laugh'd.

In this camp he teaches what he calls "the Ranger's rules," and mostly they is about fighting in a military brigade, which I will not do. He brags when he drinks, and says his "rules" is what takes the town of St. Francis, which I never endeavor to ask about because I be uncomfortable whence he is full of rum.

The most vivid rule is of the bayonet.[27] "No man sees battle without a bayonet," I remember Rogers says in his

---

"M'Dole: Hand round another Gill. You're very welcome.

"Third Indian: Some say you Englishmen are sometimes Rogues. You make poor Indians drunk, and then you cheat.

"First Indian: No, English good. The Frenchmen give no Rum.

"Second Indian: I think it's best to trade with Englishmen."

There is no evidence Rogers's play was ever performed on the stage in London at this time. Rogers, which was his custom, exaggerated.

[26] Agent 355 mentions that Rogers told her he was "Governor of Machinac" in Upper Michigan (today Machinaw City), but obviously he never told her the rest of the story. That is, he was tried for treason, stemming from his administrative work. But the case was bogus and went nowhere.

[27] In 1765 Robert Rogers published his first "Journal of the French and Indian War," which sold well in England. Afterward, he continued to keep journals on frontier warfare and to publish them. In the 1950s the U.S. Army developed a list of 28 rules from his journals for its elite Rangers. Perhaps not surprisingly they include war methods and discipline mentioned in Agent 355's diary. Obviously she was not handed a book of 28 rules by Rogers. However, there is no doubt he gave his spy trainees rules of war-fighting verbally. Also, of the raid on St Francis in 1759, Rogers wrote: "I came in sight of the Indian town St. Francis in the evening, which I discovered from a tree that I climbed at about three miles distance. Here I halted my party which now consisted of 142 men, officers included, being reduced to that number by the unhappy accident which befell Capt. Williams and several since tiring, whom I was obliged to send back. At eight o'clock this evening I left the detachment, and took with me Lieut. Turner and Ensign Avery, and went to reconnoiter the town which I did to my satisfaction, and found the Indians in a high frolic or dance. I returned to my party at two o'clock, and at three marched it to within five hundred yards of the town, where I lightened the men of their packs and formed them for the attack. At half hour before sunrise I surprised the town when they were all fast asleep, on the right, left, and center, which was done with so much alacrity by both the officers and men that the enemy had not time to recover themselves, or take arms for their own defense, till they were chiefly destroyed except some few of them who took to the water. About forty of my people pursued them, who destroyed such as attempted to make

thundering brogue. His raiding force possesses French Charleville muskets because they takes a bayonet. "A soldier with a sharp bayonet 'tis invincible," he says.

His rules be practical for fighting. Most I cannot remember word-for-word. Whence marching in the wilderness never walk close to the soldier in front because a single shot kills two. Whence ye be a force of three hundred divide into three columns, and attack from the center, left and right for best results. Each morning designate a meeting place for soldiers in case ye be attacked by a superior force and disperse. If ye attack the enemy on a river bank, leave soldiers on the other side to halt enemy escapes across the waters.

In the early days of camp, me and the men carry sixty pounds of equipment and hike in the hills and thick forests to build muscle and mental strength. The muskets and rifles weigh fifteen pounds alone and each person carts sixty cartridges as well as water and a small food pack. We drinks water only by permission of Rogers.

In camp I meets a young, quiet man named Henry Knox, a artillerist who among the men is one who does not laugh because he sees me, a female with a musket and tomahawk. We talks some nights together, and unlike other men, Henry does not desire me and becomes a friend. One night he tells me the trouble with George Washington's Army is it needs heavy guns to win.

"Howitzers be heavy," I says. "He has these."

"No, the big guns, the forty-two pounders," he says.

"Ye talk of the cannons on parapets of a fort?"

He says it is what he means.

"Washington moves much," I says. "These guns be big and cannot move with soldiers."

"Yer wrong," he says. "Wait here."

Henry leaves and runs to his tent, excited. In a while he returns with a bunch of drawings. He show'd me a picture he draw'd. "On this sled," he says. The picture is a sled with a

---

their escape that way, and sunk both them and their boats. A little after sunrise I set fire to all their houses except three in which I reserved for the use of the party. The fire consumed many of the Indians who had concealed themselves in the cellars and lofts of theirs houses."

gun on top of it. "Guns on sleds pull smooth over snow in winter." He does not like the look on me face. "It will not work, yer thinking?"

"Nay, Henry, I think it is a perfect idea," I says. "But, it must be winter. Say yer on a siege of a city in Connecticut, these guns pull'd in snow and over frozen rivers from, say Pennsylvania to Connecticut, would win the day."

"Yes," says Henry, "perfect to siege of a city!"

Henry Knox is happy about his sled idea for all the next week and then, one day he tells me he is leaving Rogers's camp to join the new Continental Army and become a Washington artillerists.

"May God protect ye," I says, and kiss his cheek, friendly. His face flushes red.

I can say this, it is ten years or more since the last war with the French who incite the Indians against the British and Rogers know'd which weapons to keep because he tells his men and me many times, "The weapons and cavalry charges of Europe's wars is made for flat battlefields and these weapons do not kill in the forests and the hills of the Thirteen Colonies." Rogers trains his men to be regulars, which is fighting in ranks of a military brigade. And he also trains us as irregulars, which is a marauder who fights behind trees and even in same, hanging from a branch, with the flintlock musket and not the older matchlock musket. The matchlock cannot be fired easy in rain; and what army is wont to call a truce because of rain? The matchlock also regularly misfires.

I remember Rogers lined up five men with old matchlock muskets which is fired by lighting a match by hand and igniting powder.

"Fire!" he orders.

Two of these matchlocks did not shoot.

"'Tis why we do not use these cursed guns," he roars.

The musket is a killer when fired at two hundred feet, though luck is as much needed as skill for the shooter. The musket is load'd down the barrel with a half-inch metal ball taken from inside a paper cartridge, rip'd open by the teeth, and powder. When this projectile strikes a body it puts a sizeable hole in flesh and bones. It takes two minutes to reload a matchlock while a flintlock musket is faster, under a minute.

"Indians be clever devils and watch for the flash of ye musket, and attack with a tomahawk down ye throat before ye can reload," says Rogers, who teaches us to charge a single line of matchlocks with tomahawks, which handle is two-feet long, once the enemy fires because his reloading time is so long. Rogers cuts the handle of a tomahawk shorter for me, and I learns to toss it with much skill.

Every day for the first three weeks of me training we do Brown Bess [musket] maneuvers and shot, and at the end of this drudgery me arms ached from the weight of this clumsy weapon, which on a lucky day one time, I score three exact hits of five shots at one hundred and forty five paces, which is shooting better than many men. Whence we finish our musket shots this day I surmise men become jealous of me as a marksman, viz., of being the only woman in camp, and these wild beasts begins to harass me over same.[28] "*Homme, homme, homme,*" they grunts it passing by me, which is French for man. It is no confusion of meaning for me. In the eyes of the brutes in buckskin I lost me womanhood in their eyes, doing such manly tasks so well.

One morning after me firing muskets like a marksman, Rogers says to me: "'Tis time me girl to shoot a man's gun."

He gives me a rifle which is almost longer than me.

"This be one long musket," I says.

"'Tis . . . a long rifle, indeed," says he. "It be accurate at two hundred yards and is the gun to snipe enemy from trees." He show'd me the barrel, and it is bored out like. "But," says Rogers, "it do not hold a bayonet."

"I cannot charge with no bayonet," I says.

---

[28] The use of *viz.* is archaic and from fifteenth century written English, although it is still used in the modern English language by stuffy professors in stuffy academia writing about stuffy subjects. The adverb *viz.* is the abbreviation of the Latin word *videlicet*, which means "this is to say" or "to wit." In other words, when you read viz. in a sentence there is more to follow to explain it. Take this sentence for instance: "Jane and I both shared the same ambition, viz. to find a rich man and marry."

"Charge?" shouts Rogers. "Charge? So yer want'g to charge now, you do?"

"I can run faster than men," says I, which is true.

In sudden anger, Rogers look'g like he is to throttle me throat. "No female wench is charge'n in a troop of Robert Rogers. Never. They'd laugh at me in every public house from Nova Scotia to London. Never!"

Rogers is not among the ones to upset.

I takes the long rifle and handles it and aims it, show'g I can hold it comfortably.

Rogers says the rifle fires straighter and farther and deadlier than muskets like the British Brown Bess or the French gun, and he tells me, it is perfect for a female.

Sixty shots a day for a month is what I fire from this long rifle on orders of Rogers, and each week he moves a board farther from me to shoot at, and finally to two-hundred yards away. He stands and I fire five shots at the board with a white spot on it, and he walks to see it. "Thrice dead middle," he yells, meaning I hit the white spot three of the five shots. "Yer fancier than me men." It is the next day Rogers sets out to prove it. He calls two dozen of the most lubberly and coarse human men in existence, and announces a "contest" for marksman shooting the long rifle.

It is no small wagon-pull of laughing when Rogers proclaims who it is they be shooting against: me. Laughing like swine in a mudpit, they bedaubed me, saying, "Git her a howitzer she cain't hit nothing with no goose gun," and "I taint shooting again no bitch booby!"

"Volunteers?" yells Rogers.

Silence. None of these vile men is doing a contest of marksman against a female, it becomes clear.

"Did I mention the prize reward for this winner?" says Rogers. He be tantalizing these brutes.

Much head-shaking, and I do not know neither.

"Why, 'tis this little creature for one night of yer pleasure," says Rogers, pointing at me.

I be so confounded by this, I cannot speak.

Shouts rise up loud from the gathered circle of lusty lubbers, which all want to shoot now. They be wavering arms and hands to be shooter selected by Rogers.

I says to Rogers, private and standing near, "I cannot do this contest if the booty is me."

He whispers in his brogue, "These men be roused up now, me dear, and if you do not shoot, I cannot vouchsafe yer living through this night in this camp."

Until this very moment I see'd Robert Rogers as me friend and patron; not now. I says, "And if I win this shooting contest which is me prize, Sir?"

Rogers is laughing like a drunken Irishman. "Yer virtue, deary, yer virtue," he says, coarsely.

The men is all still shouting to be named by Rogers and he says, "Where is Rudolf?"

Rudolf is a German Hessian who is training in long rifle and knife-throwing, and he speaks only German and stays by his self, mostly. Camp gossip is Rudolf was a Captain in the German army and is strip'd off to a private for reasons nobody know'd. It is not certain on which side, rebel or British, Rudolf fights, and nobody asks.

"Rudolf is in his tent," a voice says.

"Git Big Rudolf," Rogers orders.

Minutes pass and a man whose only hair on his body is two massively bushy eyebrows walks into the circle with a boy, who tells Rudolf in German what is being done. Rogers explains the contest to the boy who tells Rudolf, who says he will not do a marksman contest with a female. When Rogers tells the boy the prize, at first the boy refuses to tell Big Rudolf and acts embarrassed.

"Tell him or we geld ye," Rogers snarls at the boy, who immediately talks.

Big Rudolf comes alive. His bushy brows wiggle like a caterpillar and he walks over to me, his tongue swishing in his toothless mouth.

He touches me bum, and I slap his large hand away. "I not be yer whore yet, ye nick ninny [simpleton]."

Uproarious laughter fills camp round us.

"A guinea on the bitch," I hear'd a voice say.

Bitch is the worst curse for a woman and I stare this man down with wicked eyes.

Half hour later we stand in a meadow which has two pine trees close together. Rogers orders three white feathers fixed to each tree, and says the shooters will fire from fifty, one hundred, and finally, from one-hundred and fifty yards at the feathers. "The shooter who hits the most feathers wins his prize," says Rogers, and I hear'd the word "his" and I know'd who Rogers wagers on.

Rogers flips a guinea coin and Big Rudolf wins. The Big German tells the boy, "Let the wench shoot first."

I shoulder the long rifle like a trained man, and none of the brutes be laughing. I fire at fifty yards and hit the top feather on the pine tree on the right. I hear'd a lone hoot behind me and it soon falls into silence.

Now Big Rudolf must shoot at the other pine tree. This he does with nonchalance and the top feather vanishes from his pine tree.

"One and one, tie," calls Rogers.

All pace back led by Rogers to the one hundred yard marker.

I reload the long rifle, and stand, aiming at me tiny feather. "Crack," the shot explodes and chips bark off the pine, but the ball misses the middle feather.

Laughing hoots explode.

Inside I moan, and I hear'd a man say, "She's poor at the bigger distance."

Big Rudolf steps up, his chest protruding like he is the King of Prussia. He looks at me and his dirty eyes peer over me body like he just undressed me. He aims and fires – "bang," and the shot rips the middle feather off his pine tree.

"Big Rudolf is two feathers," says Rogers. "Our deary little wench is only one."

These men be dancing round like it is theirselves be shooting to win me.

With rapidity we all step to the one-hundred and fifty yard marker.

I load me long rifle, all the while seeing this ugly vision in me mind of this big bushy-eyed German on top of me body, thrashing about in rapture and me in disgust. Inside I feels sick. I must squint me eyes at the tree to see the white feather, and I aim the rifle.

"Crack!" The tiny white feather disappears. Inside me stomach untightens, and I breathe.

Rudolf struts to his firing spot. Not a sound is heard as he aims and fires . . . and misses.

"Tie, 'tis indeed, a tie," says Rogers, who gives out a public show'g of surprise. "The Missy two; Big Rudolf two."

Grumbling in the gathered men starts because nobody wins a contest in a tie and nobody pays a wager or bet without it being a winner. Rogers know'd this and orders the lubbers quieted. "Who has red rags?" he asks.

This be a sash worn by the order of the Crown to show loyalty, and four men say they do. "Give me two red rags," orders Rogers. He tells the German boy to tell Big Rudolf the contest continues by firing long rifles at red rags tied on the two pine trees."

Big Rudolf says yea to this in German.

I says it is all right, but wonder whether I be having a say in this question at all.

"At two hundred and fifty yards," says Rogers, abruptly.

"Impossible," someone shouts.

"No one shoots that good," says another.

"This is a wench not Apollo with his bow," I hear'd yelled now.

Rogers orders the red rags tied to the pine trees and then steps back to a point being two hundred and fifty yards away from same. He flips a coin and I win.

"I shoot first," I proclaims.

Some brute mutters, "She is as queer as Dick's hatband [she's out of order without knowing.]" I is told later in the world of men, I should let the other man shoot and then see where I stands. I did not know this rule then.

I looks at the pine tree and it is such a long distance from me I cannot see the red rage, just a dark spot. I can feel there is no wind, and I aim the rifle slightly high, thinking of the weight of the ball and how gravity pulls it, and I takes a big breath and holds it in.

"Crack!"

I cannot see if I hit the red rag, and Rogers tells his young Lieutenant by his side to check it.

Moments later, from the Lieutenant: "The rag is burned with a shot!"

I hear'd a few shouts of men, which quickly dies.

Big Rudolf comes up, his long rifle loaded. He laughs at me and says something in German in a muttered breath. Aiming, he fires very manly.

The Lieutenant who step'd wide of the trees, runs and looks at Big Rudolf's red rag. "Miss!" he shouts.

Big Rudolf throws his long rifle on the ground, and muttering vociferously in German, storms off, his boy following, dragging the gun along.

Rogers is laughing in his brogue, and the big bear hugs me. He turns to his men, holding out his hands. A dozen of the brutes walks up and puts guineas in his open palms.

Why the oaf, I thinks, Rogers bets on me.

Smiling, he drops gold coins in me hand, and says, "Yer the best shot on the frontier."

Me head grow'd bigger this day.

This same night I be walking past a campfire of men and is called over by one to sit. It is the first time the men wavers me to the fire, and I sit quietly, me long rifle at me side because we are instructed by Rogers to never leave our weapons in case of a surprise attack. Now Big Rudolf walks up and sits. He sees me and begins speaking in load German, which I do not understand.

"What is he saying?" I ask.

None of the men know'd.

Big Rudolf's boy is not present to ask.

The men be telling me they never see'd any woman or any man hit a red rage at two-hundred and fifty yards and they ask me name so they can tell of it.

"Miss Tabitha," I says. I do not want more said of me self and I git up to leave and I thank the men for asking me to sit with them like this, and they smile and say farewell.

Walking from the campfire I run into Rudolf's German boy.

"Yer master is over at the fire," I tells the boy, "and he talks much and nobody knows what he says, but he talks angry."

"He is angry," the boy says to me, frankly.

"Of losing; I be this way, too, if I lost the contest," I says.

"No," says the boy. "He says the 'bitch cheats.'"

"Cheats?"

"Rudolf says Lieutenant gits pay to say he misses red rag."

"I pay the Lieutenant to lie?"

The boy says yea, it is what Rudolf says.

Who is angry now?

I walks back to the campfire ill-tempered as a hornet. I says to the brutes, "Big Rudolf says I cheated in the contest. He says I pay the Lieutenant to lie and say Big Rudolf misses."

To a man, they agree, "Lieutenant Drew do not cheat!"

I takes me long rifle in me hands, walks over to Big Rudolf who acts surprised I confront same. He looks dead at me and I hits his forehead with the stock of me long gun, hard. He falls back, out like a stiff raccoon.

I says to the boy. "When yer master wakes, tell Big Rudolf this wench bests his self with both ends of this long rifle."

The next morning I gits up early and be vigilant of Big Rudolf's revenge on me, but none comes. Lieutenant Drew, a handsome man younger than me, arrives at me tent. "I hear'd Big Rudolf says I be a liar and cheat," he says to me. "Is it so?" I know'd I should not tell the truth of it, and stay quiet. "So he does," says Lieutenant Drew, figuring me out. "I will git me honor back!"

A code duello of gentleman's honor, I thinks, and runs to tell Robert Rogers. I know'd Big Rudolf is a perfect shot with a pistol, and I do not want the young Lieutenant kill'd. I tells Rogers of this duel which is on its way and he calls a handful of his best regulars to detain Lieutenant Drew, and to escort Big Rudolf, "dead or alive" from the encampment, along with his German servant boy. "Yer much trouble," he says to me. I never know'd what he thinks of me from moment to moment.[29]

◆ ◆ ◆

One morning I grasp a handful of salted game for a repast and takes a walk to the stream where we relieve the night's water. The usual earthen bank of the stream is well used and smells foul, so I walks upstream for a distance to a drier more pleasant spot.

What?

I see a dark-skinned man who sits on the bank, his knees up, and he is reading a book by a tree. In the middle of the wilderness? What a sight. In a forest of all animals is a man by his self who reads a book.

I know'd from hearing Rogers's talk, a white man does not walk towards an Indian without his know'g it, yet the man does not run or look at me. I immediately peer close to his self for knifes or tomahawks and, see'g none, I makes a pleasant time of it.

"What is it, ye reading?" I says, kindly.

"Poetry, Anne Dudley Bradstreet, more to yer point of question," comes back in the freshest voice in the finest ~~King's English I ever hear'd~~, even from Hamilton his self.

---

[29] There should not be, but if there is a reader who doubts a female was able to physically and mentally engage in battle in the 1770s, consider the cases of three women – Sally St. Clair, Anna Marie Lane, and especially, Deborah Sampson Gannett – all about the same age as Agent 355 in their middle twenties or slightly younger when they distinguished themselves as "soldiers" in the Revolutionary War. I qualify the word soldier because women were not allowed to enlist in the Continental Army. Many tried however by disguising themselves as men, some probably to fraudulently collect a "signing" bonus. Some dressed like men and used male names to join because they wanted to fight the British, like Deborah Sampson, whose military service was extraordinary. Tall for a woman of the age and as a member of an elite military unit, she fought in several battles and was wounded. She ultimately received an honorable discharge and years later the Massachusetts town of Sharon built a memorial statue of her. Sally St. Clair also joined the Continental Army using a male name and was only discovered to be female after being prepared for burial when killed in 1782 at the Siege of Savannah. Anna Maria Lane, who later received a disabled veteran's pension of a hundred dollars a year from Virginia, enlisted in the Continental Army along with her husband whom she fought alongside of in several battles, even after she was wounded. Her pension award document states that "in the Revolutionary War [she] performed extraordinary military services at the Battle of Germantown, in the garb, and with the courage of a soldier."

This be a Indian with the Indian taken out, I thinks. (I cannot write it down in this personal diary exactly as fine as he or Hamilton truly speaks, each fine word, I mean, and I asks readers of this diary to please understand this fact.)

"Read a poem for me," I says, sitting without invitation.

He does not flinch. "Upon a Fit of Sickness, 1632" he begins, "written when she was nineteen years."

I cannot believe his perfect word diction.

"Twice ten years old not fully told,
"Since nature gave me breath,
"Me race is run, me thread spun,
"Lo, here is fatal death.
"All men must die, and so must I;
"This cannot be revoked.
"For Adam's sake this word God spake
"When he so high provoked.
"Yet live I shall, this life's but small,
"In place of highest bliss,
"Where I shall have all I can crave,
"No life is like to this."

He reads for a moment longer, finishing the poem, and closes his book, carefully. He looks at me curiously, with big black eyes. "I be not aware Father recruits females."

"Ye read beautiful," says I, suddenly realizing he just utters, "Father." I says, "Father? Father who?"

"Never mind," he says sharp at me.

I do not need more from this man on the topic because he mentions his Father "recruiting" and there is one man and one man only who recruits soldiers for the Rangers and it is Robert Rogers his self. Yet this man is pure Indian.

I learn soon he is of the "Abenakis" tribe.

In weeks which follow, we meet in our secret spot, and he relishes in reading poems to me and I love how he pronounces words so well. One day I asks, "How is it a Indian reads like a scholar from King's College?"

"Father's teachings," he answers, shyly as if not wanting to be overhear'd in the woods.

I let it go; not to plunge a stick in a sleeping bear's nose. I know Rogers is cranial like Hamilton and is skilled in words and writing as he is with throw-axe and in skinning raccoons.

Our poetry readings takes place in our secret spot whence me training is in hiatus – Rogers too liquored to teach us three days straight once. One time he stops his reading of poetry, looks deep at me hair and picks nits [louse eggs] from it, and we is bemused.

"Poetic nits," I says, and he cannot stop laughing at it. I know'd he likes me.

Sometimes he reads his poems at night by a candle he brings along. Screams and growls of animals in dark times were of no bother to this one as he reads unconcerned, though, I gits nervous and miss stanzas and verses. I never cotton wild beasts.

One night I asks what his name is, and he says, "James."[30]

He gives no last name just James. When he finally asks me name, I give the same false name I is know'd by in camp, "Tabitha Baldwin . . . Miss Tabitha." How do I figure out this name? I hear'd a woman by the name of Miss Tabitha and the name of a Mister Baldwin spoken among guests at the social I attend with Alexander Hamilton in New Jersey at the estates of his King's College classmate Robert Troup. Since the days in Rogers's camp it is the name I parade when invited to social celebrations among aristocrats who associate with the British in Philadelphia and New York. In another way of saying it, there does not exist a true Tabitha Baldwin.[31]

---

[30] Of the fight at St. Francis and raids near it by his Rangers, Rogers wrote in his journal: "We had . . . taken twenty of their women and children prisoners, fifteen of whom I let go their own way and five I brought with me, viz. two Indian boys and three Indian girls." I am speculating here but I believe the Indian Agent 355 met on the bank of the stream was one of these "boys." For whatever reason Rogers decided to raise the boy he named "James" himself. The raid on St. Francis happened in 1759, and Agent 355 trained with Rogers in 1775, which could have made him about the same age as Agent 355 if taken by Rogers as a boy. Agent 355 describes him as a "dark-skinned man" not a boy, and from that information, and from what happened later, I am assuming he was in his twenties like her. Robert Rogers's father was born in the early 1700s in Ireland. Robert was one of ten children born to Irish-immigrants James and Mary McFatridge Rogers in Methuen in Massachusetts before the family moved to what is New Hampshire. Robert's brothers James and Richard served in the French and Indian War, James in Rogers's Rangers. After the war, the family moved to Vermont, where members fought for the British in the Revolutionary War.

[31] For no better reason than to put a chuckle in the day of the editor of Agent 355's diary, I conducted a Google search of the name "Tabitha Baldwin" in 2017 and came up with scores and

In these weeks of Tabitha and James on the riverbank, I never once see'd this man in camp. He does not live in camp and I do not know where it is he does. I never asks another soldier about James because I know'd Rogers will learn it, and punish me and James for becoming friends.

On days too hot to sit, read and listen we soak in the cool, flowing stream-water. One day I sees this red, blue and white bead necklace on his bare neck and says to James, "It is a charming adornment."

To which he responds, "Me Mother's."

It looks Indian and I understands.

I be curious why the Indian son of Robert Rogers is not being trained to be a great warrior by his father, and asks finally.

"He says James will never be a warrior."

"Yer body is manly," I says, "and as a Indian it is a natural thing to fight."

"It cannot be so," says he. He goes on to say his Father will not train James in the ways of fighting and using guns and knives.

I is ready to say it is a noble thing for Rogers, if he does not want a son of his to die in battle but to learn poetry and better thinking skills and oratory. Uncommon for a Indian, yet noble.

"He be affright," James says in a low voice.

"Scared? Robert Rogers? Of what?"

James falls silent. I know'd his moods by now, and whenever some matter is a trouble in his mind he does not talk.

I wait and listen to the water in the stream form a whirlpool by a rock. Overhead a bird screeches displeasure of us being close.

"Me." James says it quiet, like telling it into a unfilled space.

---

scores of hits and mentions, including 65 Tabitha Baldwins in the U.S. I also found Tabitha Baldwins in Colonial America, a fact that means once this diary is published, historians will scurry to learn all they possibly can about the era's Tabitha Baldwins in efforts to unmask Agent 355. Ironically, there was even a "Tabitha Baldwin" who applied for membership in the United States Sons of the American Revolution in the 1800s!

"Yer own Father is afraid of ye?" I says. "I do not understand this."

He goes on to tell me Rogers takes James as a boy from his tribe in a raid, and other Indians say Rogers kill'd James's mother in this raid of the same Indian camp. James cries telling me this, and I holds his body close to me for a comfort. "Father is affright. If he trains me to kill, James will kill Father in revenge."

This day ends in complete quietude. At night warm in me fur on the ground in me tent, I think how true. Poetry canst not kill.

Another afternoon Rogers is drunken, the soldiers relax, and I goes to our secret spot and find James a lazy lot. We go swimming in our nakedness as platonically and as carefree as Adam and Eve before the Serpent. In looking at what I was unaccustomed of looking at, I gain knowledge of our compatibility instantly, and one afternoon, as if I bit the Apple me self, I says to James: "Meet tonight and bring a soft coverlet for the damp ground."

It is this very night I creep quickly from me tent, avoiding any noise to disturb the vigilant Rogers, and hurry to the secret spot where James sets a candle aflame, and on the ground is the largest fur bear hide – it is a grizzly's – I ever see'd. He cuddles into it warmly when I walks into the light.

Can a woman attempt the chastity of a man?

I admits it to all readers, forthright, I is the aggressor this night; hadst missing innermost feelings of nights with Hamilton in his bed. I untie me galligaskins [breeches] and lie naked by James, who is startled to see it, outside the stream of water for swimming. I is not a "poxy" as we call whores, nor ever charged with "carnal copulation" or fornication, but this night I puts his hand on me commodity [private part], and I know'd this: sex is instinctual in animals and it is no different with human beings because James performs his task like Adam after the Serpent slithers off. It be his first time. His way is shy, gentle and tender in touching and in lying atop me, careful of his slender bulk on me, and me guessing about our compatibility in the views I see'd when swimming, bears out. I never feels this way previously with Hamilton who is often of sullen spirits and preoccupied with his own needs. Me heart pumps and pounds with love and joy with James and I shakes in his arms and I know'd he shares me feelings because I see'd it in his dark eyes.

This night, if mother ever asks, yea, the answer is he is the man for me for the years ahead. I be in love, agreeably.

On nights that follow this we meet whence practicable on the furry grizzly-hide, and our hearts beat at the same speed.

◆ ◆ ◆

I write down earlier in this diary of wishing never to meet Robert Rogers. I now with hard difficulty present the unsavory story of why. One night late – he stays up all hours of night, drinking and carousing in camp – he comes to me tent, and I hear his rough manner outside, which wakes me. "Have it here," he says, pouring rum in a tin cup, it sloshing on the dirt of the floor in the tent.

"I be tired for early foot-march in the morrow," I says.

"Tis better to march tonight," he says, with a sinister laugh, and he takes and drinks the rum he pours out for me.

I sleep in my breeches, which is camp rule in case of surprise attack, and he pulls the cover off me, and grabs me legs. For a moment, and only a moment, I think of screaming. In the camp of Robert Rogers, Robert Rogers is King and monarch, and not a weakly one like George in London. More to the point for a female like me, what is a woman for, if not fornication and procreation? It is what menfolk say. Screaming me head off will bring naught, and I be so aware of same, I shut me mouth tight. He lustily unties me breeches and pulled them from me body.

I lie in me own suit of skin on me thin fur on the ground, looking up at Rogers.

It is a half-moon night and light sinks into the tent through the door. Corned [drunk], Robert Rogers staggers momentarily from the rum, and unbuttons his leather breeches, and there he stands in the tent light. This is no human man. This be a plowhorse, I says to me self in utter surprise at what I see'd hanging.

"'Tis so pretty, 'tis so fresh," he says, forcing me legs open and lying atop me. "But I not be the first, I know this."

Me brain comes even more alive, and I shiver with a dread thought: James tells his Father this? Of our intimacy? It cannot be.

Then Rogers strikes in me. It is pain like I never feel in me life, and he spends the minutes thrusting his self thus inside me, and it hurts me horrible yet I do not dare utter a baleful sound, for none alive will aid me.

He grunts noises of a wilderness animal devouring its prey. Each utterance sends the fearsome breath of a cow locked in a barn for weeks, a stench I can never forget, from his drooling lips. Tears stream down me face from its vicious painfulness and it takes so long for Rogers to end up where he wants, I think to me self: "He is busy on me, and his head is crazy with lust, and me arms is free. How easy it is for a woman in this state to stick a knife in his fleshy neck. In passion a man is never more vulnerable."

I just write Tabitha Baldwin's Rule No. 1 of self-preservation.

All this night I crave opium for the pain of a cut he leaves inside me, which makes it painful to relieve me self in the morning, and for days. A quotation from me reading sweeps over me. Vice to be hate'd, needs but to be seen.[32]

The next day Rogers is nice to me. Contrition comes when lust leaves, and Rogers is even dumbfoundedly shy around me, but he says nary of word by way of being sorry for his brutality and sexual rape. He never touches me in the same way again, and in days me discomfiture disappears as me body heals.

After Rogers's attack I never see'd James. I visit our secret spot and it lacks James, poetry book, candle, bearskin. James is disappear'd. I be wont to ask Rogers, and fear it does nothing but imperil James. But I remember well what drunken Rogers says to me: "I not be the first, I know this."

---

[32] Her inexact quotation is from "Essay on Man, Epistle II" by Alexander Pope, 1688-1744. The actual quote is: "Vice is a monster of so frightful mien, as to be hated, need but to be seen . . . ."

On the last day of me training, which lasts months, Rogers, presents me with two gifts. One a Navy dagger with a four-inch blade. He is fortunate I do not possess it the awful night! Two, the light dragoon pistol, which I mention I carry under me cape at the Great New York Fire, and kill the young Redcoat. It be unloaded, and a dozen large shots for it, he gives me in a box. Camp rule says all muskets must be loaded and ready. I thinks, Rogers keeps this pistol un-loaded to stop me from killing same for molesting me.

The morning I is to leave camp, I find the poetry book James reads on me fur bed, along with his Mother's red, blue and white bead necklace. Taking these in hand, I runs to our spot to return same and cannot find James for this chore.[33]

Is James his self run off?

On banks of the stream I cry for me lost love. I scream his name up the water and down the stream in the wilderness. The meadow grass is flat where we lain together nights and join'd our bodies as one on the Grizzly skin, and I lie me self alone on the very spot and weep and weep and weep for James. Me sweetheart leaves and I be in torture and torment forever.

Before taking a wagon from the camp to Philadelphia, Robert Rogers says: "Will you take an oath to kill for the King?"

I says I be willing to kill for same.

"Willing?" Rogers is astute, digging out ambiguity in words.

"Yea," I respond, quickly, too quickly.

Rogers gives a hand signal to his regular who carries a finely built wooden box forty-five centimeters long with a tomahawk carved on the top and puts it in the wagon for me. I see'd by the man's labor the box is heavy, indeed.

---

[33] As soon as I read reference to the book and necklace being given by James to Agent 355, I called John Spivey in Setauket to ask if these items were found in the wooden box with the manuscript, and he assured me they were not. "What do you think happened to them?" Spivey asked me. "We will never know for certain, of course, but my learned assumption is James was a true love and these things were probably buried with her."

Rogers looks at me father-like and grins. "Prove your loyalty and go to Philadelphia and kill General Gage."

I be all-a-mort,[34] but contain me rapture of surprise at his words and hide same inside me. Rogers pats the box again, and with his awful, dead serious grin, says, "Kill this bloody general and 'tis yours." He puts his face close to me, and I smells his foul mouth. "Do not end the blackguard, and 'tis box is mine for return. If not returned, 'tis ye in a bigger box."[35] There be required no Irish translator. If I do not assassinate Mister Gage, I is dead me self. And Robert Rogers know'd all the ways of pain to do it.

"I understand," I says.

What a curse on me. Here I be: A Patriot spy working for Alexander Hamilton, close advisor of the general leading the Continental Army against the King; being trained as a Loyalist spy by the head of His Majesty's elite Rogers's Rangers which fights this general leading the fight against the King; and I be bribed by the leader of the Rogers's Rangers to murder the general who is fighting for the King to defeat George Washington.

Betwattled [confused]?

I want to scream, and hide.

Me head fills with vulgarity for Rogers.

1. Back biting villain.

2. Fire prigger [robber who acts friendly].

---

[34] *All-a-mort* is from the works of Shakespeare and means "confounded or struck dumb" by someone's actions or words.

[35] When I read her description of the box I knew it was the exact same wooden box in which John Spivey had found her manuscript. It is about 18 inches long and had a tomahawk engraved on the lid. (Once Agent 355 revealed contents of the box Rogers had given to her, much of what happened in her life afterwards made sense to me.) Of course Agent 355 had no way of knowing of Rogers's bitter animus for General Thomas Gage. They were enemies fighting on the same side. When Rogers was named Governor of Michigan, Gage, who also hated Rogers's good friend, Jeffrey Amherst (Amherst College is named after the town in Massachusetts named after Lord Jeffrey Amherst), plotted against them. Gage, commander of all British forces in North America, intrigued against Rogers and saw him as a social climber who was too sensitive to the Indians (proof his play about Pontiac) while Gage and his aristocratic cronies saw Indians as savages, and not a noble one. Thus Gage had Rogers spied on and worked to find a way to remove him from the Michigan governorship. He finally came up with a way to dump Rogers. It came in an affidavit by Rogers's own secretary who claimed Rogers had threatened to turn Michigan over to the French. Rogers was arrested and charged with treason in 1767. In shackles he was taken to Montreal for trial. Gage's mistake was thinking he could win in a trial in Montreal, where Jeffrey Amherst had powerful friends. With his influence, Rogers was acquitted.

3. Dunghill [a coward].

4. Bastardly gullion [bastard's vile bastard].

5. Jackanapes [ugly little ape].

I be gallied [fatigued like a galley slave]. What is it I gits me self into?

I think of a rhyme from me childhood:

"Look out for thyself,

"And take care of thyself,

"For nobody cares for thee."

Following the excruciating experience of Robert Rogers's wilderness camp, I vanish to lick me wounds, in me head and body. Body humors be unbalanced, and me blood is let twice, which, the surgeon says is a danger not a help.

It is fall of 1775 and I seek no part of this spy'g for Alexander Hamilton, nor of the clowes [rogue] Robert Rogers. I blame Hamilton, who thinks me a gudgeon [person easily imposed on], for me woes.

Then for me immediate unnerving, I learn't General Thomas Gage who Rogers covets to kill, leaves, going back to England in October, and lately is replaced by General William Howe over all Redcoats in the North Americas.

I cannot kill a man across the sea.

But would I kill Gage, could I? Nay. I be rickety, and cannot act upon it. In me sleep I hear'd his words: "Do not end the blackguard, and 'tis box is mine for return. If not returned, 'tis you in a bigger box." It is Rogers in me nightmares, and I fear he is angry and vengeful over me not killing Mister Gage, after he fills me dirty breeches with a kingly sum.

Oh, the box which is so weight'd? Inside is a Lionheart's Ransom of English tokens and Spanish gold. I be a chicken nabob![36] This box contains seven hundred pounds in London bank tokens and gold bullion.[37]

---

[36] The Colonial slang expression "chicken nabob" refers to a person who travels to the East Indies with a fortune of fifty thousand English pounds. The phrase is borrowed from the chicken turtle.

[37] In using the phrase "Lionheart's Ransom" it is assumed Agent 355 means the amount of ransom, about 100,000 pounds sterling, sought for release of King Richard I of England, known as Richard

Heedfully I takes a circumbendibus [roundabout] route from Rogers's Indian camp and visit Setauket for a time, and talks with Anna Strong and Selah, who meets again in December as a delegate to New York provincial congress and the same next year in May. I encourage her, and gift her money for her cherubims [peevish children]. Anna cries in being so blessed and thankful.[38] I must hide in secret the gold bullion, and I risk arrest if it is discover'd on me.[39] I stay a short visit on Long Island.

---

the Lionheart, after being captured by Austria's Leopold V in late-1192 as he returned from a crusade in the Holy Land. The amount of money she found in the box given to her by Robert Rogers, based on some methods of monetary calculation, is estimated to be $107,000, enough for "Tabitha Baldwin" to live on for the rest of her life.

[38] If nothing is certain but one fact after reading Agent 355's diary, it is this: she is a very resourceful and clever woman. A New York newspaper story in 1948 which reported that historian Morton Pennypacker, author of the original *General Washington's Spies*, was writing a second book on the topic, also mentioned Agent 355. The newspaper writer called her "a plucky young woman who took many daring risks for the American cause." Plucky for sure. But what she wasn't is a disambiguator. By mentioning she went to Setauket, which I believe, and then adding that she met and talked with "Anna Strong" there, she might be bamboozling the reader. Obviously if she is visiting Anna Strong she cannot be Anna Strong. I have already expressed the opinion that this is not Mrs. Strong's diary, and I'll happily live with this scholarly decision. However, I add, warning readers, that when it comes to Agent 355, nothing is ever as it seems, never completely true or completely false. (She was a spy, after all.)

[39] Since the first edition of his book, I had to expand this footnote because nothing in this whole saga of John Spivey finding the wooden box with Agent 355's manuscript in it has caused him more headaches than her mention of hiding the gold. Here is the original footnote in the first edition: "The gold paid by Robert Rogers to Tabitha Baldwin (Agent 355) has never been found, and it seems reasonable to assume that over the course of her lifetime she spent it." Obviously the statement was inadequate. A month after the first edition was released, Spivey wrote to me and was livid. "I have had people come to my home all hours and ask if they can look for the gold – inside my house! I've chased them off, but in the past week I have had two attempted break-ins, and have had to alert authorities. The gold is not in the crawl space in my home or any place else. I hired a crew with high-frequency metal detectors to search for the gold in every inch of my home. It came back negative. I didn't give a hoot about the gold itself, I wanted to be able to announce that the GOLD ISN'T HERE! I have done so and still it has not stopped gold-hungry intruders. I petitioned the zoning board of the Town of Brookhaven for permission to install a security system with outdoor closed-circuit cameras. They denied my request on the basis that my home is in the Historic District, and such "modern" apparatus isn't allowed. They threatened me with 15 days in JAIL if I put in the cameras. In a compromise with the town, I hired a full-time security guard for my property (actually three of them)." It was after reading his e-mail that I called Spivey on my cell phone. "You mean you have muscle-bound dudes dressed in army fatigues and carrying nine-millimeter handguns and sporting jackboots on patrol each night?" To this remark, Spivey, always a man with a sense of humor, responded: "No the local zoning didn't allow it. So I dress them in authentic 1776 British redcoat uniforms and they march with Brown Bess muzzle-loaders over their shoulders. Fitting for Setauket." We had a good laugh.

I makes me way south and westerly to a spot I think an Irish Catholic is not to think me at, Pennsylvania; Lancaster, location peopled by Amish and Mennonites, who settled in 1720. I lodge in rooms near the Philadelphia Pike, and a day each week, I help with chores in the large, two-story brick home of Quaker Caleb Cope, a non-combatant, and his wife Mary, and their son John, of twelve years.

What better place to hide from rogue Robert Rogers?

I take tokens from the box and do not require more money, yet I know'd most Quakers be Loyalists and thinks that if I to be a spy, what better place to listen than in the home of Loyalists?

Days after arriving in Lancaster I hear'd of the barracks prison for British troops. Caleb Cope tells me the barracks keeps low ranks of Redcoats. British officers, upon a providential promise of not escaping, can stay at taverns in town, such as George Gibson's who paints a hickory tree on his tavern signage because this town be settled on the site of the Hickory Indians.

In me work for the Cope Family, I meet Lancaster's fine residents. Some be Whigs who stop and argue with Caleb Cope over his support of the King. I also see'd such personages as be on the Lancaster Committee of Correspondence, like Edward Shippen (later father-in-law of Benedict Arnold), Matthias Slough, William Henry and Charles Hall. Cope advises me last year [1774] the Committee of Correspondence meets and both expresses loyalty to the King and denies Parliament's right to tax Colonies. This committee calls "for a close union of all the Anglo-American Colonies to resist oppressive acts of the British Parliament." Cope tells me when word of bloodshed at Lexington and Concord, Massachusetts, reaches Lancaster on a Tuesday, April 25, 1775, it is only two days later at Grape Tavern, the house of Adam Reigart, people meet and then post handbills of defiance of the Parliament, and call to form military companies to defend rights and liberties with their lives and fortunes. From what I see'd of the militia being raised, they look stout boys.[40]

I be happily surprised on a day I arrive at Cope's for me chores, and sees a handsome, British officer in the parlor. He is finer in manner than even Alexander Hamilton, and I do not speak to this gentleman. Caleb Cope is not present to tell me his particulars so I go to me rooms this night without knowing the gentleman's name, yet see'd by his regimentals he is Lieutenant. Two days later I see'd Caleb Cope on the Pike and asks of the young Lieutenant. He tells me tavern owners git proper pay for lodging British officers who be prisoners. Mister Cope says he offers his fine home to the Lieutenant and he accepts, along with another officer. He says the officers be captured by General Montgomery at Fort Saint-Jean in Quebec, Canada, and can walk freely in town on a pledge of not escaping.

It is a cold November, 1775.

♦♦♦

"Lieutenant John André," the stranger says to me the next week upon arrival at Cope's, and his voice is of a gentry cove [gentleman]. I be for a short moment embarrassed because I forgets me false name, Tabitha Baldwin, and hesitates, and I be certain he notices. Then I thinks this is because he believes me shy. He kisses me hand, softly, in welcome.

There is no way to say this and sound good. He is dimber [pretty]. John André is the fairest face I ever encounter not on a woman. A pretty gaze from dark eyes, small mouth for a man and perfect nose. He enjoys talking of his self, and I

[40] In August 1775 an officer described his Pennsylvania men this way: "They are remarkably stout and hardy men; many of them exceeding six feet in height. They are dressed in white frocks or rifle shirts and round hats. These men are remarkable for the accuracy of their aim; striking a mark with great certainty at two hundred yards distance. At a review, a company of them, while on a quick advance, fired their balls into objects of seven inches diameter, at the distance of two hundred and fifty yards. They are now stationed in our lines, and their shot have frequently proved fatal to British officers and soldiers who expose themselves." But everything wasn't rosy, as another officer from Pennsylvania describes an unruly incident in Massachusetts with his men: "They had twice before broken open our guard-house and released their companions who were confined there for small crimes. On Sunday last the adjutant having confined a sergeant for neglect of duty, the men began again, and threatened to take him out. The adjutant seized the principal mutineer and put him in also, and coming to report the matter to the colonel, we were alarmed with a huzzaing, and upon going out, found they had broken open the guardhouse and taken the man out . . . It was in vain to attempt stopping them. . . Sent word to Gen. Washington, who reinforced the guard to five hundred men with bayonets and loaded pieces."

see'd why. He is intelligent and one afternoon speaks to me in French, which is not uncommon, and in German and Italian, which be. He is so talent'd, too, and paints and draws pictures of beautiful things. His voice is like a songbird's, and nights after me chores we sit in the parlor and sing a quiet chaunt [song], as we be in the home of Quakers.

I be vague when he asks about me, saying only me father is a seaman and is gone to his reward and me mother is a "Loyalist and Tory" in New York, where I be among five siblings. None of this is true, but so it be in this spy business.

A favorite of André is Irish conny wabble, which I learned to cook from Robert Rogers by mixing eggs and brandy together. André of French lineage never one for praising anything Irish or Scot, yet he praises the eggs and brandy and asks for same on many occasions, which I makes for his breakfast.

One day I walks into the parlor and Lieutenant André is teaching young John Cope how to draw on paper, and to paint. I remember André telling Caleb Cope this about his son's progress in art, speaking of a "figure" the boy drew with ink: "He must take particular care in forming the features in faces, and in copying hands exactly. He should now and then copy things from the life and then compare the proportions with what prints he may have or what rules he may have remembered. With respect to his shading with Indian ink, the anatomical figure is tolerably well done, but he would find his work smoother and softer were he to lay the shades on more gradually, not blackening the darkest at once but by washing them over repeatedly, and never till the paper is quite dry. The figure is very well drawn."

This same day I peer'd at art paper on a table near André. It is a fine drawing of a British officer, with a pudding face, and I say, "Who is it here?"

"A dear friend, Captain John Graves Simcoe," says André. "It is for yer pleasure." He gives the ink drawing to me.[41]

---

[41] John Graves Simcoe, 1752-1806, was a friend of John André and served as a British army officer in the Revolution, heading the Queen's Rangers. He ultimately achieved the rank of general and, in 1791, was appointed Lieutenant Governor of Upper Canada, where many Loyalist American

"It is fine, I cannot accept," I says.

"In a moment's passing I will draw another," says he.

I takes this fine work to me rooms.

1776

Early in this year I gits word of the death of a friend on Long Island who is a widow and is mother of four children. Quakers Caleb and Mary Cope tell me to go to help these children find homes among families, and I do.

Fighting brigands and British Redcoats is one thing, but fighting the children's kinsman to take a new mouth to feed in fosterage is another kind of war. I ends up giving each of four kin of me dead friend three pounds to take one of her children, and promise another two pounds each the next year. I never hear'd of such uncaring kin, but it is this war which upsets society this way. Me friend's husband dies in 1775 in a rebel militia and these kinsman all be Loyalists. Gold, not blood, is the only flag of truce which crosses these enemy lines.

Faugh! These greedy kin be damned.

At this time I gits a message waiting for me at me uncle's house which says Hamilton wishes to see me, with urgency. For days I ignore this request and work to find the children shelter. But, I know'd I must see Hamilton soon, and travel his way in snow and cold.

At Hamilton's near the city of New York he brags to me of his capture of cannons at a British stockade at New York harbor in August 1775, and says he forms a militia group from friends at King's College.[42]

"refugees" fled following war's end in 1783. Among his achievements in Canada were efforts to abolish slavery in Canada and founding the city of Toronto. He also served in Parliament. In the AMC drama, TURN: Washington's Spies, Simcoe is portrayed as a sadistic villain and murderer whom viewers learned to hate more with each TV episode. However, given real historical events, this portrayal is over-the-top and has been called "character assassination." One thing certain is of all those who fought for the British, Simcoe was one of the most interesting. He even faked being insane once when captured and later released. His memoir published in 1844, *Simcoe's Military Journal, A History of the Operations of a Partisan Corps Called the Queen's Rangers by Lieutenant Colonel J.G. Simcoe, During the War of the American Revolution*, makes for fascinating reading.

"Have you hear'd the glorious news of Boston?" Hamilton asks. I says I be traveling and hear'd nothing of battles and war. "General Howe's abandoning Boston!"

I says, "He surrenders without a fight?"

Hamilton is laughing and slapping his hands together in joy. "Bunker Hill, of course," says Hamilton. "But when His Excellency General Washington put big siege guns from New York on Boston heights, Howe figures he cannot defend it, and says he is leaving."

"Big siege guns from New York?" says I.

"Amazing feat," says Hamilton. "A young officer puts the guns on snow sleds at Fort Ticonderoga and moves eighty cannons and thousands of shot pull'd by oxen to Boston in January. Ends eight years of British rule in the city."

I is laughing and slapping me hands together now, and Hamilton gazes at me, wondering why.

"Henry Knox," I says. "Henry Knox builds these sleds." I then tells Hamilton of Knox and his sled drawings at Rogers's Indian camp. I never see'd Hamilton so much impressed by another man.

On this visit, me and Hamilton find intimacy in his bed, and it takes all of me mental strength to let Hamilton touch me after Rogers's attack on me womanhood, which I do not tell Hamilton of, as he will think less of me for it. In the bed Hamilton tells me this: "Yer beautiful soft body taken to Robert Rogers's camp is now yer beautiful body of muscles and callouses." I takes me arms around his bare chest and squeezes air out of his body in fun. We laugh happy like at King's College in 1774. Me body does not feel this pleasurable since being with James on our spot next to the stream at his father's camp.

James? Where is he gone?

Hamilton tells me Washington wants his skills on his staff as a aide, and he says I can help by still spy'g.

---

[42] Commanding a volunteer force of King's College members Hamilton commandeered twenty-one cannons from the British stockade on Manhattan Island of New York, although there was no real fighting because the stockade was guarded by only a British Royal Navy ship which really could not prevent the raid by his foot-soldiers.

"Alexander," I says, "I cannot do this now. I need time to settle private affairs arising from months at Rogers's." It is a lie, small one, a necessary one.

He agrees.

I do not tell Hamilton Robert Rogers will hunt me down and kill me for not kill'g his enemy, General Gage.

We part, and I say I return in a month.

◆ ◆ ◆

I travel back to Lancaster and take up duties in the home of Caleb and Mary Cope, who I come to cherish.

Again, I see'd John André and we talk as friends do. One evening we be in the parlor and André is writing a letter, and I asks him if it be a letter to a sweetheart?

Nay, he says, no sweetheart presently, and he adds he be engaged years ago.

I asks her particulars.

"Honora Sneyd," he says, and corrects his self, "Honora Edgeworth, she married two years ago."[43]

We spends an hour talking of her qualities, her writing, her kindness and her love of children. André is most praiseworthy of her, and says he remains her loyal friend and servant. Lieutenant André speaks in aristocratic diction, even more so than Hamilton, and he begins reminiscing of Honora Sneyd, and recites what I takes as a letter he once pens from his heart to her. When he completes reciting this, I say, "John André, this be beautiful. Can you write this down for a keepsake for me?"

André is so dear, he says he will do this.

I keeps this note from his hand all these years, and I share it now in this diary, in John André's own words:

"The idea of a clean hearth, and a snug circle round it, form'd by a few sincere friends, transports me. You seem combin'd together against the inclemency of the weather, the

---

[43] Honora Sneyd, 1751-1780, was a minor English writer known more for being friends with writer and poet Anna Seward, who would write an ode to John André after his death. Miss Sneyd married Richard Edgeworth in 1773, his second wife. She was known as an advocate for educating children and was a member of the Lunar Society, a social club of intellectuals including Erasmus Darwin, who wrote a seminal book on evolution, *Zoonomia*, and was grandfather of Charles Darwin. Honora Sneyd ended her engagement with John André because, according to historian Alexander Rose, she believed he lacked "the reasoning mind she required."

hurry, bustle, ceremony, censoriousness, and envy of the World. The purity, the warmth, the kindly influence of fire, to all for whom it is kindled, is a good emblem of the friendship of such amiable minds. Since I cannot be there in reality, pray imagine me with you; admit me to your conversations, think how I wish for the blessing of joining them! Be persuaded that I take part in all your pleasures, in the dear hope, that e'er it be very long, your blazing hearth will burn again for me. Pray Keep me a place; Let the poker, tongs, or shovel, represent me."

Even now, as I write this diary, his words bedazzle me like excess light.

In the parlor André says of me eyes: "Such beautiful eyes I never see'd, as if Cassiopeia's Andromeda's herself." Then he mentions why one as lovely as me is not betrothed, or as he says it to me subject of the "cropping drums"?[44] I say thanks for the flattering words. Then he asks me the same about ever having, as he says it, a "Valentine," and I says I once loved a kind boy and he leaves me.

André says in the most sensitive, caring and loving voice I ever hear'd: "No man should leave one as lovely as ye, Miss Tabitha."

I cherish these words all these years passing.

In the spring Lieutenant André is taken by Continental soldiers to Carlisle, Pennsylvania, sixty miles distant from Lancaster. Our farewells be tender and pleasant and the gracious and chivalrous André presents me a inked sketch of a May flower, and it is exquisite as ye expects from a artist like André, so talented and witty of detail. It is not many weeks which André writes to Caleb Cope to describe his quarters at a stone tavern in Carlisle and asks if young John Cope is ready to continue his art studying under the excellent tutoring of André his self by a journey to Carlisle. Caleb Cope

---

[44] In London military drummers earned money by playing at weddings, and they were called cropping drums.

tells me he is not accepting of it, and writes this to André stating same.

It is months since I arrive in Lancaster, and in autumn I travel to Setauket to attend to a business I cannot mention in this diary lest I reveal me name and family particulars. The business is not the New York fire when I burned the city into dust. Thinking as I write this diary, I remember the business in Setauket like it happens yesterday. I know it saddens and angers me today, all these years later, and it touches me then into a randy [unruly] state. I thinks this is the why of why I crept like a howler in to New York with me compatriot to set it aflame.

It is uncertainty, and I do not know this answer.

On this visit to Setauket I see Anna Strong and talk with Abraham Woodhull, her neighbor, who returns from New York. Before disembarking to Lancaster, I hear'd news of Nathan Hale's hanging for being a spy, and curse the British for it because I know he is a friend of Benjamin Tallmadge, and because, I be a spy me self. I hand me friend Anna money for her children and travel back to Lancaster in November. On the road I thinks: Doing chores in the household of peaceful Quakers, Caleb and Mary Cope, who treat me as a cater cousin [good friend] is restful. Yet I pine for fresh adventures after see'g Anna and Abraham Woodhull in Setauket. The spy for Hamilton inside me blooms to life again.

Upon me return, Caleb Cope says André sends a second letter about his son John's art work and the proposition of tutelage by André. Caleb says it is thought André does not receive his former letter on the matter. It is a common matter for letters to waylay in the post created by King and Queen William and Mary in 1692. Letters when delivered proper go to taverns. We hear'd Congress last year [1775] promises better routes because of the war trouble, but I be doubtful over this.

I volunteer to journey me self to Carlisle for delivery of his vital response in the matter to Lieutenant André. Going to Carlisle is personal business as well as I want to find how me friend is these days in captivity, and secretly learn word from Carlisle Loyalists on British movements.

For the journey to Carlisle sixty miles distant I hire a two-horse, open tumbril [cart] not already requisitioned by the Army and leaves on a sunny, cold November morning to escort Caleb Cope's letter to handsome André.

On the road in a bend, trees blind in all directions. A skinner [highwayman] sneaks from the woods and stops me horses in step. He is fast at it, and I cannot unsling me pistol for defense and kill this vermin.

"Me fine bitch booby what's it to be?" he says, and his musket points at me face. I see'd he is a rouge soldier, using the military word for wench "bitch booby," which I hear'd much in Rogers's camp. "Yer boung [purse] and budget [wallet] and tumbril or this here'n musket ball in yer pretty face?"

His teeth is black and eyes sunk in dark in the two sockets of his skull. I smells his body stench from in the wagon.

"Me pocket book with dollars is in the wagon, sir, hand me down and I fetch it for ye."

He thinks me a lady, and sets the Brown Bess against the wagon wheel, to aid me. I steps off the tumbril and he braces me.

Me feet secure on the dirt, I fast as a lightning crack pulls Rogers's dagger from me winter cape and stabs the rouge in his black eyeball. The blade thrusts down and comes out his cheek. Blood gushes back at me in a spout, and the marauder reels and screams, jumping and fussing, and pounding the dirt like a drunken Indian. I see'd the wound is not fraught with fate and he is not entering death if the blood stops letting. Ugly scarred he will be, as it is. I turns the Brown Bess on the rank rider [highwayman] and says as brutish as Rogers his self, "Git, or I end ye, Beelzebub!"

This devil stumbles like a mad-struck man into the woods, crying and moaning and blasting [cussing] at me every word for whore like "biter" [female ready for sex] he ever know'd.

Packed up I goes quietly on to Carlisle, many hours distant, having cleaned the dagger blade on wet tree leaves aside the muddy road. It is on this lonely journey I thinks I be certain training at Rogers's camp stays with me, because I be thinking what he hath taught. "The blind snake is soon under foot."

◆◆◆

I find lodging in Carlisle and once in me rooms I venture on the outside to find Lieutenant André and deliver Caleb Cope's letter from Lancaster. I find the stone tavern on the corner of Chapel Alley and South Hanover Street and inquire of the Lieutenant. Our meeting is joyous, and he introduces me to his friend and roommate Lieutenant John Despard. To André I be a Tory and Loyalist and he tells me relations in Carlisle is not the same as relations in Lancaster, and he is subject to harassment by townsfolk who hit them with stones and garbage. André says a resident raised a hatchet at his head to show "its agreeable effect on the skull." He tells me the two lost liberty of walking in town and of hunting because of ill-will in town directed at same.[45]

I stay for days in Carlisle because André is me friend, although in a sense he is also me enemy, and I love him as a kindred brother. After he tells of his woe I say the barracks in Lancaster is in disquiet, too, and some British prisoners say they be venting anger by burning the town down.[46]

---

[45] André might not have told Agent 355, or the woman he knew as Tabitha Baldwin, the whole story of how they lost the privilege of hunting up to the six miles from Carlisle, as "long as they wore their uniforms beyond the town limits," according to a favorite story in Carlisle. On a hunt the two officers, André and Despard were seen talking to two Tories, and the local Committee of Safety thereby revoked their privileges. The Tories were arrested and searched, and later imprisoned after letters written in French were found on them. Because André spoke French it was assumed the letters were for him. Contents of the letters were never learned. The situation got so heated against the two British officers that a man identified only as Thompson showed up one night with members of a militia and threatened to lynch André and Despard because they were treated better than the British were treating American prisoners who were "dying by starvation." A Mrs. Ramsey told her husband who knew Thompson to stop him and he did, and the next morning André and Despard sent Mrs. Ramsey a note expressing their thanks "for saving them from the hacking sword of the redoubtable Thompson."

[46] Many British prisoners were confined at the Lancaster barracks, beginning in 1775, including Hessians captured at Trenton in 1776, and after the surrender of British General John Burgoyne at Saratoga in 1777.

Lieutenant André is silent on the matter and knows the situation of the barracks well, and so I asks him what is to be done? He says he does not want wounded to result at the barracks. "I worry they be shot by nervous rebels in miscalculation," he says.

Nervous rebels, I thinks. The name angers me. André sits in a red chair and takes paper to write a verse, and I says: "British dragoons miscalculate as well as Patriots."

"Rebels," he says the word again.

"Human people," I says in correction.

"The human who wields the hatchet at me face?" he says.

"Angry of ransacking Patriot farms by Redcoats."

André looks at me for the longest time, and I be thinking is me colors wavering too awful brightly? He says nastily Carlisle is a town of a "stubborn, illiterate crew called the Scotch-Irish, sticklers for the Covenant . . . . A greasy committee of worsted-stocking knaves." He bucks up, stops his verse, and is not liking what I opine of Redcoats to cry havoc and pillage Patriot homes and farms. "Royal fusiliers kill in battle, not merchants on street corners with petitions of grievance."

"But the King hangs spies," I says.

The Lieutenant looks at me with his dark eyes again, figuring it, and I thinks how beetle-headed [dumb] be me for saying it. I be careless when glimflashy [angry].

"When is this?" says André, who is surprised of this hanging.

At first I stammer, thinking is this right? "Perhaps the hatchet-man is angry over it," I says.

"What spy is this?"

It comes out like in a flood from me. "In September Nathan Hale, a Captain and Patriot, went to the gallows a spy in New York. General William Howe sent him to the hangman near the Dove Tavern."[47]

---

[47] Historian Rose makes a point of writing that Colonel Benjamin Tallmadge had lost some mental acuity at age 80, when in 1834 he wrote a letter to historian Jared Sparks, telling details of his conversation with André as they rode together, following the arrest of André for spying in 1780. Colonel Tallmadge told Sparks that Andre said he knew about Nathan Hale's hanging but "you surly do not consider his case and mine alike." Tallmadge said he told André the two cases were "precisely similar, and similar will be your fate." Historian Rose contends that "Tallmadge's aged

The name General Howe stirs a bellicose smile from André who folds his hands on his lap, and knows why. "If he is a soldier and is reconnoitering out of uniform he is considered an illegal combatant, a spy," he says with a confident raise of his head. "But I did not know the case of Captain Hale. There be a exchange of prisoners considered, and I will inquire when transferred."[48]

It is the first I hear'd of a release, and it covers me with sadness. As we talk for minutes more I think of what I did not reveal to John André. It is what Abraham Woodhull tells me of Nathan Hale's capture. It makes me body shiver with fear in thinking of it. It is Robert Rogers his self who catches Captain Hale in New York.

When the end of 1776 is come, Lieutenant John André is traded for Continental Army prisoners back to British lines. Yet it is not to be the last I see'd of me beautiful John André.[49]

1777

In this year I return to the arms of Alexander Hamilton, who can protect me from Robert Rogers and his madness and wrath and who, upon me reaching Hamilton after these

---

memory was playing him tricks." His proof is that "Andre, being a prisoner in Pennsylvania when Hale was hanged, was hardly likely to have 'remembered' the details of an obscure spy in New York." Hale was an "obscure spy" because only two American newspapers mentioned his death during the war. Oddly, a news item about his hanging also appeared on the front page of *The Edinburgh Evening Courant* in Scotland on December 2, 1776, although Hale's name was not given. Agent 355 says in her diary she told Andre about Hale in 1776. If her recounting were fact then at age 80, Colonel Tallmadge's mind was not "playing him tricks." It would mean his conversation with André is spot on. The Continental Army was told of Hale's execution on the night after his hanging when a British aide to British General Howe met with Colonial officers about exchanging prisoners. Washington aide Captain Tench Tilghman later wrote: "General Howe hanged a Captain of ours belonging to Knowlton's Rangers who went into New York to make discoveries. I don't see why we should not make retaliation." Perhaps this letter to Washington sealed the fate of John André.

[48] After this remark isn't it ironic that four years later André would be out of uniform and caught as a "spy" after obtaining maps of defenses and other information about West Point from turncoat Benedict Arnold. As a result he was tried by a military tribunal and found guilty of spying "under a feigned name and a disguised habit" and ought to "suffer death." Agent 355 provides details on this event later in her diary.

[49] Agent 355 is obviously smitten with the dashing John André. What she doesn't know is that André might have found himself a girlfriend in Carlisle, but the relationship ended when he was transferred.

many months of hiding by the waters of the Sound, he says to me, "We believed ye truly dead all these months."

I is dead inside me. *Cave, Cave, Deus videt! Absit.* I cannot continue and tell in this diary of this personal event which haunts me forever. It remains between me self and God.[50]

◆ ◆ ◆

Walking at night toward Hamilton's house where he waits for me, I sense but do not see a presence behind me. It is strange, I do not hear steps or noises just a sense of a presence, a lurker. I puts me hand up into me cape, unhooks the pistol off its sling, and turns quickly, pointing it to fire.

Nothing but bare night!

The air is cool and the road wet from a light rain and I smell a foul odor – probably dog dung in the street. I hide the pistol, and walks on. Now again, I feel it. By God, it is behind me! I turn and see'd a dark hulk in a hooded cape duck away down a alley. It is someone or thing follow'g me!

---

[50] *Cave, cave, Deus videt!* is an Ecclesiastical Latin phrase in the Roman Catholic Church meaning, "Beware, beware, God sees!" The word *Absit* is Latin for "God save me." This is the first indication that Agent 355 might be Catholic, which was rare in the Thirteen Colonies. Only one and half percent of two-and-half million white people were Catholic at the time in predominately Protestant America. Additionally, by using these phrases of religious anguish she signals she is greatly troubled by something she isn't telling us. To be sure historians love to gossip, and by this I mean "speculate" about people long dead who have no rights of redress in libel courts. Maligning an historical figure, no matter how beloved by his countrymen, as a "crook," "homosexual" or "drunkard" is in the historian's everyday playbook. It is in this spirit of speculation that I submit this: Agent 355 was likely with child in "autumn 1776" when she left the Quaker home of Caleb Cope for Setauket "to attend to a business I cannot mention here in this diary lest I reveal me name and family particulars." We know she is sexually active at this time, she has relations with Rogers's Indian son James and is raped by Rogers himself, and she had been the lover of Alexander Hamilton. Because she leaves a time gap in her diary, from the time she last sees John André in Carlisle, Pennsylvania in November 1776, to the time she reappears and works for Caleb Brewster in the spring of 1777, it isn't unreasonable to speculate she might have been carrying a baby during some of these months. Her remark that her business in Setauket "I cannot mention" because it might reveal her identity is revealing, nonetheless. Agent 355 is worldly enough to know that she can be identified through the names of any children she might have. It is possible that she ventured to New York City where prostitution was rampant and had an abortion. Abortion by using abortifacients to cause a miscarriage were common in North America from 1600 to 1900. After the Revolutionary War, however, abortion was frowned upon and found unacceptable by many. Her statement, "I am dead inside me" is enigmatic and might harken back to Rogers's brutal sexual attack. But it also might relate to a lost child. Getting an abortion certainly would have caused her to write "God save me" in Latin. Of course Agent 355 might have just as well gone to Setauket to bury her mother, and did not disclose the fact because it might identify her by way of some future snoop looking up death dates on headstones in Setauket.

Fear grips me. Is it Robert Rogers here to kill me? It is a large thing which hides. Then, I thinks: Big Rudolf? Is it this Hessian stealthily seeking vengeance on me for besting his rifle shots?

In fast-steps I come to Hamilton's, and tells of me being follow'd. He immediately calls a guard, and sends same down the street to check alleys. Half hour later the guard returns and talks privately to Hamilton. "He says there is nothing to be concerned with," Hamilton tells me. Then he says, "Perhaps there is no caped phantom at all, just imaginary, in yer mind. Perhaps this 'Shadow Man' is none but stress, mental pressure and want of rest."

"Nay," I says. "A lurker is out for me."

Hamilton smiles the way he does when he does not want to talk or hear further of a matter, and we talk about spy'g British sails on the Sound. He is on Washington's staff and His Excellency needs "eyes and ears" on Long Island. After two days of intimacy, I be on me way to the Sound.

At the Long Island Sound I send messages to Hamilton, telling same of British ships sailing up and down the brackish waters, and I know'd he is telling Washington for his own plans. Then for a month Caleb Brewster who pilots three stout whaleboats at Black Rock harbor in Connecticut hires me for a sentry, as me long rifle shooting is deadly from two-hundred running paces and he is being harassed by Loyalists privateering against rebels. I do not tell Caleb of me spy'g actions for Hamilton; and as he calls me an article [handsome girl] and his bleached mort [female with a fair-complexion], I like Caleb Brewster for he is fearless and of honesty; though, lo, he is no Hamilton in appearance.

Oar'd by eight seaworthy lads, his whaleboat is long, easy and fast in the seas and slips in and out of shallows in the Sound, never with a splash or hubbub [noise]. On one night in the dark, we ferry into a shallow which Caleb says a man waits with a wagon of goods for Patriots in Long Island. A musket shot roars from the bank and kills this oarsman dead, outright. Caleb shouts, "Lumpers" [thieves who lurk at wharfs to steal goods off ships], and I takes up the long rifle.

Robert Rogers is a brigand yet he is a skilled fighter and trains me to watch the flash of the muzzle and quickly return a shot "into it." In the dark I fire at the powder flame. We hear'd a gurgling, ugly noise on the bank. The lumper rolls in the dirt, and is in the process of becoming dead.

Caleb says he ne'er seen such firing by a woman, and asks where I learn't such fine work with the long rifle.

"Me father," I lies.

"A democratic man," says he.

This wagon of goods for Patriots is load'd and we sets out again.

On this stay on Long Island I see'd me friend Anna and learn't how stories about a person's peculiar skills gits around, and it be a warning of how easy it becomes for an enemy spy hunter to watch me. Says Anna as we sits in her house and takes a fine tea: "Caleb Brewster says yer the best long rifle shot he ever see'd. How can this be?"

"Caleb Brewster talks too much," I says, and me answer is a surprise to her. Me problem is I cannot lie and tell Anna I be show'd how to fire the long rifle by me father. Anna Strong know'd the truth about me father and family. So I says: "Anna yer a sister to me and for this I love ye; because I love ye I cannot say today, maybe later in years when life is becalm'd."

From this day forward I know'd me friend Anna Strong is well aware I be involved in secrets which I cannot share, and I know'd she prays I be working for Washington's Army and not the King's.

◆◆◆

The French King Louis XVI wants to support the Colonies in the fight against his enemy King George, but cannot announce it, and so, Hamilton tells me, one Pierre August Caron de Beaumarchais, confidante of the French Monarch, is secretly sending war goods to America by way of the West Indies.

These goods is on three ships, *Le Romain, La Seine and L'Amphitrite*, and ready for sail from port of Le Havre in northern France. In confidence Hamilton says goods is: 200 field pieces, 300,000 muskets, 100 tons of powder and ammunition, 3,000 tents, and blankets and shoes for 30,000 men of the Continental Army, along with buttons, needles and threads, knives and raw wool and silk.

"What glorious bounty," I says.

"We desperately need this armament to win," Hamilton tells me. "But, a mercenary spy for King George in the West Indies by the name of Guillory has learn't of this voyage and is on his way to New York to sell the same information to British General William Howe. He looks seriously at me, and says: "Hamilton's spies must stop him." Hamilton never tells me who his other spies be, only Milligan and his slave boy is known to me.

"How will I know this Guillory?"

"His repulsiveness of appearance. The Frenchman has a scar face and spends much time in brothels," is all Hamilton can say of Guillory. His good looks turn solemn. "Lacking Beaumarchais's supplies for the army," he says, "our effort comes to naught but chains and the King's gallows."

I is sent back to the decrepit and foul section of New York. What of the irony? I takes rooms in the district of which I burnt out. What a city in distress. What hath I wrought?

It is stench'd with the odor of a piss-pot. The very air breathe'd feels burnt and reeks with disease. I gits sick of it in two days thence arriving. It is hard to see building after building and dwelling after dwelling burnt into black ash-heaps and streets thick with besmeared, marshy soot. Many of 30,000 citizenry is in the cold and others long move'd away. Inhabitants, all these months afterwards, tack sheets of canvas to the remnants of charred walls and standing chimneys and form a city of tents to be bivouacked for shelter. Children run in stink'g mud and this sea of wet ash makes permanent stains on children who become blotch'd in blackness, both of face and feet.

It is in truth as I once hear'd a "city of canvas" of old ship's sails and inside is pots boil'g for heat. Yet in this wicked place call'd "Holy Ground" by Trinity Church and King's College I must stay because it is a full covey [collection of whores] in which the spy of the name Guillory will land and seek a bat or a crack [whores of varying social standing].

◆ ◆ ◆

On the third night of me vile vigil, it happens again, which curls the hairs at the nape of me neck. For a long distance I walk on a narrow street and hear faint footsteps behind me, and when I turn, nothing is behind me to see. This happens twice more, and the last time I turns, I sees this shadow in a hood and cape jump into the alcove of a doorway. This thing is tall and big, and I slips me pistol from its sling under me cape, ready to wreak close-fire hell on it. Renew'd terror shudders in me: is it Robert Rogers, here to collect his box of gold or me life in payment? No, I thinks; if it is Rogers I be dead this instant. Yet, if this is Rogers I be no match for his kill'g skills. Or, I thinks again: Big Rudolf? No. I best this man in a rifle contest and hits his head. A man does not kill for such as this.

Then I thinks, is it the spy Guillory his self track'g me! No, this cannot be. How does he know of me?

I turn back and hurry on me way. At a corner I meets two watchmen on patrol, and tells these well-behaved gentlemen a sneakish man in a hood and cape who follows me in the dark is down this narrow street, and these watchmen go in search of same in a strut. I gits in haste back to me rooms unmolested, and keeps the pistol, dagger and tomahawk close, and waits. I name this caped phantom what Hamilton calls it, "The Shadow Man." Is it what Hamilton also calls it? Me mind playing tricks in the dark?

I cannot go astray with fear. Hamilton's mission for me is find Guillory, and this I must. The next night I hire three brute tars [ex-British sailors] to hunt public houses for the man I say is so scarred of face he is hard to rest eyes upon, and I pay them two guineas for each as they say Congress dollars be worthless. These tars walk the district keeping a sharp eye out for a week, and one evening me short brute named Angus comes to me rooms, and says: "He's at Smith's Tavern at the bloody Wharf, and talk'n' to a bat [low-class whore]."

"Show me," I says, and takes me cape. The pistol is on its sling; dagger in me smicket [smock].

"Balsam?" says Angus. He holds out a dirty hand, the grubber.

"Money's in your pocket when I sees his scarred face, cove."

♦♦♦

In the window of the tavern I sees Guillory by his marked, ugly face. He is boisterous and coarse and moving about wickedly inside from rum, and I watch for a time. Outside I sees a stout man who is the town bull [pimp or whoremaster] and he waits for his wench inside to settle on whoring business with Guillory. I says to the bull pander: "Three guineas and fifteen shillings to call out the bunter [low-class prostitute]."

"What sauce box [bold person] is this?" he asks, and pokes his face into me.

"Ye one who puts money in yer pocket," I says, and shows the money for his eyes to see.

It is more than he sees in months.

I looks the bull in the eye. "I want the Good Man [vigorous fornicator], for me self."

The town bulls laughs at me lusty countenance.

"He be yers," he says, and I pays the coinage.

The town bull goes inside the tavern and tells his wench to leave, and tells Guillory, "The best wench for ten shillings waits outside for his pleasurement."

I sees Guillory pay the town bull and in minutes he greedily guzzles his grog and stands outside, looking me over with his eyes and hands, like'g what he is see'g. "Yer a fine crack [whore]," he says in English accented in thick French. He smells the aroma around me, and it is scented with spice and lavender and he says, "Sweetest of the ladies."

He talks with his face close to me and I know'd he is Guillory. I talk pleasantries, and ask if we can meet tomorrow, too, and he says he cannot. "Why," I says. "Ye be a Good Man."

"Business," is all he says.

Guess-work is he has not contacted British officers at this time about the coming of Beaumarchais's three ships of war goods, yet might on the morrow. I thinks to me self, should I git his secrets, or send his body to its demise, as Hamilton orders. Me task is to stop Guillory from telling his secret about Beaumarchais's ships, and I already know'd what he knows.

Guillory points round the corner.

"Nay," says I. "This is the whore of fine gentlemen and this one is no alley wench."

I say I have rooms and Madeira with brandy and rum, and a bed as soft as a loft of hay which is the scent of rose pedals.

His ugly face makes a ugly, lusty grin.

We walk from the Wharf to the rooms. He is full of keen desire and he touches me arse on the stairs to the rooms and laughs. Inside I pour rum, and his rough hand is on my breast and he drinks in lavish gulps.

"Take off yer breeches, Good Man," I says, and I hides Roger's dagger beneath the linen sheets. I lays me self on the bed and pulls up my cotton smicket, show'g me private self.

"*Non*," he says. He pulls me off the bed and slams me against the wall.

"Do not harrow me like a wolf is in yer stomach [monstrous appetite], Sir," I says. I be out of breath. He slips his whore's pipe [penis] inside me with a jolt to me body, and starts thrusting up me against the wall. It sounds like a cannonade, and a picture hung on the wall falls in a crash on the floor.

"This will not do, Sir," I shouts. "A British captain is in the rooms next, and he will be ireful of waking."

"Which?" says Guillory, stopping his racket?

I make up a name, and wiggle from his grip. "André, Captain André, an important and weighty Royal officer," I says.

"Wake this Captain, I want to speak," Guillory says. "Wake this man!"

"I be mistaken, Sir," I says, trying to step out of a hole I slide in. "This Captain returns at ten." Guillory looks for his timepiece, and closes it. "Say," I invites him to the bed, and pulls up me smicket for unfulfilled desire. "I need a Good Man."

He removes his shirt, takes a long drink of rum and lays on top of me on the bed. Soon he is thrusting his self in me with lascivious grunting, his head on fire with lust, muttering words of able seamen I never hear'd a fore. Me left arm is bound by his right hand, and his left arm is hard around me torso, and he squeezes me so muscular me chest is unable to breathe. I screech a wench's utterance and he thinks I be ecstatic by his manhood. Beneath the coverlet, in stealthy motion I takes the dagger tightly into me right hand. His eyes are closed and his nose and chin dig into me breasts and drivel leaks from his mouth on me pink skin.

Swift as the bite of a rattlesnake, I plunge the knife deep into the side of his rouse'd vein neck. It cuts so far inside his throat, the hilt is stop'd by the flesh of his neck. Guillory screams, and jumps up, gasping for breath. Hot blood from his throat streams onto me naked skin and falls on the bed. His eyes stare wide as a cup of black tea and he grips me throat with his large hands, and I feels fingers of his right hand claw and cut into me smooth skin, and, in a blink of an eye, Guillory collapses his body on me, a deadweight.

Soaked is me in his viscid blood.

I hear a knock on the door, and a voice.

"Mistress!"

It is Angus, me swamper and whiddler [informer], say'g he hear'd screams. "So what is it?" he shouts.

I look in Guillory's clothes and find papers in French, and put them in my cape, and open the door for Angus, who is trepid at what he sees. The body is bloody on the bed, and me self is full of his blood. "The cove tried to hush [murder] me," I says, the dagger in me hand.

Brainless, Angus runs harum scarum from the rooms.

I clean the knife on the bed, gits me cape and pistol, and in minutes be light-heeled [running] me self away from the dead body of this bloody spy.

♦♦♦

Hamilton is pleased with me and with his self when the papers from Guillory be turned into English, and he tells me it is all written: the war goods, ships' names, date of sail from La Havre. "Yer the best," he says, and uses me real name.

Later, it is April 1777 and I be in Portsmouth, New Hampshire with Hamilton when Beaumarchais's three vessels land and unload war goods for the His Excellency's Continental Army.

When yer business is spy'g, it is not know'd if it is of weight in the bigger sense of a war. So this is what I read years later, and I writes it down as I reads it: "The ammunition, guns, and the complete military equipment for twenty-five thousand men, amounting in value to no less than five million French livres, were landed on the American coast. The joy of the colonists knew no bounds, for by this time they were not only practically destitute of all munitions of war, but they were quite without means of securing them. The timely arrival of these immense cargoes permitted the vigorous carrying on of the campaign of 1777 which ended in the decisive victory of Saratoga."[51]

Me spy'g makes a difference.

I need time to wash the spy Guillory's blood off me body in a figurative sense, and I tells Hamilton I must return to Setauket. In Setauket I see'd a much-troubled Anna Strong. "They threaten to take Selah," she tells me of her husband because he served as a delegate to the provincial congress in

---

[51] Incredibly British General John Burgoyne surrendered nearly 6,000 men to General Washington at the battle of Saratoga, New York, which, when adding another 1,300 British soldiers killed and wounded in the months prior to the battle, it amounted to 25 percent of all British troops in America at the time. It was a devastating loss in October, 1777. It had two major impacts which changed the rebellion markedly. First it was the first major victory for the Continental Army and went a long way in convincing Americans they could actually win this war against the much strong mother country. After Saratoga volunteers enlisting in militias and regular army increased many fold. In addition and of larger significance, the victory convinced the French king to openly support the colonials, ending the need for Beaumarchais's secret shipments of war goods to America, although these also continued. Agent 355 laments that she never knew if her espionage really helped the war effort in the "bigger" sense. There is no question that her act of stopping spy Guillory from informing the British Royal Navy of Beaumarchais's vessels was very significant.

New York in 1775 and 1776. "They have ghastly prison ships at Wallabout Bay where the only way you leave is in a coffin."

I tells Anna of me condolences over the death, murder by the British really, of her kin Brigadier General Nathaniel Woodhull last September [1776], and she swears profanely at the British for stab'g the general with a sword many times for refuse'g to say "God save the King" on his capture. The General's wife is daughter of Anna's step-mother's sister. "I know'd the murder of his cousin, the General, is what boils inside Abraham Woodhull against the British," I tell her, and Anna says to me, "Abraham loved the General as we all did."

Anna is the only person in Setauket who know'd I be doing something secret, and she is wise and never asks me of what I be doing. She see'd the small red mark on me neck from Guillory's powerful fingers and she raises a smile at me, and I sees what it is which makes her animated, and I says, "I be Frenchified by a passionate top diver [lover of women]."

Anna shrieks with laughter.

I know'd she thinks I be couple'd with a French soldier because I say I be "Frenchified," and I leave it thus. In the spy'g trade I be learning the less which is said of it, even to a dear friend, is wisest.

Before I leave I tells Anna I be paid for me work and I give her twenty guineas for her children.

"I cannot take this," she says in protest.

"If Selah is taken, yer children be require'g it," I says, mindful of British General Howe's edict of putting any person who even sneezes like a rebel in gaol [jail].

She accepts the money, and hugs me.

This money is not from Hamilton, but from Robert Rogers's box of gold. Bestowing this gift to her children puts a warmth in me, which is need'd at this time of this woman's young life. It be all I can say.

Then Anna takes out a small cask of Madeira wine, and pours a cup for each, and we toast "our families and ancestors," the "United Colonies," the "Congress" and "His Excellency General Washington." Finally, I say, "And to our feminine friendship! May we drink again when older and freer."

With it, Anna weeps.

She know'd the danger of me endeavors.

Two nights later I see'd me Uncle in Setauket with me Aunt. Me Uncle be asking why is it his niece is away all these times. I can see his anger build up, and finally he says, if I be attach'd to the "rebel cause" I be no kin of his. Me Uncle is a strict Loyalist to the King, and says he know'd I be friends of Alexander Hamilton and asks me about "this skelm [scoundrel]."

I hast not seen Mister Hamilton since Yale College, I lies, and do not know his activities.

"He is a traitor to his King," says me Uncle.

"They be shooting traitors and hanging them on chains as examples to be avoid'd, is what I see'd," I says of being in New York these last years.

"Doing what at?" he insists.

"Cook for a regiment of General Howe," I lies again. Spy'g on yer mentally damaged King is what I want to say, but hold me self fast.

"A sensible trade, cook'g for the fine gentleman, Viscount Howe," says he.

I hold out me open hand of gold guineas. "General Howe pays good," I says. I see'd me Aunt's eyes in surprise at the abundance of coinage. "Take it, ten guineas," says I.

Me Uncle says nay; me aunt takes it.

"Any news from Howe's camp on the war?" asks me Uncle.

"I cook and do not listen," says I.

"We hear'd General Washington's army is supplied by the French King's ships," says me Uncle, and his face turns a sour look. "The bloody . . . ." Me Aunt instantly scolds me Uncle for swear'g, and he continues, "From France the Continental Army gits cannons and muskets and powder to carry on this rebellion, and this war might go on years because of it."

Inside I swell with pride in killing Guillory.

"Before I forget," me Aunt says, remember'g, "Stephen Kent comes by to see you months ago, on his way to Georgia."

"To Georgia? All the way from Setauket?" I says.

Me Uncle speaks a hint of pride in his voice. "Stephen's gone to join Colonel Thomas Brown's King's Rangers which is beating the tar out of the rebels in the Southern Colonies."

I remember fondly Stephen Kent. His memory fills me mind pleasantly, and I recall the morning he oars his father's fishing skiff into the choppy waters of the Sound. We is both teens, and we decides to let the boat drift of its own will as if there be not a care in the world but git'g songs right in the hymnal.

Lying with our bare feet up and catching the warm breeze, Stephen says, "Where'd we go if we drift forever?"

"Where do ye want to go?"

"Constantinople."

"How do ye spell it?" I asks.

Stephen says he does not know.

"Cannot go if ye cannot spell it."

"You spell it," he says.

"It is not me which wants to go there."

"Where is ye drifting to, then?" he says, talking into the sky.

"Black Rock."

"That is nothing; it is just across the Sound." He sounds frustrated with me.

"It is why I go to it," I says. "It is doable and I can spell it."

Stephen uses me real name and says he thinks I can be a hard personage to figure out.

"I be pragmatical, that is all."

He raises his head, and looks at me funny.

So I spells it out – "p-r-a-g-m-a-t-i-c-a-l."

"Girls," Stephen mutters.

Now a large white and gray osprey flies low over us in the skiff, and we both jump up to watch it. On this clear, sunny day we stand in the boat in the gently rolling water, watching this osprey dive feet-first into the black water, lift'g a fish out with his talons.

I clap me hands for the tenacious bird.

Suddenly, something hits the skiff and it nearly swamps, and Stephen loses his balance and falls into the cold water.

He shouts like he cannot swim and is splashing round.

I know'd he is a perfect fish in the water, and I know'd this by swimming in the Sound with Stephen many times. I laughs at his antics in the sea. Now I looks at Stephen and his eyes grow wide open and he stares at something in the water behind me and points and splashes, seriously.

I turns. "Aha," I yells.

It is the tail of a giant whale feet away from me. The animal makes a big splash and I falls in the skiff so I not be toss'd in the sea. "He is a humpback," yells Stephen from the water. He swims to the skiff and I help Stephen into the boat. In awe we watch this humpback swim by, and Stephen figures this whale brushed the skiff, plunging his body overboard. Now we sees a whaleboat with sixteen oarsmen rowing like they be returning home from two years at sea, chasing the whale. Standing at the bow is a stout-chested sailor with a harpoon aimed at the humpback, and I screams, "They be kill'g this whale!"

"They be whalers, they kill whales, don't they," says Stephen.

"Not this particular whale. Besides, how can anybody kill?"

I takes the oars and tells Stephen to stay still. I row with all me strength and stamina and put the skiff in between the whalers and the humpback. All this time the harpoons man and oarsmen be shouting profanities, and saying they be harpooning me instead, and I do not care. The harpoons man cannot get a good toss at the whale because me skiff is in the way. His spear is made with a blade wide like a flat spoon and is so sharp a man can shave his beard off with it, and I know'd it would takes me head right off.

Amidst the yelling of profanities, the big mottled black fish dive'd, and the giant white of his tail slaps the sea with a thunder of sound, and the whaleboat oarsmen wait for this massive animal to splash up and out of the water again so they can chase and kill it. The giant creature never does.

Aye, aye, me whale is at the bottom of the Sound, safe.

All this time Stephen hides in the skiff, afraid to show these rough sailors his face. I stand up in the boat and takes me hat off and wavers it like the ensign of the winner in a battle. "A bloody female," I hear'd one shout in jesting disgust. The whole bunch of crewmen begins to laugh because they must be thinking they be bested by a mere girl, of all lives and lubbers. I turns the skiff to return to shore, and Stephen comes close to me.

"Ye be a grand girl, too," he says, with pride, and he kisses me mouth long enough to feel his lips, which be warm.

Until this day, I never been kissed a fore.

For a moment as I sit with me Uncle and Aunt, me mind sticks on "how can anybody kill," which is what I tells Stephen in the skiff that day. I think of spy Guillory. I must be in a trace because suddenly me Aunt is uttering me real name and asking me if I be ill.

"Nay," I says, waking and coming to me senses.

"We mention Stephen Kent who is gone to join Colonel Brown to fight in Georgia," says me Aunt, looking at me like I be certainly sick.

"Stephen," I says. "A handsome boy who kissed me on his father's skiff out on the Sound."

Me Aunt looks surprise'd.

"Just one time," I says to settle her mind.

"He is sweet on ye, still," she says. "I know'd this when Stephen asks about ye so politely."

The sentiment makes me heart smile.

"The Sons of Liberty tarred and feathered him," says me Uncle.

"Stephen?" I says quickly.

"Old Colonel Brown," he says. "The Sons burn'd off toes from his feet to git his pledge and old Colonel Brown still curses them and keeps his Loyalty for his King. Young Stephen Kent is in good hands with Colonel Brown against these rebels."

I stay to share a meal, and listen to me Uncle talk of neighbors who harass his family Loyalty to his king and country, and, finally, I say I must go, and kiss them both good-bye.

◆◆◆

It be June 1777 and Hamilton, advising General Washington, says to me: "I will kidnap a British General, and we need yer help."

I thinks I just murdered a British spy and now yer seeking me to kidnap a General? Like I be a glutton for buggery? But I says, "How is me service to be done?"

"He is a whore-monger," says Hamilton, his beautiful blue eyes light on me in a big smile.

Moral virtue is distant to a spy.

So, I sets out on this journey.

The General is garrisoned on a farm in Rhode Island when I arrive, expressing me self as a Loyalist wife whose husband deserts me for the Pennsylvania militias, and the General takes his pity on me. Soon, I begins washing the General's clothes and cooking meals for his officers. In a week I sleep in the General's apartment, first with him and second, after it is done, with his aide in his rooms, a young Major. The General perspires a plentitude in bed and his foul odor is unpleasantness. In this farmhouse I hear much from this General, Richard Prescott, of movements of Redcoats in Rhode Island for Hamilton's ears.

When I cook for officers, complaints of Generals is plentiful. One is General William Howe's decision to invade Pennsylvania rather than join General Burgoyne's Northern Army at Saratoga, which the officers complain, causes Burgoyne's surrender to "the blackguard" Washington, and these British officers call Howe a "Tallywags" [man's testicles]. These traitorous complaints is conduct'd in quiet, yet I hears them all.

It is why women make perfect spies: men thinks we be stupid in military matters, which is untruth, particularly of me after much time with Robert Rogers, who knows fighting better than His Excellency Washington his self.

One week Hamilton sends me a contact, a Anglican Reverend know'd to General Prescott, and this Reverend picks up me information in code for Hamilton. To wit: He sleeps without a guard outside his rooms and at the house, in which a quarrelsome landlord lives, only one sentinel is post'd outside. This be like walking into a schoolhouse.

It is not long when Lieutenant-Colonel William Barton of the Rhode Island Militia is task'd with taking the General.

On July 10, 1777, this is what I see'd at General Prescott's farmhouse at midnight.

After Colonel Barton withal forty men land a oar-craft a mile from the General's quarters, he takes his men to a safe distance from the house. Colonel Barton and a Negro, the pilot of the oar-craft, and a second soldier walks towards the house, and the lonesome sentinel sees the Colonel and hails him to stop.[52]

"I come for the rebel prisoners," Colonel Barton says to his guard, and moves closer in the dark. A second time the sentinel orders a halt, and says the Colonel needs a counter-sign. Colonel Barton walks closer and says he hath no counter-sign and is come for prisoners. The bold Colonel walks up to the sentinel's bayonet, punches it aside and seizes him. "Be silent," Colonel Barton says, "or it is instant death."

If only the whole body of the British army is taken thus!

The rest of his men surround the house, and the Negro called "Prince" and Colonel Barton forces the door open. Colonel Barton and the Negro enter. Inside the farmhouse is the quarrelsome landlord and he says "nay" and is shaking his head such and will not say the direction of the General's apartment. I know it yet cannot say; Colonel Barton is not told I spy for Hamilton.

Colonel Barton says the landlord will die where he stands if he will not soften his resolve, which he soon does.

---

[52] Agent 355's use of "Negro" to describe a dark-skinned person was prevalent at the time. Even black writers in describing other African-Americans at the time used Negro. The editor has left Agent 355's use of "Negro" untouched. She could have just as well used the word "black." In examining the entomology of the word "black" to describe a person's ethnicity or race we learn that black connoting a "dark-skinned person, African" was used in 1620. Black as a color is from Old English.

They discover the General's bedroom door locked. "Prince" instantly thrusts his beetle head through the panel door and seizes the General in bed in his nightgown.

They seize the young Major in his bedclothes, too.

The Negro is the first militia man who is not a white man I see'd in a fight with the British, and it is done good, and I thinks why is it persons in Virginia say no to Negroes in the army ranks. Many Negroes fight in militias, so I say what is the difference in it?[53]

The flaw in this perfect kidnap plan is me.

Hamilton tells me not to reveal me self as a spy to Colonel Barton. "Leave her," says the Colonel, and he takes General Prescott. I is left in the house with the landlord who is bound up. I gits me clothes and follow the Colonel and his men at a great distance. They is like a night wraith. They is all gone on the oar-boats when I gits to the shore's water.

British ships sulk in all shapes in the waters and mope around me.

"Halt in position," comes from behind me.

I do not possess my dagger or pistol this time and turns and shows me self prettily to three Redcoats.

"What business it is?" the shortest Redcoat says.

"I be taken by raiders who capture General Prescott and they surrender me here," I lie, convincingly. "Miss Tabitha

---

[53] Even while Washington and his inner circle tried to keep the ongoing bitter arguments between leaders in the Northern Colonies and the Southern Colonials over the issue of blacks serving in the Continental Army contained, this female spy of the time is very aware of it. Not only did the South not want blacks in its army brigades it surely didn't want to give them guns. This rift got so bad that the British tried to exploit it by encouraging blacks to enlist in the King's army, and many did. Still, many, many more African-Americans served with distinction in both the French and Indian War and the Revolutionary War. These black soldiers were overlooked by historians until 1890 when Joseph T. Wilson, a black war hero of the American Civil War, published The Black Phalanx, which told their stories and bestowed the honor and praise they deserved. By the way, Colonel Barton was rewarded for bravery in General Prescott's abduction. As author of The Black Phalanx wrote in 1890: "Congress voted Col. Barton a magnificent sword, but the real captor of Gen. Prescott, so far as known, received nothing." The black soldier "Prince" has been identified as Jack Sisson, 1743-1821. Colonel Barton also got a Fort named after him in Rhode Island, and its earthworks still exist today. Beginning in 1778, all Northern colonies enlisted African-Americans, which amounted to 5,000 blacks or five percent of the Continental Army. Agent 355 didn't mention why the Americans wanted to abduct General Prescott. The reason is they wanted a high-ranking British officer to exchange for Major General Charles Lee, who had beaten back a British attempt to take Charleston, S.C. in 1776 and was later captured by the British. This exchange, General Prescott for General Lee, took place in 1778.

Baldwin," I say and curtsy, "General's cook and maidservant."

They locks me in a room in the farmhouse and say a British Colonel travels to investigate seizure of General Prescott, and tells me they will catch and kill his kidnappers. When he arrives I know'd this Colonel is a mean cuss. And when they takes me from the room I see the landlord talking with the Colonel. Then a Redcoat brings in the Anglican clergyman who carries the secret message to Hamilton.

"Ye be a rebel spy, Miss Tabitha Baldwin," says the Colonel. "You will go to Newport for interrogation by the Generals."

I thinks it is me time to befriend Nathan Hale in Heaven.

They binds me hands with twine, and I be placed in a wagon, and made the charge of a young British Lieutenant who I see'd and know'd thinks I be a lovely little thing to gaze upon.

We starts our travel to Newport and me demise. On this troubled journey the Lieutenant tells me of his family in London and how it is fruitless for rebels in the Colonies to continue being traitors to the King, to which he says, "God save the King." He looks at me, serious. "Ye say it!"

"God save the King," I says, without hesitation. I know'd General Nathaniel Woodhull dies by not saying it, and I be untroubled with lying.

We journey a short ways. I thinks about Nathan Hale as we pass a tall oak, and I dream of General Howe's hangman's toss of the rope over the bough and the noose falls around me young neck, and is tight, and I weep.[54] The young Lieutenant asks me what is wrong in me and I says, "Yer home is beautiful, I long to be in London."

He smiles in kindness at me.

Hours and hours in the wagon and I says a stop is needed for personal micturition, and I see'd he does not understand this, and I point me bound hands at me self where the body forks, and he stops the wagon. I ask to free-

---

[54] Actually it would have been rare for Agent 355 to have been hanged for spying because such punishments were reserved for men, and besides, the male chauvinists of the time viewed women as more of a nuisance than a threat.

bound me hands and he says nay, and I says for defecation and cleansing with leaves on the ground. He gits out of the wagon and helps me down. He takes his musket from the wagon. He cuts the twine, and me wrists hurt red. "Flee and I will be forced to kill ye," says the Lieutenant. "Stay in sight."

This is me precise plan, I thinks.

I walks ten steps, stops and ducks, and he observes. Wavering me hand so the Lieutenant turns his self for modesty and decency sake, and his answer is will not do it. I lifts me smicket full and the breeze is cool on me nakedness, and he takes notice of me. Like men he is not cool to it, and is lustful in his heart. Finishing, I step towards the wagon and lifts the smicket and says let us lie and rest, and the Lieutenant stows his Brown Bess in the wagon. He steps to me, his face like a chopping [lusty] boy for his trollop [slutty woman]. I lay on the ground of soft greens and he pulls off his boots and breeches.

Just then I jumps and kicks his ballocks [testicles] as hard as the strength and wrath ever mustered in me. He squeals like a penned swine and bends his body, and I throttle his throat with me clenched fist and the lusty lamb falls, retching. I gits the musket by the wagon. "Git to the woods," I says, "or this Brown Bess makes ye a bloody eunuch."

The Lieutenant takes his breeches and reaches for his black boots, and I say, nay, leave the boots and run, which he instantly does. In the wagon I bolt, and in days I secure a place with a rebel boat's man who takes me to safe harbors, not ready to meet Nathan Hale.

1778

In May 1778 I be smuggled into British Philadelphia on a task from Hamilton, who recruits, as I report a fore, a spy by the name of Hercules Milligan, a Hamilton friend and his New York tailor, a man who outfits British officers in his establishment and keeps ears in the direction of their talk.

Mister Milligan talks to friends who sneaks me into Philadelphia occupied by British with no suspicion.[55]

It is all a spy scheme.

Hamilton, George Washington's trusting aide, has His Excellency pen a letter of introduction to his good friend Benjamin Chew in Philadelphia about me by the name of "Mary Fletcher" of the prominent Fletcher Family, and says I be the fine daughter of the New York family of his acquaintance and prays Benjamin Chew "will offer me courtesy of safety and succor." I makes his acquaintance and stays at his fine mansion and meets his daughters, among them, Peggy, 17, and Sarah, who is me age and soon becomes me fine acquaintance and friend.

Hamilton's plan is bearing fruit because I be asked to attend the festivities of General Howe's embarking to England on May 18. This event is a name I cannot say and will not try, yet it is the biggest party of British army, Royal Navy, patricians and finest families in Philadelphia history, all gathered as one.[56] On the day of this farewell banquet for General Howe which is a afternoon gala, I wear'd a gown as full and lovely as any off a ship from Paris. Because Hamilton is concerned that I might be know'd to British prisoners from Lancaster and Carlisle who won release, he order'd a long and beautiful Rocco French wig of black hair for me to wear in disguise. It is up high and flows down curls at the ears. In this hair I fail at being me, and looks like a bourgeoisie personage of Paris affluency. I be mentally certain I will not be know'd by anybody present.

---

[55] Hamilton recruit Milligan, time and again, funneled information to Robert Townsend and the Culper Spy Ring. Mulligan's clothing store near Townsend's business was popular with members of the British military.

[56] The elaborate party was called a "*Mischianza*," which is the Italian word "*mescolanza*," meaning medley. It was the climax of the city's social season, and Agent 355 is right, the city had never seen anything as spectacular as this event in the Colonial era or any other era. She mentions women dressed up like peacocks in plume and men attended in their finery and shining shoe-buckles. She was struck by this because at the time colonies boycotted English goods and many groups supported the effort by refusing to wear anything from England. Some women went so bold as to stop serving tea – quite a revolutionary act! One popular poem at the time went: "Wear none but your own country linen; of economy boast. Let your pride be the most; to show clothes of your make and spinning." It is fact, however, that most items boycotted by patriots were of a luxury nature, such as wine, fine textiles, silver buttons, diamonds, clocks and watches and jewelry. This greatly impacted shop owners handling such goods.

In fashion at this grand party, among the beautiful women there be a great deal of dress and much swallow-tail, and, for the gracious gentlemen, they be in exquisite cravat. I suspects the ban on import of British fabric and jewelry is broke by each personage who walks in foppish attire at this spree [party of pleasure]. Carriages arrive and we travel to Knight's Wharf on the Delaware River in the city, and form a regatta of boats with flowers and banners and we float down the waters south to Walnut Grove of Joseph Wharton, a prominent merchant, thence to a field for jousting and games.

Then a salute of ships' guns by British man-of-wars rings out for General Howe, and triumphal arches, surmounted by effigies of Fame, display inscriptions commemorating glories of the departing General.[57] Jousting matches of knights who fight for damsels who be ladies of fine Loyalist families, sweet lovely young Peggy Chew is one, commence. At this joust, there is a glorious long parade with the medieval tournament, wherein the seven silk-clad knights of the Blended Rose and seven of the Burning Mountain did amicably break lances in honor of the fourteen blooming damsels in Turkish costume. Following this is plays with harlequins in costumes rich in the spender of colors. The banquet party of four hundred guests is a pleasant gleam of silver and china and a lovely disposition of fruit and flowers and a fine, delicious procession of dishes, marched on and marshalled off, for the requisite number of hours and during which I eat I know'd not what and taste wine and nibbles of confectionery. This meal finished with coffee, and all waited on by twenty-four Africans wearing turbans and sashes. After dinner and before dancing I see this stately young man astride a gallant white steed. He is in full headdress and color-fabrics and I ask Sarah Chew "who is this fine gentleman of royal bearing?"

"Ye did not see this beautiful man at the joust?" she asks, and I say I did not. "I see ye be taken, and so is everybody," she says, pleasantly, and is smiling at me like I be see'g this

---

[57] General Sir Henry Clinton took General William Howe's place as commander-in-chief of British forces in North America.

dreamy gentleman as a frequenter [suitor]. She says, "I be so happy and thrilled to introduce ye, Mary Fletcher of New York." She laughs a girl laugh so endearing. "Yet yer competition for his admiration is the whole body of this city of ladies, and Miss Margaret Shippen, in particular, the prettiest of all."[58]

"His name, if it pleases ye?" I says.

"No other than Captain John André, of course."[59]

---

[58] Future wife of Benedict Arnold.

[59] Captain John André was stationed in Philadelphia without Agent 355's knowledge and was in charge of providing "entertainment" for British soldiers "wintering" in the city. Along with Captain John Montresor, an engineer, André planned the whole elaborate show. I thought it interesting to have André himself describe part of extravaganza, the jousts between knights fighting for the honor of their ladies. His lavish prose reads like a magazine's coverage of a fashion show. In a letter to young Peggy Chew, the "damsel" saved by the gallantry of "knight" André in the mock jousting, he wrote this "intimate" account on June 2, 1778: "The Ladies selected from the foremost in youth, beauty and fashion were habited in fancy dresses. They wore gauze Turbans spangled and edged with gold or Silver, on the right Side a veil of the same kind hung as low as the waist and the left side of the Turban was enriched with pearl and tassels of gold or Silver and crested with a feather. The dress was of the polonaise Kind and of white Silk with long sleeves, the Sashes which were worn round the waist and were tied with a large bow on the left side hung very low and were trimmed spangled and fringed according to the Colors of the Knight . . . Seven white Knights on Horses of that Color entered the Quadrangle from the left proceeded by a Herald and three Trumpets. Their device which the Herald bore on his Coat and with which the Trumpet banners were blazon'd was a white and red rose with their Stalks entwined. The motto was "we droop when separate." themselves. Of the blended Rose, their dress was that worn in the time of Henry the 4th of France: The Vest was of white Satin, the upper part of the Sleeves made very full but of pink confined within a row of straps of white satin laced with Silver upon a black edging. The Trunk Hose were exceeding wide and of the same kind with the shoulder-part of the Sleeves. A large pink scarf fastened on the right shoulder with a white bow crossed the Breast. A pink and white Sword belt laced with black and Silver girded the waist. Pink bows with fringe were fastened to the Knees, and a wide buff leather boot hung carelessly round the ankles: The Hat of white satin with a narrow brim and high crown, was turned up in front and enlivened by red white and black plumes . . . The Horses were caparisoned with the same Colors. The Esquires of which the chief Knights had two and the other Knights one were in a pink Spanish dress with white mantles and sashes . . . The first defiance was then pronounced in the following Words, "The Knights of the Blended Rose, by me their Herald proclaim and assert, that the Ladies of the Blended Rose, excel in Wit, Beauty and every Accomplishment, those of the whole world, and, should any Knight be so hardy as to dispute or deny it, they are ready to enter the lists with them and maintain their assertions, by deeds of Arms, according to the laws of ancient Chivalry" . . . Seven Black Knights now appeared within the Quadrangle. They were in black Satin contrasted with orange and laced with gold according to the style of dress of the White Knights; Their Horses were black and likewise ornamented with black and orange. The Esquires were in orange colored silk with black mantles and Trimmings: They styled themselves Knights of the Burning Mountain, and their Herald had that device on his Coat with the motto, "I burn forever." They shewed themselves to contend for the superior Worth of the Ladies of the burning Mountain and to disprove the Assertion of the White Knights. After having moved in procession round the Quadrangle, exchanged a Salute with their Antagonists, and paid their Compliment to the distinguished group of Spectators, they took their place opposite to the White Knights . . . Their defiance was nearly in the following words. The Knights of the Burning Mountain enter these lists not to contend with words, but to disprove by deeds of Arms the

My insides git sick immediately with illness, and I says to Sarah Chew the excuse of the *bourdaloues* [to urinate]. I in a hurry leaves the festival grounds. Now I thinks I see'd André looking at me from his horse. The black wig and curls hides me yet I know he admires me eyes in Lancaster and says same to me many times, and I worry he know'd me eyes from sight. In the darkness, I run from the party like running from Rogers.

I cannot let John André see me!

I flee to my rooms in the city for transport to New York and I thinks of what John might say if he recognized me eyes: "A chore-woman named Tabitha Baldwin one day in the house of Quaker Caleb Cope and, by all surprise, ye be a young lady named Mary Fletcher of fine society and taste, hosted by a Loyalist family in Philadelphia on the next. And wearing a disguise by changing yer appearance with black curls. A spy like Nathan Hale. Off to the three-legged mare [gallows] with her!"

Oh, the shame.

The dagger Rogers lays in me hands in the camp days is not with me in Philadelphia. It is certain if it were, the Great War would be won this day because every British General, Admiral and bloody back soldier in North America turns out for this grand party in Philadelphia. I, dagger in ready, could kill each and every Redcoat in existence there at this festival, but for the want of me dagger. To witness: in front of me,

---

vainglorious assertions of the Knights of the blended Rose and to shew that the Ladies of the burning Mountain as far excel all others in Charms as the Knights themselves surpass all others in prowess . . . The Signal for the Charge was next sounded [and] with great rapidity and dexterity, each Knights Spear appeared to be shivered against his Antagonist. The Charge back again was immediate and with the pistol, which was fired in passing, the other pistol being produced, a third Charge was made; The Knights then drew their Swords and rode again at each other striking as they passed. The Whole now advanced against each other at once and closed, each Knight to his adversary, fighting hand to hand, and circling rounds to direct their blow, till on a Signal they desisted to admit of a Single Combat between the Chiefs. These whilst fighting furiously, were parted by the interposition of the Judges of the Field, who doubtless deemed the Ladies so fair and the Knights so brave that it wou'd have been impious to decide in favor of either. The Knights of both colors thus reconciled by a happy compromise formed in one Line at the bottom of the Field, alternately a black and a white champion, and advanced in Line to salute the witnesses of their Feats; they then filed so as each to ride by his Opponent, and being preceded by their Trumpets and Heralds and attended by their Esquires moved in procession to martial music [and] formed themselves on either side of the avenue leading to the next; The Company passed between them towards the house and were saluted by Each Knight as they came opposite to him."

only paces off, is General William Howe, his brother of Royal Navy Admiral Richard Howe and General Henry Clinton and all of the aide-de-camps sucking the monkey [drinking liquor] all night and git'g boosey, corned and nazy [drunk]. They all be easy kills for want of me dagger.

◆ ◆ ◆

Because of John André's celebration roads of Philadelphia is fill'd with Redcoats and Loyalists and I be smuggled by a henchman of Hercules Milligan to Christ Church, a church with a tall spire and rooms off the main congregation hall. It is here in a room I first see'd Robert Morris, a pleasant man of his mid-forties who tells me I is a beautiful young woman, words of which I never hear'd since falling in love with young James Rogers at his father's Indian camp. Mister Morris tells me a story of a Sons of Liberty plot to blow up His Majesty's ships in dock, and never know'd if it is carried out. It concern'd large kegs filled with gun powder which they float on the Delaware and hit British ships and sink same.[60]

I like Mister Morris. He not handsome like John André who any available woman would love and respect, but Robert Morris is smart, mostly of money matters, and like André he carries a manner of aristocratic certitude and grace. Morris is kind to me and we git intimate and, in doing this, I learn't he is a man of fierce passion. After a two weeks of this, the henchman of Hercules Milligan comes to Christ Church and says it is time to smuggle me as fast as a barrel of grog back to New York, and we leave; I never git time to say farewell to Robert Morris, which makes me sad.

In New York I is inform'd to see Alexander Hamilton, and I know it is to be a abusive scolding of me failure in Philadelphia to dagger to death every General in the King's

---

[60] This so-called "Battle of the Kegs" took place in January 1778 and involved the Sons of Liberty filling barrels with gun powder and floating them down the Delaware River in hopes of hitting and sinking British ships of war at the Philadelphia wharf. These keg "mines," designed by a Yale College graduate, were spotted on the river and fired upon by British ships, exploding many. It caused quite a ruckus and many people gathered in the winter cold to watch the "battle," with some making fun of the situation because it looked like the Royal Navy's gunners were shooting at floating garbage. Unfortunately, it has been written, two "curious" boys were killed by exploding kegs. In 1777 powder-filled kegs sank a British barge, killing four sailors.

army. It never happen'd. I tell Hamilton I be recognized in me black wig by a British officer I know'd in Lancaster, and this smart man I meets in Philadelphia by the name of Robert Morris save'd me from arrest and worse. I tell Hamilton Mister Morris is the smartest man I ever talk to of money, coinage and banks, and Hamilton says he will look him up one day. But now, he says, General Washington wants all spies to stop sending Hamilton information (he is naming another officer in charge of spies). Hamilton then tells me of a task tonight in New Jersey.

Tonight?

I ask Hamilton if time is there to "sog me dew beaters" [soak her feet]?

"One of them," he says, and laughs Hamilton's way.

He says General Sir Henry Clinton is moving his army from Philadelphia, and says I will git information of strength, arms and things equipped.

"Aye," I says, being quippy, "and I walk in to Sir Henry's midst like the King's Mother?"

"Like a fine woman merchant and peddler," says Hamilton. "In a cart of wares of gold and silver buttons, and British textiles and watches and jewelry, needles and threads, combs and knives and fifty jars of sweet molasses. All stolen from the warehouse of a patriot merchant guilty of hoarding illicit goods."

"Me a King's army camp follower?"

"A peddler," says he. "Tell me a selling pitch."

A moan comes instead.

It is worse this night.

Hamilton orders me hair shorn short like a sheep's, and says I will tell British this lie: I be punished by a Patriot mob for being a Loyalist.[61] Looking more a boy than a girl in hours, the peddler's cart of goods and the spy by the name of Mary Fletcher of New York is aboard a small, swift boat and moving along the shores of New Jersey. The next days the sun is the hottest all year and rain is soaking the fields when

---

[61] Cutting a woman's hair short was a form of punishment normally carried out by the military, which rarely ever punished females with harsher punishments.

I be stopped in me cart by Redcoats.[62] "General Clinton bars peddlers," the British officer says. "Turn this round."

"And deny yer boys these'n fine goods," says I.

"How do we know ye is not a 'Molly Pitcher' from the rebels?" he says.[63]

I spew spit on the dirt. "Rebels burn me husband to death in Pennsylvania," says I. "Hate these rebel dogs!"

A Redcoat steps forward and says to the officer. "Sir, she wears the red rag of protection from the King's oath, and she seems harmless, suitable. Let us see her peddler's wares, if it is yer pleasure."[64]

Seeing a chance, I takes a handful of silver buttons from the cart and says, "What mother wants a son to march to battle without fine trimmings as these?" I shows the buttons and they shines now in the sun, with the rain gone. Three Redcoats gather and takes a look. "How 'bout a jar of sweet West Indies molasses for yer sweetheart?" A haver of bewitching charm, I be.

I is allowed to follow the British soldiers and to sell to all takers, most of them young Redcoats and Scots in kilts. In three days all jars of molasses is gone from the cart, and all silver buttons. In days I see two wings of the British army, and note the 37th and 44th Regiments. The left wing of 8,000 British soldiers, grenadiers, Scots under command of Lord Cornwallis is at Monmouth Courthouse on the road from Allentown; the right wing of Hessians under General Knyphausen is beyond the courthouse on the road to

---

[62] In a letter home British General Clinton said it was "96" degrees "in the shade." It was also rainy and the humidity must have been stifling for the troops on both sides.

[63] "Molly Pitcher" was a common name given to Patriot woman who carried pails of water to clean cannons during battles. Interestingly, in the battle of Monmouth and in the Battle of Fort Washington two "Molly Pitchers" took over firing cannons when male gunners were killed and wounded. One was Margaret Cochran Corbin, 1751-1800, a nurse who was with her gunner husband John Corbin when he was killed at Fort Washington by Hessians in November 1776. Witnesses say she began loading, aiming and firing the cannon herself after he fell. She was wounded in the same battle, and became the first woman to be awarded a military pension by Congress.

[64] After the British took control of New York, residents were called in to take a loyalty oath to the King. Once a resident pledged allegiance he was required to wear a red sash or rag to show his support publicly. Problem was that once word about wearing red rags got around many people wore them, including Patriots to fool the British. It appears that Agent 355 had picked up on this rouse and wore a "red rag" to Monmouth to spy on the British.

Middletown, and General Clinton is amount with its 7,000 men. I note the British and Germans carry bayonets and the Scots broadswords. I count ten field cannons and two large guns.[65] Washington is afoot, word in camp is, and I plan to escape to his lines.

On the fourth day with the British army it rains so they cannot march and General Clinton orders encampment at the Monmouth Courthouse. The air is wet to breathe, and sight is gone this night. It is this time fate frowns on me, harder than any soaking from Heaven. From the wet dark a officer's shinning boots step to me peddler's wagon, and I be under it, and he says, "Peddler, Miss Mary Fletcher, I be told ye possess fine English watches, and I be in need of one."

I know'd I hear'd such as this elegant gentleman's voice a fore, and me thinks it is the officer that buy'd five jars of molasses and the last of the silver buttons, and I says, "Watches, the finest of watches from London," and I leant me head from under the cart.

Me heart stops beating with a gasp.

In the dark is the face of Captain John André. His surprised declarative is "Tabitha Baldwin! What happened to your beautiful hair?" John André, wonderful John André. His worry is me head is shorn. Not why is yer name Mary Fletcher and not Tabitha Baldwin? Or where is it you git such goods and what is yer business in the King's brigade? Or, what spy papers do ye have in yer wagon? (I do not say these things but keep same in me mind.)

He invites me to his tent, and I tells André a lie of being in Lancaster when the barracks prisoners riot, and the rebels say I help'd prisoners, and punish me by disfiguring me hair in disgrace. I tells him rebels keep me head shorn as example to Loyalists. I leave weeks ago, I tell him, with help of Caleb Cope and Quakers who grant me cart and wares to sell to git me to me family in New York.

"Me poor Miss Tabitha," says André. He holds me hand, and is tender. He asks why I be Mary Fletcher, and I say the rebels say they will kill Tabitha Baldwin if I is a betrayer

---

[65] The "large guns" were likely five-and-a-half inch Howitzers. These guns were mobile and had an effective range of about 750 yards, firing bombs or cannon balls.

again, and by selling banned goods this way, I must use the false name of Mary Fletcher. "It is too dangerous for ye here," says André, "rebels march this way." He tells me he will have me escorted towards Allentown in the morning. I leave the next day and a Redcoat rides with me cart, and before this I give me friend André a gift.

"A watch," he says, much pleased, and offers payment for same, and I says nay to it.

It is not the English watch he seeks but one made by French watchmaker Pierre August Caron de Beaumarchais,[66] who I meets months ago at New Hampshire, and who presents the watch to me with Hamilton.

Captain John André holds the watch and kisses me hand.

Thusly I go, a Redcoat astride his horse in lead of the cart going towards Philadelphia, which the British abandon'd to take New York. A ways on the road and shots ring, and the Redcoat falls from his mount dead in the road. Two raiders arm'd with new French muskets run at me from trees and I know'd they is Continental Army jagers [sharpshooters] and I raise me arms to show I be having no pistol.

"Git from the wagon," one with no teeth says, and I do as he orders.

Another says to me, "Troy wench!" and slaps me.

"Take me to His Excellency!" I demand.

"Oh, a blowen [whore of a gentleman]," says he.

I is forced to say what I never say, and I shout it with spittle on me cheek it is so shrill. "I be a spy for General Washington and unless ye take me to His Excellency in this moment in time, he will hang ye in the fork of yon live-oak or marshal a gunning line for ye if this battle is lost because he lacks me information on General Clinton's strength and equipment."

They looks nervous, and the two parley amongst themselves.

---

[66] Pierre August Caron de Beaumarchais was not only the savior who delivered the weapons used in the Battle of Saratoga, he was a talented playwright who penned the French comedy *"Le Barbier de Séville,"* which inspired the famous opera of the same name. He was also renowned as a master watchmaker.

"If I not be a rebel spy why is it I say take me to General Washington?"

Sometimes men is stupes [stupid].

Now I see'd the one with no teeth is winning this quarrel, and the other soldier gits their horses and the one says to me, "Mount the horse-flesh and try to run I shoot ye in the back." I git on the dead Redcoat's horse and we move in a leaping gait to Washington, who hears the count for Clinton's army and details. I is told after the fight His Excellency order'd added men into battle at the Monmouth Courthouse and farm fields and equip'd his men with bayonets when he learn't it from me.[67]

In camp I see Hamilton, and he says his horse is shot out from beneath his self in the fighting. He tells me as a confidante, Washington is taking his spies away to form a new group in Setauket, Long Island. "A land," Hamilton says, "which is well known to ye."

Me only regret in the Battle of Monmouth, as I write this diary today, is that I ever helped kidnap General Richard Prescott in Rhode Island to be exchanged for General Charles Lee.[68]

---

[67] The Battle of Monmouth was a draw between the armies and after the first day's fighting on June 28, 1778, losses to the Americans numbered 362, while the British loss was given at 416. Washington's own account states that his men buried 245 British dead on the battlefield, and estimated that the number of British dead and wounded at around 1,200. Many deaths were caused by sunstroke from the heat, including Washington's horse. The battle ended after one day when the British lit bright fires to make Washington think they were spending the night and instead fled in the darkness.

[68] Agent 355, because she was there with Washington (and Hamilton) at the Battle of Monmouth, knew about the treachery of Washington's General Charles Lee. The account of his traitorous acts at this battle was immanently told by historian John Fiske in his wonderfully detailed history, *The American Revolution*, published in 1891. "Sunday, the 28th of June, was a day of fiery heat. Early in the morning [General Sir Henry] Clinton moved cautiously. [General Wilhelm von] Knyphausen [commander of the German Hessians] made all haste forward on the Middletown road, and the left wing followed till it had passed more than a mile beyond Monmouth Courthouse, when it found itself outflanked on the north by the American columns. Lee had advanced from Freehold church by the main road, crossing two deep ravines upon causeways; and now, while his left wing was folding about [General Charles] Cornwallis on the north, occupying superior ground, his center, under [Colonel Anthony] Wayne, was close behind, and his right, under [General Marquis de] Lafayette, had already passed the Courthouse, and was threatening the other end of the British line on the south. Cornwallis instantly changed front to meet the danger on the north, and a detachment was thrown down the road toward the Courthouse to check Lafayette. The British position was one of peril, but the behavior of the American commander [Lee] now became very extraordinary. When Wayne was beginning his attack, he was ordered by Lee to hold back and simply make a feint, as the main attack was to be made in another quarter. While Wayne was

Many years gone by and André is oft in me mind. This day of me giving the watch in camp, he takes pity on me, with me shorn head and me selling wares. I depart the camp on his order and his man takes me to safety from battle because John André is a friend, with heart of an artist; he be gentle, kind, and allows me to escape the British, his British camp, with suspicion of me being a Patriot spy. André know'd his own spies wear peddler's dress in Continental Army camps. Tabitha Baldwin is rebel spy, he thinks, I know'd it. He must. But, gentle John André lets me take leave. It is why I cry for André today late in life. A soul

---

wondering at this, the British troops coming down the road were seen directing their march so as to come between Wayne and Lafayette. It would be easy to check them, but the marquis had no sooner started than Lee ordered him back, murmuring about its being impossible to stand against British soldiers. Lafayette's suspicions were now aroused, and he sent a dispatch in all haste to Washington . . . The army was bewildered. Fighting had hardly begun, but their position was obviously so good that the failure to make prompt use of it suggested some unknown danger. One of the divisions on the left was now ordered back by Lee, and the others, seeing this retrograde movement, and understanding it as the prelude to a general retreat, began likewise to fall back. All thus retreated, though without flurry or disorder, to the high ground just east of the second ravine which they had crossed in their advance. All the advantage of their offensive movement was thus thrown away without a struggle . . . To the amazement of everybody, Lee ordered the retreat to be continued across the marshy ravine. As they crowded upon the causeway the ranks began to fall into disorder. Many sank exhausted from the heat. No one could tell from what they were fleeing . . . They hurried on, with increasing disorder, till they approached the brink of the westerly ravine, where their craven commander [Lee] met Washington riding up. The men who then beheld Washington's face and listened to his outburst of wrath could never forget it for the rest of their lives. It was one of those moments that live in tradition. People of today, who know nothing else about Charles Lee, think of him vaguely as the man whom Washington upbraided at Monmouth . . . Not many words were wasted. Leaving the traitor cowering and trembling in his stirrups, Washington hurried on to rally the troops. There was not a moment to lose, for the British were within a mile of them . . . The retreating soldiers immediately wheeled and formed under fire with as much coolness and precision as they could have shown on parade, and while they stopped the enemy's progress, Washington rode back and brought up the main body of his army . . . After a brave resistance, the British were driven back upon the second ravine which Lee had crossed in the morning's advance . . . After the battle, the behavior of Lee was the theme of discussion among the officers. Washington put Lee under arrest, and after a trial, he was found guilty and suspended from command for one year . . . Lee had no faith in the principles for which the Americans were fighting, or indeed in any principles. He came here to advance his own fortunes, and hoped to be made commander-in-chief. Disappointed in this, he began at once to look with hatred and envy upon Washington, and sought to thwart his purposes . . . Should Washington be defeated, Lee might negotiate for peace . . . Washington won a victory to Lee's disgrace . . . In October 1782 [Lee] died in a mean public-house in Philadelphia, friendless and alone." As an aside on Washington's uttering profanity when Lee retreated, I offer this story of a "College Divinity Professor who always held up Washington as a model for his morals": "One day he labored to convince his [students] of the wickedness of profanity when one of them said, 'Professor you told us to take Washington as an example and you know he swore terribly at the Battle of Monmouth.' The Professor was nonplussed, but finally stammered, 'Ahem? Ah, well, if ever anybody did have an excuse for swearing it was Washington at the Battle of Monmouth!'"

troubled is me. It is me own wicked hand which ties the noose on André's sweet neck as much as any spy of the Culpers, and it is for André I weep.

He let me live at Monmouth, and I let André die at Tappan. Like irony in books.

◆◆◆

After Monmouth Hamilton sends me to Boston aboard a sloop, with a secret message for the American fleet.

I be not feeling well when I board the ship and by the time I arrive in Boston, I is not a sulker [soldier who fakes sickness] I be a grunter [groaning like a hog from illness]. I be most feverish and faint. But, I deliver the message which says all materials taken by the British after the evacuation from Boston must be turn'd over to the Continental Army. This is because General Howe order'd all inhabitants of Boston to give the British linens and wool which could be used by rebels. On this order these good be thus collected by Loyalist traitor, Crean Brush, and placed on British ships. Before these can leave the harbor they be stopped by rebel ships, and this booty is return'd to Boston. Hamilton's message states these goods remain property of Congress for use of Continental soldiers as war prizes.

Because of the smallpox epidemic in Boston I takes rooms in the separate town of Dorchester close by, which is founded by Puritans in 1630. On the very day I deliver Hamilton's message to the commander in Boston I be walking to me rooms when I feel hot and begin to shiver with cold and me head and body is perspiring, wet. I be so tired with fatigue I can no longer walk, and me stomach heaves about. I sit on a short wall of stone in front of a house by a river and . . . .

Blackness.

. . .

"Where I be?"

Me question is asked of a nurse attending me in a bedchamber I never see'd a fore, as I wake from a unrestful slumber.

"In the household of Mrs. Perez Morton, the poetess," says the nurse.

I be wearing fine bedclothes of linen and covered by a silky coverlet, and I be looking about in surprise and disbelief, and I says, "How it is I be here?"

"The Mistress finds ye fainted in the road and gits the coachmen to put yer body in the carriage, and she brings ye home to her house on State Street in Boston."

Me head hurts like it is pounded by a war club. "Oww," I says, touching me head, and the nurse says, "From the malaria."

"Malaria?" I squeals in a raspy whisper.

The bedroom door opens and a fine-dressed, tall woman steps inside. "I be so happy ye be awake," says she, with a broad smile for me. "I trust Margaret is taking good care of ye." She walks to the bed and holds me hand. "I be sorry, I do not know yer name?"

For a moment I stammer, and nearly say me real name. "Miss Tabitha Baldwin of New York," I say, and she presses me hand in friendship.

"I be Mrs. Sarah Morton, wife of Boston's finest lawyer Perez Morton, but you may call me, Philenia."

"Philenia," I nod at her.

"It is the name she writes poetry by," says the nurse.

"Let us not discuss poetry, Margaret," Philenia says, correcting her. "How ye be feeling this morning, Miss Tabitha?"

"Tired and achy and hungry," I says. She is a beautiful person. She is of dark curly hair, broad eyes which sparkle with curiosity and a rather pointy nose, which does not detract from her allure. Her voluptuous lips form words slowly, and she is of the whitest skin I ever see'd on a woman.

"The doctor says the fatigue will be with ye for days," says Philenia. "He says it is mild malaria and ye should be fine in another week. I will have breakfast sent up."

"When did ye find me on the road?"

"Six days now," she says.

"Thank you for bringing me to yer house, Philenia," I says.

She smiles in the affirmative and leaves the room.

Over the next days me self and Philenia become friends
and she asks me what I be doing in Boston from New York. I
tells her I be sent to this city by a merchant, Austin Roe, who
will open a dry goods shop after the war, and asks me to
reconnoiter same for his prospects. I tells her I find it a fine
town and will say it is a good place for his business.

On a table I see'd books I never hear'd of a fore. One
published in 1740 is by Samuel Richardson called *Pamela;
or, Virtue Rewarded*; a second book is by Henry Fielding,
with the title, *Joseph Andrews, or The History of the
Adventures of Joseph Andrews and of his Friend Mr.
Abraham Adams*. This book is published in 1742.[69]

"Ye be in possession of many fine books," I tell her.

She says she is a writer mostly of poems.

I immediately thinks of James, me Indian sweetheart
who reads me poems, and it makes me sad besides sick. I
tells her of me enjoying the poems of Anne Dudley
Bradstreet, and Philenia says: "Her poem *Deliverance From
A Fever* is apropos," and she recites:

"When sorrows had begirt me round,
"And pains within and out,
"When in my flesh no part was found.
"Then didst Thou rid me out.
"My burning flesh in sweat did boil,
"My aching head did break,
"From side to side for ease I toil,
"So faint I could not speak."

I clap me hands and say, "Well done, Philenia!" This is
when I says someday I might write poems, but I do not know
how.

---

[69] We get a fairly good idea that the Morton household is liberal, certainly in its reading habits, based on the titles of books Agent 355 saw on the bedroom table. Both of these epistolary novels were broadly denounced by Puritan preachers from the pulpit as "forbidden" reading for parishioners. Author Samuel Richardson, called the father of the novel in England, wrote the especially offensive novel, *Pamela; or, Virtue Rewarded*, which Agent 355 mentioned. In it a country landowner tries to seduce and rape a 15-year-old servant and later marries her. The second book, *Joseph Andrews, or The History of the Adventures of Joseph Andrews and of his Friend Mr. Abraham Adams* by Henry Fielding, contains bawdy humor and was also banned in Boston. If they wanted bawdy reading they could have turned to much earlier literature, such as works by Middle Age English poet Geoffrey Chaucer, for instance, or Italian goldsmith Cellini's sex-laced, *The Autobiography of Benvenuto Cellini*, written in 1558.

"Miss Tabitha, I know ye can do it and never let a man say ye cannot!"

This night she shows me papers with a poem titled, *The African Chief*, and says it is hers which is not published about being against slavery of people from Africa, and I tells her I will read it. The next morning I tell her I agree with her, and slavery is bad.

She tells me the doctor says I will be able to leave the next day, and she asks if I will read part of a book she is writing which is not poetry, but a story of letters. I spend two hours reading the story which is not titled.[70] It is a story of intimacy and morality and female suffering, with characters Thomas Harrington and his sister Myra and Harriot Fawcet, illegitimate sister to Harrington and Myra, and a Maria who is Thomas Harrington's mistress.

The morning comes and I tells Philenia it is a very interesting book, and the writing of it is lively and colorful like a poem itself.

I dress in me breeches, hunting shirt and gray cape, and now realize me pistol and dagger is not in the bedroom. I fight with me self on if I should ask for same from Philenia.

Later in the parlor we embrace farewell, and she says, "Please wait here." In a moment she returns. "These be found on yer person," she says, and gives me the French pistol and Navy dagger which I gits from Robert Rogers. I be embarrassed a moment, and she says, "Nay, do not explain; we all be doing what we can for liberty."

---

[70] As editor of 355's diary I didn't think much of this divergence from her action-packed spy narrative. I was even tempted to omit it from the published manuscript. That is until I researched writer Sarah Wentworth Apthorp Morton and learned she was a poet involved in a minor literary controversy, perhaps only interesting to bookworms and bibliophiles. In addition, her husband, Perez, was involved a sex scandal in Boston. In the book controversy, a neighbor of Sarah Morton, William Hill Brown, published a novel, *The Power of Sympathy*, about a sex scandal in which a husband fathers a child by his wife's sister, and the husband ends up committing suicide. In the book characters are named Thomas Harrington, Myra and Harriot Fawcet, among others. These are the same character names Agent 355 mentions, which probably means Sarah Morton allowed her to read a draft or a chapter of *The Power of Sympathy*. This is only important when you consider that there is a literary dispute whether William Hill Brown or Sarah Morton actually wrote *The Power of Sympathy*, published years after Agent 355 stayed in the Morton home. It would not have been unusual in this era for a man to act as "stand-in" for a woman wanting to publish a book she had written with a sex plot. Based on this anecdote by Agent 355, Sarah Morton appears to be the true author of *The Power of Sympathy*, which might be a fictionalized version of her husband's indiscretion.

On me way back to Hamilton aboard a sloop I think of this: of all the time I be in Philenia's house in Boston, I never see'd her husband, Perez Morton, Boston lawyer. When I return'd to Hamilton, he tells me Mister Morton is his self a fighter for freedom from George III, and a rebel thinker.

I do not mention being struck down with malaria to Hamilton. But always did I ponder it: did I git this malady from spy Guillory who is from the West Indies?

DIARY

Second Part, 1779-1781
Written Down
May 12th to October 18th, 1810

1779

If this spy'g ever makes the realm of discourse and is printed in the gazette, Alas! Pamphleteers be treating it unfavorably because spy'g on yer neighbor is never worthy, whether Tory or Whig. Setauket is heavy Presbyterian and many is in favor of the fight. In close distance, Episcopals, Quakers, Anglicans and Papists be Loyal to the Crown, which makes quarrelsome neighbors. All say spy'g is unsavory. Work of blackguards and brothel maids. It paints a stain on all who follow it.

I be positive in mind to say if such disclosure is done, as say in a memoir by Colonel Benjamin Tallmadge or in speeches by His Excellency George Washington, also President Washington, 1789-1797, then these two men will bow and accept credit for success of the Culper spies. It is the way men treat women.

Oh, Agent 355? A lady spy? Who she be, the people will utter in surprise? It is why what I write is important for history's sake, for the dignity, distinction and renown of females in this fight.

♦♦♦

I wrote of me month with Caleb Brewster's whaleboats on the Sound in 1777, and a story which happen'd then I must tell, thus all formation of the Culper Spy Ring is told.

We is at rest at Black Rock, Connecticut, and Caleb is using a stone to sharpen two tomahawks and I says, "Can you toss them into a target?" and Caleb says, "Like a Virginia Algonquin."

He stands and pitches it at a tree, and it sticks, dead.

Caleb marches to the tree and gets his tomahawk. He steps back to me, and says, "Algonquin, see."

"Dollar, I toss it straighter."

"A girl?" he utters in cachinnation. Then he thinks more on it, and says, "I know'd ye shoot the long rifle straight, but the tomahawk. Nay, it cannot be for merely a woman. It is a man's weapon to throw."

"Whore's pipe [penis] or no whore's pipe, I can beat you, Brewster," I says, with gritty force as he gits me blood up. I know'd me words angers Caleb, and he takes his knife and marches to a stout pine tree forty paces out and peels bark, which shows a square white spot on the pine. He yells back: "Five throws for us, and the most in the target wins." He returns and hands me a tomahawk. He is ignorant of Robert Rogers's Indian training on the tomahawk for me, and I grips this heavy weapon like an Indian.

I toss me wood-handle hatchet at the tree and miss it.

Amused by it, Caleb is laughing so hard he cannot lift his tomahawk, and I walks into the trees and gits mine. "This long handle is strange to me," I says, walking back and showing the tomahawk handle. His cachinnation all a new, he dances like a rum-liquor'd Indian round a fire.

Caleb holds out his hand. "Put the dollar there, Missy."

"Four tosses to go," I says, and slap his hand with mine.

Caleb takes a short run at the tree and pitches the tomahawk and it strikes the carved white spot. He yelps like a crazy man, and gits his hatchet from the tree.

I runs and throws the tomahawk, and it hits the mark.

Caleb stops yelping. He tosses, missing the target, and curses.

I says, "Show me yer dollar."

He walks to a leather bag and pulls it out.

I runs and tosses the axe and it strikes the center of the white spot. I amble towards the tree, unstick the tomahawk, and step to the side. Caleb throws his hatchet and it sails past me head and hits the white spot.

I wait for him to git his tomahawk.

"Caleb, do not toss again towards me lest you want yer ear shave'd off by this axe," I says in a scolding way. I toss and hit the spot, dead in the middle.

"I believe ye could do it," he grumbles.

When the contest ends he is three dead centers and mine is four, and he hands me the dollar.

"Keep it," I says. "When I need a fine thrower of the tomahawk, I will seek yer pay."

Caleb shakes me hand like I be a gentleman, and asks where I learn't to toss the axe this way.

I know'd I can trust Caleb Brewster with me life, and I say from Robert Rogers of Rogers's Rangers his self.

I see'd Caleb is impressed by it.

I stick out the handle of the tomahawk for Caleb to take it, and he says, "Keep it, ye earned it."

Since, this tomahawk see'd action and blood.

This night we sit and talk and Caleb tells me of his frustrations with General Washington's war tactics. "The British take Philadelphia, and Washington winters at Valley Forge, and his leadership is in doubt. His men starve and desertions mount," he says. "Washington is beaten at Brandywine and in springtime it is talk he will not attack Howe because he did not in Jersey."[71]

"Maybe Washington does not move because he cannot see the direction to go," says I to Caleb, who appraises the remark a moment.

"He does not wear spectacles," says Caleb.

The callous-hand Caleb Brewster is best in fisticuffs, and I want his self by me when a brawl erupts. In subtle brain work he is a loggerhead, yet a better friend there never can be. I says, "I do not mean he cannot see, only he needs more eyes and ears on the British Navy in waters of New York,

---

[71] On his march to take Philadelphia in 1777 British General William Howe beat back an attack by the Continental Army under General Washington at Brandywine Creek in September 1777. This is just before Washington spent the horrible winter of 1777-1778 at Valley Forge.

where this war is Washington's to win or lose. Spies in Setauket see ships in the Sound, and tell Washington."

Caleb looks at me long, and says, "You throw a tomahawk and thinks not like any woman I ever know'd."

◆◆◆

Much happens before I see'd Caleb Brewster again: I kill the sot Guillory and save Beaumarchais's ships from British; kidnap General Prescott from Rhode Island; in Philadelphia I masquerade as a lady of fashion and see'd John André at his jousts and ball; and turn into a peddler for Hamilton at Monmouth and spy in the British ranks.

When I see'd Caleb again it is in Setauket.

I meets Caleb as he walks from Roe's Tavern, and he is excited to say something, and takes me aside in private and shows me a letter from Washington his self. He tells me he writes his self to His Excellency General Washington and propose'd to spy on British in waters of the Sound, "like ye idea," remember.

"When we do a tomahawk contest?" I say.

His excitement lessens, and he says, "This very day, it is." He reads this letter from General Washington: "White plains, August 8, 1778. Sir: I have received your Letter of Yesterday from Norwalk. Let me entreat that you will continue to use every possible means to obtain intelligence of the Enemy's motions, not only of those which are Marching Eastward, upon Long Island, but others. In a more especial manner, I have to request, that you will, by every devise you can think of, have a strict watch kept upon the Enemy's Ships of War, and give me the earliest notice of their Sailing from the hook. To obtain speedy and certain intelligence of this matter may be of great Importance to the French Fleet at, and the enterprise on, Rhode Island; for which reason, do not spare any reasonable expense to come at early and true information; always recollecting, and bearing in Mind, that vague, and uncertain accounts of things, on which any plan is to be formed is more distressing and dangerous than receiving none at all. Let an eye also be had to the Transports, whether they are preparing for the reception of Troops. Know what number of Men are upon Long Island;

whether they are moving or Stationary; what is become of their draft Horses; whether they appear to be collecting of them for a move. How they are supplied with Provisions; what arrivals; whether with Men, or Provisions. And whether any Troops have embarked for Rhode Island or elsewhere within these few days."

I listen and express congratulations to Caleb.

"This is your glory, too," says he. "It is yer idea."

"Nay, to vainglory," says I.

"His Excellency should know ye name."

"Caleb, if you seek a long life, do not utter me name in this spy'g ye be doing. Never."

"I use me own name to General Washington."

"Then yer self is all he needs ever know; not of me."

Caleb gits angry if it is not the way of it he wants, and I know'd this when he walks and leaves me. For history's sake:

---

[72] On March 15, 1792, Caleb Brewster wrote a letter to George Washington from Fairfield, Connecticut, about compensation for his service and spying during the war, in which he was seriously wounded. Here is the letter: "Sir: I have presumed upon your Excellency's known love of Justice, and upon the generous interest you take in the misfortunes of your old faithful military servants, to address to your Excellency the following representation; and I hope that the peculiar circumstances of my case and the unusual Sufferings that have attended my situation will be received as an apology for thus soliciting your Excellency's aid and support. I will, with your leave, submit to your Excellency a simple and short detail of the facts on which I ground this application. In the year 1777 I was honored with a commission of Captain in the line of the State of New York and was placed on a detached service, commanding an armed boat for the purpose of cruising in the Long Island Sound, and for the more important service of obtaining and conveying intelligence from the Enemy. Under this commission I acted till the close of the late war. Of the services I rendered in this capacity your Excellency who was acquainted with the details of these secret operations at that period, is a competent Judge . . . On the 7th of December 1782 while in the aforesaid service in a bloody engagement with two armed boats of the Enemy I received a wound by a ball through my breast. With this wound I languished and was confined two years and a half under distressing chirurgical operations and a most forlorn hope of cure. The nature of these wounds together with the impairing of my constitution by the long continuance of my confinement have rendered me incapable of any labor that requires a considerable exertion and have reduced me to the melancholy condition of an invalid for life. These are the facts on which I claimed a place on the invalid list of the United States. . . I humbly entreat your Excellency to take my distressed case into his benevolent consideration . . . I am with profound respect Your Excellency's most obedient and most humble Servant. Caleb Brewster." Washington mentioned Brewster's 1782 injury in a letter to Colonel Benjamin Tallmadge, stating, "I see nothing irreparable, [and] little occasion of serious regret, except the wound of the gallant Captain Brewster, from which I earnestly hope he may recover." After writing to Washington, Brewster joined what would become the U.S. Coast Guard and served in the War of 1812.

Caleb Brewster propose'd spy'g from Long Island Sound to Washington, an idea from a tomahawk contest.[72]

It is not long following this which Hamilton his self tells me he is gone from running spies. He says His Excellency names Colonel Benjamin Tallmadge for the business to set in motion a network of spies on Long Island. I says to me self, General Washington listens to Caleb. It is good.

In summer 1779 I be in Setauket to take care of personal business and I secure a store of gold from Robert Rogers's box.

Two happenings at this time need to be told.

In Oyster Bay I walks by the stately house of Robert Townsend's father, shop proprietor Samuel Townsend, and this home is called Raynham Hall. At the door I see'd a British Major I know'd I see'd a fore, but cannot remember when, where or how.

This night I find the picture draw'd by John André at Caleb Cope's Quaker home in Lancaster. I look close at the man's pudding face in the India inked picture and I can hear André say, like it is yesterday, he be his "dear friend Captain John Graves Simcoe."

In 1779 it be Major Simcoe and he is quarter'd in Townsend's Raynham Hall.[73]

The second happening is this. In Setauket I see'd Abraham Woodhull at a stationers and he walks with me and tells me of Colonel Tallmadge's spy group, and he asks if I be in a mind to assist his spies. He says he knows I work'd for Hamilton but Hamilton works for General Benedict Arnold at West Point now and cannot spare time to work with spies. Benjamin Tallmadge will welcome one as me into his group, says Woodhull, with me "especial training." I know'd then Caleb Brewster is telling Woodhull of me tomahawk training with Robert Rogers and of besting his own tomahawk throwing, and of me accurate long rifle shooting on his whaleboat.

---

[73] Colonel Simcoe, head of the Queen's Rangers on Long Island, often billeted in the Samuel Townsend home in Oyster Bay near Setauket and his friend John André was a visitor, according to Samuel Townsend's son, Robert, who is quoted in Alexander Rose's book, *Washington's Spies*.

Woodhull looks at me in a stern way. "If Loyalist informants learn who we be, Tallmadge says we can take action to keep ourselves secret, and stop them before they tell," Woodhull says.

"I kill these Loyalists, yer saying?"

Woodhull says it is so with his eyes without saying it.

"Me training with Robert Rogers is know'd by ye?"

"Yea," he says. "There be no one else like thou in Setauket." Now I see'd he looks for a knife and pistol in me breeches, and I laughs. Immediately, he says, "Washington promises compensation."[74]

"I do not kill for money, Abraham."

"I know, I speak of expenses for journeys."

"Then, yea," I say, "I be joining yer spies."

"Great, I will tell Tallmadge."

"I want to see yer note to Colonel Tallmadge," I says. "What yer saying of me."

It is agree'd and two days more Abraham Woodhull finds me, and he hands me a message. "This is what I will send to Benjamin." I look at it and it is numbers. "It is code," he says. He says he is writing to Tallmadge about being stopped by a British patrol which could have discovered a secret letter on him. And he says he is also telling Tallmadge about me, and he reads the message from the code: "I think by the assistance of a 355 of my acquaintance, shall be able to outwit them all."

"A 355?" says I.

"A Lady," says Abraham. "355 is code for Lady."

"Tabitha Baldwin is a lady?" I says it and laughs.

"Who?" says Abraham who know'd me true name.

"Tabitha Baldwin is me spy name," says I. "It is the only name ever say of me to Tallmadge or Washington."

Abraham Woodhull agrees.

---

[74] At the end of the war Abraham Woodhull submitted a bill for spying "expenses" to George Washington – mostly for travel expenses – which included money for himself and other members of the Culper Spy Ring, including four pounds for Anna Strong. While amounting to a little more than 150 pounds, Washington complained about the bill, saying in the last two years of the war the Culper information wasn't worth the money. Omitted from Woodhull's bill was any compensation for Agent 355, apparently in accord with her wishes.

I then says, "Do not use Lady 355 again in letters to Tallmadge. If Benjamin Tallmadge needs to talk to me he can see me his self."

He agrees.[75]

To show me serious mind on this I pull the pistol Rogers gives me and looks at it. "This is serious with me, Abraham, yer certain you understand me."

Woodhull is not a brave man or a person of military war, and he stares for a long time at the pistol. He then looks at me. "You will never be talked about by me again, and God has hear'd this pledge," says he.

And, with it, like a wavering of a wand of magic, I is a member of the Culper Spy Ring.

♦♦♦

Months follow and I be warming me feet by the fire and I hear'd a crashing sound. I takes me pistol outside in the dark and find Abraham Woodhull. He be roughed with blood and bruises on his face and is crying like I never see'd a man off the gallows, and he stumbles with lack of breath.

"Connecticut skinners," he gasps all affright.

"They be many about these nights," says I. "Not a Loyalist be safe."

"Took me goods and saddle," says he. "I must git the saddle back."

I walks to a coat and gits money so he can buy a saddle, and enough for a horse if he desires, and puts it on the table. "Take it," I says. "Buy a saddle. Done with it."

"You do not understand," says he. "A secret letter for Tallmadge is in this saddle. If it is discovered the Culper spies will be exposed."

"They be Patriot marauders not Cowboys," I tells Abraham. "They do not deal with Loyalists or British. They attack them, rouse Loyalists."[76]

---

[75] Agent 355's insistence of not being mentioned again in Abraham Woodhull's secret dispatches might explain why there is only one mention of an "Agent 355" in all correspondence of members of the Culper Spy Ring, including Washington's papers and Tallmadge's. She also is not mentioned in Alexander Hamilton's papers

[76] Freebooting marauders were common in the war, with groups called "Cowboys" raiding and pillaging in the name of Tories and Loyalists, and groups called "Skinners" who claimed allegiance to the rebels and General Washington, wreaking havoc among Loyalist families. They often

"I cannot take the chance," he says. "I must have the saddle back. This letter will send Redcoats to me door. Hanging is a cold bargain."

I tells Woodhull to describe the robbers and he says there is three, and he tells me how they dress and what two of same look like. "Caleb will take me across," I says. "Git yer saddle, I do."

The night Abraham comes to me beat and bruise'd he gives me a letter from Tallmadge for "a person of his interest" and it tells me to seek out the spies of Colonel Beverley Robinson in the Hudson River country, and gives details. This mission is on me mind when I be moved to help Woodhull.

Two nights pass and I be on swampy shore with Caleb Brewster who takes me across the Sound. He says one of the skinners ore'd on his boat and he lives in a cabin in from the swamp, and he calls this man an ornery cuss, and says he should go with me, and I says no. "I bring the Woodhull's saddle back, you git the letter and take it to Tallmadge," says I. "Then, business up the Hudson calls me."

Caleb watches me put on me belt of weapons, black me face with soot, pull me hat over me hair and put on me quiet Indian moccasins, and leap from the whaleboat. In me breeches is me pistol and tomahawk on a leather belt, and

---

operated in the no-man's land between British and American lines. In truth these raiders had one interest – booty for themselves. However, the British enlisted marauders to prey on patriot civilians. In a book about Loyalist marauders written in 1887 by William S. Stryker, he wrote: "We learn from General Howe's Narrative that at the beginning of the campaign of 1777 General Cortland Skinner had been able to recruit but five hundred and seventeen men of his (Loyalist) complement, but in November, 1777, he had eight hundred and fifty-nine men on his brigade rolls, and in May, 1778, after several months of active exertions, he had enlisted one thousand one hundred and one men. But at that time the nucleus for six battalions had been made and the officers commissioned. During that year five hundred and fifty additional volunteers, mostly from New Jersey, were enrolled for service, and afterward sent to Charleston, South Carolina. It is then apparent that General Skinner recruited about two-thirds of the quota first assigned to him. All of these soldiers immediately on enlistment were placed in active service, and they began to distinguish themselves at an early day in their great zeal to annoy, intimidate and injure their former patriot friends and neighbors." On the other side, some skinners were under charter of Colonial governors. The situation got so bad on Long Island that the Culper Spy Ring worried that marauders attacking the British-controlled settlement of Setauket would expose them. In other words, it would amount to the downfall of a very significant *rebel* spy ring by raiders who had pledged loyalty to the *rebels*.

inside the linen hunting shirt is me four-inch dagger from Rogers.

"They shan't know of the coming whirlwind," he says.

I slip into the darkness of the woods, a sleek, soundless hoplite in Indian shoes.

The cabin is lively in voices when I creep softly to a window. Inside three men at a table play cards and drink grog, bought, I thinks, from selling Abraham Woodhull's goods. If they sell'd the saddle me task is lost, I know'd. Pistol in left hand and short-handle tomahawk in right, I kick in the door with a clatter.

Stunned by surprise of it, one man falls back over in his chair on the floor.

"I not be here to molest ye," I say, the pistol staring firmly into a man's eyes, proving me a liar. "I comes for the saddle ye marauders takes in Setauket."

"Saddle?" says the one on the floor.

"It is property of me gray-hair grandma," says I, "and she'n wants it returned."

The skinners laugh at me.

"Yer a wench," says one who laughs most, "a bloody whore and wench." He laughs like what is this, a woman in petticoats comes to beat us down? "Yer a whore and so is yer gray-hair grandma."

Instantly without a word I split his head with the tomahawk. He falls dead and his blood spills on the table of strewn cards.

The other skinners scream and go backwards in horror.

"Any more of ye vermin think me grandma's a bloody whore?"

These brave skinners turn tongueless.

"Now, tell the whereabouts of the saddle ye thieve'd in Setauket. Tell me, and ye live."

The skinner who fell on the floor when I kicks in the door wavers to a bed in a corner and says, "Saddle at foot of bed."

Now I see'd it.

"Pick it up and move by the door," I says, and the pistol is pointed at his head. I see'd the second skinner move the other way, and I know'd he be flanking me.

I shoot this man dead in the heart, and he falls like a heavy spring melon.

The other skinner grabs the saddle and runs at me with its leather wide in front of him, and hits me hard. The saddle is tossed aside and his strong blow knocks the tomahawk from me grasp. I falls on the floor, and in seconds the skinner is atop me, his dirty hands round me throat, squeezing, enraged, and coursing, "wench! wench! wench!" and gnashing his jaws.

I fight hard with me arms and legs and rips the dagger from inside me shirt. But, I feel me mind going into dizziness and darkness from his potent grip. With every muscle tense'd, I thrust the knife into the skinner's side, and I feels his hot blood immediately on men hand. Like killer Robert Rogers teaches us, I yank'd it round in his inside humors and organs, and the dirty skinner screams and his hand goes loose on me neck. He tries to stand and falls on me dead of body, his blood soaking sticky wet and warm on me shirt.

I push this man off me like a bad lover.

I collect me weapons and with much exhaustion I takes the saddle back to Caleb near the swamp. He rips Woodhull's secret letter from the saddle for Colonel Tallmadge, and says the drop point is far up the Sound.

Near unable to breathe and as bloody as a slaughtered hog, I tells Caleb me business is far up the Hudson, and I be on me way.

I do not git far.

◆◆◆

All the way back to 1776, the rumors being so vast in number of His Excellency General Washington being subject of plots and treachery against his self, and by his own house-guard, it is with skepticism I gits the message by express rider in 1779 from Colonel Tallmadge.[77] It says I must ride

[77] It seems likely Agent 355 is referring to the case of Continental Army soldier Thomas Hickey who was hanged in June 1776, the first hanging in the Continental Army in the war. In a plot apparently hatched and financed by the last Royal Governor of New York, Hickey is alleged to have been involved in a plot to kill or kidnap George Washington in New York. Hickey, who had been a member of Washington's personal guard at Richmond Hall before the British took over control of the city, was later jailed for the common crime of passing counterfeit money. In jail Hickey told another inmate he was prepared to defect to the British side once the King's army landed in New

tonight to a town I never hear'd of, Parsippany, New Jersey, to protect New Jersey Governor William Livingston who has a reward put on his head, dead or alive of 2,000 guineas.[78] Tallmadge says he does not trust the loyalty of the New Jersey Militia which guards Governor Livingston. He says Livingston agitates Loyalists and rebels, and it is unknow'd which might attack him. Tallmadge says he agitates rebels for "niceness" and "being placable" to Loyalist families in New Jersey. As for me spy cover, Tallmadge also sends me a letter from Washington his self to Livingston, with His Excellency's "compliments," making a housemaid available for the Governor, one "Miss Tabitha Baldwin of New York." This letter I present to the Governor upon arrival.[79]

York. His cellmate snitched him off and Hickey was tried for sedition and executed. While passing counterfeit dollars was a capital offense, rumors circulated that Hickey had been involved in a plot to kill Washington – perhaps by poison – and this was the real reason he was executed. At Richmond Hall, Washington's meals were provided by tavern owner Samuel Fraunces, who in 1785, sought payment from Congress for his wartime services to the commander-in-chief and filed an affidavit which stated he had discovered the plot and had exposed it, saying, "That [Fraunces] was the Person that first discovered the Conspiracy which was formed in the Year 1776 against the Life of his Excellency General Washington." Congress agreed to pay him 2,000 pounds in expenses for Washington's meals at Richmond Hall and noted he was "instrumental in discovering and defeating" the plot. In his *Biographical Sketches, Loyalists, of the American Revolution*, Lorenzo Sabine, (1864), wrote of Thomas Hickey: "In 1776 a plot of the disaffected to the Whig cause extended to Washington s own camp, and part of his guard were engaged in it. Hickey was one of the number. He was tried, and having been convicted by the unanimous opinion of a court-martial, was executed on the 28th of June of that year, in a field between McDougall's and Huntington's camps, near the Bowery Lane, New York, in the presence of nearly twenty thousand spectators."

[78] During 1779 General Cortland Skinner offered a reward of 2,000 guineas for the capture of Governor Livingston of New Jersey, dead or alive. "This excited the cupidity and the reckless zeal of many of the Jersey loyalists," stated a history of Monmouth, New York. "A very spirited correspondence ensued in March and April, 1779, between the Governor and Sir Henry Clinton in reference to this attempted exploit." General Skinner was the last attorney general under the Royal Government of New Jersey. He made a brigadier general in 1776 and was told to raise a loyalist army called the New Jersey Volunteers. Skinner ran an extensive spy network in New Jersey and New York but rarely led any of his volunteers into battle. He fled America for England in 1782. The most dramatic British raid to capture Livingston came in February 1779 when a thousand British troops, guided by local Tories, landed in darkness near the governor's home Liberty Hall in Elizabethtown to capture him and surprise the Continentals stationed nearby. Sentries detected the British soldiers, and Livingston escaped. Two of his daughters stayed behind in the house to mislead the British. The British withdrew when the Continentals came to the governor's aid.

[79] Washington wrote to New Jersey Governor William Livingston about what he considered the poor state of the New Jersey Militia. In a letter to Livingston on January 24, 1777, Washington wrote: "Sir. The irregular and disjointed State of the Militia of this province makes it necessary for me to inform you, that unless a Law is passed by your Legislature to reduce them to some order, and oblige them to turn out in a different Manner from what they have hitherto done, we shall bring very few into the Field, and even those few, will render little or no Service. Their Officers are generally of the lowest Class of people, and instead of setting a good Example to their Men, are

After weeks in his house, I thinks Governor Livingston is forceful in his tone to staff, and I likes what I hear'd of his way of training his female children in the skills outside the house. I like kindheart'd Mrs. Susannah [French] Livingston who lives for safety in Basking Ridge with brother-in-law, Lord Stirling, and visits Parsippany one time. Then she tells me they be thirteen children "as many children as there are states in the Union." She says her daughter, Sarah, is wed to John Jay. I thinks it is Benjamin Tallmadge which tells me John Jay's brother is investor of invisible ink of which Washington writes secret messages. I do not tell Mrs. Livingston this, but I be amused by this thought.

Instantly I did not like the house in which Governor Livingston rents for his residence in Parsippany, which he is forced to live in because British troops often attack his home, Liberty Hall, in Elizabethtown, New Jersey, and ransack it much. This house has many window which can be shot at. A long veranda or porch at front of house is easy way to climb to uppermost windows and bedrooms. House is at end of this dark road, Old Parsippany Road, which is easily attack'd at night by marauders and Loyalist Cowboys who will escape into denseness of nearby forests.

I tell this to New Jersey Militia Captain Edward Drake of Governor Livingston's personal guard, and he laughs at me and says, "Wenches should stay out of military thinking and affairs." He laughs at me, calls me a "crazy" woman.

"When they come, Sir, this wench might save yer life."

These words ignite more laughing from the Captain, and he tells me to go to the cook house and prepare meals.

---

leading them into every kind of Mischief, one Species of which is plundering the Inhabitants under pretense of their being Tories. A Law should in my Opinion be passed to put a stop to this kind of lawless Rapine, for unless there is something done to prevent it, the people will throw themselves of choice into the hands of the British Troops. But your first object should be a well-regulated Militia Law. The people, put under good Officers, would behave in quite another manner, and not only render real Service as Soldiers, but would protect, instead of distressing the Inhabitants. What I would wish to have particularly insisted upon, in the new Law, should be, that every Man capable of bearing Arms, should be obliged to turn out, and not buy off their Service by a trifling Sum. We want Men and not Money. I have the Honor to be with the greatest Respect Sir Your Most Obedient Servant." Livingston wrote to the New Jersey general assembly, calling attention to the "well-known Defects of our Militia Law" and to ask them to pass a new law, which the assembly did. Still, both Washington and Livingston thought the new law inadequate. A separate letter introducing housemaid "Miss Tabitha Baldwin" has not been found.

Today Captain Drake is not laughing.

He is dead.

This happen'd at two o'clock on a moonless night on June 22, 1779. I awakes and hear'd musket shots outside, and jumps from me bed inside the house and hooks the pistol on its sling, and gits the tomahawk which is under blankets in a corner of the room. I hear'd voices on top of the porch, and I runs to the Governor's room, which the door is open and inside Governor Livingston is on the floor and a Loyalist raider is astride his body and holding a knife high to stab his chest.

I fires the pistol and it knocks the Cowboy off the Governor, instantly dead. Now Captain Drake, dress'd in his hunting shirt, which he sleeps in and this makes him nake'd, runs in carrying his sword. From the window, a Loyalist marauder there to kill or kidnap the governor shoots Captain Drake in the chest. He falls and drops his sword. I see'd the Cowboy at the window and he see'd me, a lowly wench, and he steps in the bedroom anyhow and without caution to kill the Governor. I throws the tomahawk and it misses me mark, which is the Cowboy's head.

I gits the Captain's sword and swings it in the dark room and I hear'd the Cowboy screech in pang, and I know'd the blade cut deep into his face. He dives like off a rock into a pond right out the window, and rolls off the roof of the front porch on to the ground.

Outside, a New Jersey Militia patrol scares the raiders away, and later, I do not find the one which I cut, dead on the ground. Outside, I hear'd our militia men say, "Moody's out. It is Moody."[80] This name I never know'd, yet will see again.

---

[80] The Parsippany attack of Loyalist James Moody and his Tory raiders revealed in the diary is similar to one that happened about the same date, and could be the same event. This raid on Governor Livingston's house was written up in *The New Jersey Gazette* on July 28, 1779. The story about the attack on "June 22, 1779," stated: "A number of villains (says a correspondent) in the vicinity of Parsippany, Morris county, having for some days before been suspected of being concerned in a conspiracy to take or assassinate Governor Livingston, as soon as he should return from the General Assembly; a son of the Governor's having previously induced one of the persons suspected to believe that His Excellency was looked for on June 22, caused a report to be propagated towards the evening of that day, that he was actually returned. As the young Gentleman suspected that the conspirators would, in consequence of the report, attack the house that night, he had concerted proper measures for their reception. Accordingly, at about two o'clock

In the Governor's bedroom is poor Captain Drake prone in his blood on the floor.

"Are you wounded?" Governor Livingston asks, and I say nay to it.

Days pass and Captain Drake and two more militia men kill'd by the Loyalists outside the Governor's house git entomb'd in a solemn service of God-fearing men. The Governor greatly adds the number of militia soldiers on patrol at the house, and I begins to think it is time for Tabitha Baldwin to leave.

One evening I is in the small house which is a kitchen at the back of the big house and Governor Livingston calls to me. He is with a militia Lieutenant by his side. "Where does a housemaid learn to shot and fight with a tomahawk like ye did to save me?" says the Governor.

I cannot say from notorious Robert Rogers, for it will cause the Governor's Soul itself to shiver. "Taught by me Uncle Ebenezer, Sir, who learn't it from his grandfather who fought in Queen Ann's War with the Rangers organized by Benjamin Church in 1676."[81]

"The famed Major Church?" says Governor Livingston, impressed I can see. "A fine teacher, indeed. Most daughters like mine git training in embroidery and song but in firearms, nay! It is left for sons. Why is it a man teaches a female such things as pistols?"

In quick thought, I says, "Me Uncle is unlucky in children and did not rear a son. Me thinks of it thus: because it is so, he puts his want of a son on me, a female, and teaches me skills of a son." This be a lie, too, and me skill of lying rivals me skill of spy'g, and ye cannot have the latter without the former.

---

the next morning the ruffians were discovered within fifty yards of the Governor's house; but being fired upon by one of our patrols, they instantly took into the woods and fled. The person however, who was suspected to be at the head of the gang, and who had for some time past taken up his residence in that neighborhood to facilitate the conspiracy, disappeared the next morning, was pursued and taken. He is committed to goal in Morris-town and has already made considerable discoveries." As we know from the diary, however, Loyalist marauder James Moody was not captured.

[81] Major Benjamin Church is the organizer of what was to become the United States Army Rangers in modern times. Church was a Colonist who lent his military talents to the King in several wars in North America before the American Revolution. He died in 1718.

The Governor thinks on this, and nods. "I do not disagree with yer unusual training because I want me own daughters to think their own thoughts, even if new ones," he says. "Yer Uncle is a man of enlightenment."

"Of course, Sir," I say, feeling happy to end this lie which coils tightly round me stomach.

"Well," says the Governor, "ye require a proclamation, Miss Tabitha. You save'd the Governor's life. The public must be told. I will send the proclamation to the Assembly."

A terror overcomes me.

"Nay, please, Sir, do not," says I.

The militia Lieutenant's eyebrows raise in deep question.

What trouble this is? I cannot say, "But, Governor Livingston, Sir, I be a spy and cannot be named in *Rivington's Royal Gazette*. The Assembly will find there is no real Tabitha Baldwin." Here is what I say: "Governor Livingston, His Excellency the Commander-In-Chief is me employer, and it does not suit me to be a public personage until I gits his blessing and approval. I will write and ask for it, Sir."

"So be it, I will wait his pleasure."

The statement settles down the Lieutenant, and me stomach.

This very night I write a secret message to Colonel Benjamin Tallmadge. I tells of the Loyalist plot to kill Governor Livingston who seeks to call me a martyr; (this cannot be the right word); or I mean to say a brave hero for public approbation. This proclamation cannot be, I tells Tallmadge. Days later Governor Livingston gits a letter from General Washington his self which states his housemaid, Miss Tabitha, must return to New Windsor [N.Y.] and no public announcement be made of her actions.[82] I know'd this same Lieutenant looks at me with suspicion after this letter, thinking why is this wench so favor'd? I gits this urge to say,

---

[82] A check of Washington's and Governor Livingston's surviving correspondence during this period turned up no letter mentioning "Tabitha Baldwin." It is possible that Agent 355 was wrong about the letter or that the letter was destroyed. n any event we know she left Parsippany soon after the raid by James Moody and that no official proclamation was ever issued by the governor thanking Tabitha Baldwin for saving his life. Like the true identity of Agent 355 herself, this letter, if it ever existed, remains a mystery.

"I is a spy and a good one, Lieutenant, is it disagreeable to yer ears?"

I say none of it.

With a grand "God be with ye" from Governor Livingston, I leave the house in Parsippany two days later with two stout militia men, privates, as me escorts. In new breeches and hunting shirt and round hat I looks like a boy, and go northerly on horses towards New Windsor, a Continental Army depot and hospital where Washington stays in the home of Colonel Thomas Ellison.

On the ride I talk to New Jersey Militia Private Edward Fenton, escort, and I asks who is Moody?

"Moody is killer Moody," he says. "He is Ensign James Moody of First Battalion of Skinner's Loyal Corps. Once a farmer and now a killer. His very name is terror to Patriots in New Jersey, and the cry, 'Moody is out!' is a call to arm and be prepare'd for death. Ye never hear'd of Moody, ma'am?" He is surprised by this lack of knowing.

"Never till this instant," I says.

"Ye sure been sheltered from this war, ma'am." I cannot hold back a laugh at his words, and he says what is the humor?

"Tell me more of Moody, Private Fenton," I says, and the private tells me this: "Moody requested a Tory friend named Hutchinson, with six men and some guides, to join them in a raid into Monmouth. In all Moody and sixteen men. They starts from Sandy Hook for Shrewsbury, and elude the rebel guard, and gain a place called Tinton Falls. There they surprise and takes prisoners: one Colonel, one Lieutenant-Colonel, one Major and two Captains, others of lesser note, and without injury to private property, they destroy a considerable magazine of powder and arms. With these prisoners and such public stores as they could bring off, Mister Hutchinson is in front whilst Moody brings up the rear with his sixteen men. They is soon pursued by double their number and soon overtaken. But Moody keeps up a smart fire on his assailants, retarding them till Hutchinson with his booty gits ahead a considerable distance. He then advances on the shore at Black Point where the enemy cannot flank them. But just at this time the enemy is reinforced by ten men, now near forty strong. Hutchinson with one man crosses the inlet. Now a warm engagement ensues with Moody which lasts a hour. By this time all Moody's ammunition is exhausted. The bayonet is Moody's only resource, and this the enemy cannot withstand; they flee, leaving eleven of their number kill'd or wound'd."

Private Fenton stops his narration, and waits for me to look into his face. "Moody kill'd nine his self with his bayonet." Now the Private continues: "Unfortunately for Moody, his small but gallant party cannot follow up the blow, being in a manner utterly exhausted by a long harassed march in hot weather. His men is captured, but not Moody. Our troops find Captain Chadwick dead, and the Lieutenant expiring on the field. There is something peculiarly awful in the death of the rebel Captain. He is shot by Moody whilst with the most bitter oaths and threats of vengeance. After having miss fired once, Moody again fires at the Captain. Moody escape'd and is indict'd for murder of Captain Chadwick."

"He be sought for murder?" I asks.

"He be hang'd when captured," says the Private Fenton.

We ride for hours farther north, and suddenly shots burst from a copse of white oaks. Private Fenton falls dead from his horse and the second Private kicks his horse in the flanks and races off back towards Parsippany.

The horse I ride falls dead under me, shot through the shoulder by a musket ball, and I is spill'd on the ground with a yowl. Before I can raise me pistol, a musket lashes me ear.

"What I should do with this one, Moody?"

"Kill, for the one which rides off," is the answer.

The Cowboy rips off me hat, and me hair, which is grow'd longer from Hamilton cut'g it short, falls down. "Moody, it is a female wench!" the marauder shouts.

The man with the name which is terror to people in New Jersey walks over, and spies me close. His face is bandaged, and he squints with beady black pupils at me, and I see'd his mind calculating. "Take her," Moody orders.

Whilst another Private guards me with his musket, the first Private takes me pistol and finds the tomahawk in the saddle, and shows same to Moody. Moody yells, and walks like a man on fire back to me. He lifts me off the dirt by me hair and rips the noisome bandage off his face. His cheek is caked with black blood and he snarls at me, with green teeth. He pulls me nose into his bloody gash, and snarls, "I know ye . . . I know ye. Yer at Livingston's." He taps his finger on the ugly caked-over wound. "This be yer gift to old Moody." He laughs a bellyful. "When I be done with ye, wench, ye be want'g that sword to kill yer self."

I is put in chains and it is off to Ensign James Moody's encampment. On the long ride to Moody's, which is a property he abducted from a Whig farmholder in Westchester county [N.Y.], I thinks many times if this be the last ride for me, I will take Moody and his men to Hell, too.

◆ ◆ ◆

Moody is not the clever one he thinks. Robert Rogers teaches to cover eyes of enemy capture so he does not know his location, and how to proceed to git to it if he escapes and goes for his army to return. I be free to gaze about, and I know which is north and which is south, and which way is the rebel lines and which is the Redcoats. The land is no longer farms, only spindly stalks of old brown hay and grain, decaying and in ruin. We pass apple orchards, fruit rotted at bottoms of trees.[83]

---

[83] Before the war this region of Westchester County, N.Y. was a scene of rural affluence, with rich farm fields and fruit orchards. By the time of Agent 355's capture the land had been plundered by numerous bands of foraging parties which bore off hundreds of loads of its hay and grain. "The land was in ruins," a resident at the time wrote. "Most of the farm-holders had fled, and such as remained were not permitted to reap where they had sown. The fields were covered with the tangled harvest-growths that decayed ungathered on the ground, and in the neglected orchards the fruit rotted in great heaps beneath the trees." The American who describes the scene attributes all the devastation to the enemy for he considered Cowboys and Skinners as renegades alike, and all villainous Tories. He recites the tortures they employed to extort from the inhabitants. "The wretch would be hanged till he became insensible; then cut down and revived, and again hanged. The case of an aged Quaker makes it probable these ruffians were nominally Whigs; for the Quakers were generally loyal. This poor old man had given up all his money, but more was required. To be sure that he was secreting nothing from them, his captors first inflicted the torment of scorching. They stripped him naked, immersed him in hot ashes, and roasted him as one would a potato, till the blistered skin rose from his flesh. Then he was thrice hung and cut down; nor did his oppressors leave him while life appeared to remain." When Arron Burr took command of Malcolm's Regiment in Westchester County after the Battle of Monmouth, he noted that the

I asks a Moody Cowboy why the land is depressed, and he says, "Skinners and rebel skunks," and spits on the ground from his horse.

"Farmers run off in fear," says I.

The Cowboy confirms it by a belly grunt.

"But, is this not Whig homesteads?" I says, because I know'd a little of Westchester allegiances by then. He spits at me, and rides away from me.

Everybody lies these days.

At this farm, which is among many tall white oak trees, Moody lives in a cave blast'd with powder in a hillock, and his men, I count fifty-three, sleep in a house and a shack a long ways from the old, decrepit hut without windows I is tossed inside with chains bolt'd to me wrists. In the corner is a cot and in another a chair. On the chair is a guard with me, none outside.

It is a benefit of womanhood in a fight; men think yer weak, do not require a strict watch as men do.

It may be so – usually.

The guard's name is Willard Hall, and he speaks as an educated man I say I is "Miss Tabitha, housemaid."

"Housemaid?" says he. "We kidnap housemaids, for sin? Old Moody is lost his mind."

"Yer not from Westchester, I can tell by yer voice," I says.

"Massachusetts . . . Westford, Massachusetts," he says, pleasantly. "Reverend Willard Hall."

"Reverend! I see yer speaking is richly schooled."

"Graduated at Harvard, 1722," says Hall, with pride in his fine voice.[84]

---

region was being plundered by lawless bands of Loyalists and rebels and by undisciplined soldiers from both armies. The brutality got so out-of-hand that Burr said, wishing for arbitrary power to halt it: "I could gibbet half a dozen good Whigs, with all the venom of an inveterate Tory."

[84] Records show a Reverend Willard Hall of Westford, Massachusetts did graduate from Harvard University in 1722, but there is no record of him riding with James Moody's bunch. Records show Whig complaints against Rev. Hall were numerous in May 1775, and a "final hearing" on his case was held on June 4, 1776 before "the Committees of the towns of Dunstable, Littleton, Westford, and Acton" and that the decision was that in "divers instances, he hath shown himself unfriendly to the cause of the United American Colonies.'

"Why ride with Moody, he is infamous?" I know'd he sees how shock'd is I at this.

"I do not share his killing," says Hall, who is armed with a pistol and a long-knife. "I share his dislike of people who take our freedom."

"Is it not what King George does?"

"Not to me, and I do not care to speak of it," Hall says, probably thinking he is talking too much to a prisoner he guards.

A meal is brought to the shack by a woman, who, Hall tells me, is a Quaker which cooks for Moody. The wood bowl I eat from is encrust'd with dough, dirt and grease and holds broth with a few peas. Hall takes his pity on me and hands me a piece of his bread biscuit, and I thank his kindness. It is hard to eat with ragged chains bolt'd on me wrists, which is git'g sores, and I spill broth thrice.

After this supper Hall leaves the shack to see Moody, he says.

I takes this time to relieve me self in the dirt floor of the hut, and I figure Hall is urinate'g outside, after he locks the door hard and he leaves me. He stays gone, and inside I looks for ways to git out. Alas! It is a thick wood shack without loose boards. Then I spy it. A stout wood post by the wall next to the cot I is to sleep upon. A hole is bore'd through this post. I stick the iron bolt which holds the chains on me wrists and it fits inside the hole. I work the bolt up and down with all of me strength and it gives. I hear'd talking outside the hut and stop, and sit on the bed. The door opens and in walks a tall man I never see'd a fore, and Hall is behind and says, "This is Captain Lippincott to look at his wares."

I thinks "wares?" and stay silent on the cot.[85] This man Lippincott is worse in looks than is Moody his self, and smells like a grease-pot a week old. He pulls me hair from me face, holding it tight in his giant hand, and takes a knife with

---

[85] Nearly as "infamous" as James Moody himself was Captain Richard Lippincott who started his military career with Moody's First Battalion of New Jersey Volunteers, and later was in the service of the brutal "Board of Associated Loyalists" in New York City, which was responsible for many Whig civilian deaths and executions.

the other and cuts the top of me hunting shirt and me breast is expose'd to the cold, and he cuts me mammary skin with the blade, and I hits his arm with me chain'd hands. Lippincott slaps me face hard and laughs at me, and says he is to return at two o'clock to "ravish this whore."

He slams the hut door.

"Me fate is to be rape'd this night," I says to Hall.

Hall makes it affirmative with "uh," and says, "Captain Lippincott is victorious for ye in a card game." Hall looks shy in saying it, unable to keep his eyes upon me. "Moody did allow his officers to play cards for yer virtue."

"What is the time?"

"Midnight, and the Captain takes the guard in two hours," says Hall.

". . . And violates me . . . ."

"It is not the worst of it for ye, Miss Tabitha." I asks Hall what is meant. "Moody says ye cut his face and he is to cut yer face and scorch you when the Captain is done."[86] His head shakes. "I do not agree in it, but I is without power to stop it, Miss."

It is set in me mind; I must escape within two hours or be rape'd and cut and burned. I immediately tells Hall I is too cold and he leaves and brings back a long coat for me. I put the coat like a tent over me ready to work on the bolt. Hall sleeps on the chair and I work'd the bolt into the hole of the post and push up and down with all of the strength in me arms for what feels like hours but it may be only minutes. With a powerful push of me whole body the bolt snaps in two parts, and chains fall from me wrists. I creep to the chair, and with a heavy blow hit Hall in the head with the chain. He falls on the dirt floor, out. He is not dead, but cannot move. Another enemy I would kill, but not Hall. He takes pity on me, and for this, I takes pity on Reverend Willard Hall.[87]

---

[86] Scorching was a kind of torture in which a person was stripped naked and rolled over smoldering ashes until the skin blistered and bubbled up from the flesh. If a person survived he was disfigured for life.

[87] Agent 355 says Rev. Willard Hall, mentioned in Note 75, was knocked out but alive when she left him in the hut. Official records also show that Hall died in 1779. If this is the same Willard Hall who served as guard of Agent 355, it might not stretch credulity to assume that he was killed by Moody himself as punishment for her escape. This is informed speculation based on Moody's penchant for

With his pistol and long knife in hand, I use the knife to
break the door lock. Outside I hear'd talking up by the house
where the men sleep. It is a black night and so dark and I
cannot see men where the voices is coming from. Now I
hear'd footsteps, and lay on the ground with the dark long
coat over me. A soldier passes me. It be Captain Lippincott
on his way to the hut.

To rape and ravish me.

I wait, and then bolt into a field, heading, I think
northerly but in this darkness I do not know with certainty.
Behind I hear shouts and yells and men all a stir, and know'd
they find poor Hall on the floor of the hut and me fled. I
come to a stand of white oaks and immediately feels the bark
of one, as I know'd what Indians know'd from me training at
Robert Rogers's camp. The bark of a white oak is rough and
unpleasant to the touch on the south side, but on the north
side it is smooth. By occasionally touch'g oaks for smooth
bark I continues to head north in the dark forest. I know'd to
the north is Continental Army lines.

I hear'd a noise, and I crouch behind a tree. I see'd the
outline of two of Moody's Cowboys, and it is a distance away,
and I cannot fire the pistol which is a signal to bring the rest
of his men down on me. I lay on the ground in the dark and
puts the dark coat over me body, and the two men walks by
me, and limbs crack and twigs snap. I slither quietly like a
snake out of the long coat, and, with the knife in me right
hand, I slink in the darkness behind these two soldiers.
Walking in line, I jumps on the back of the soldier behind the
other, and he shouts, and I thrust the knife into his neck with
so much force I thinks his head will be decapitate'd. The
other soldier turns, raises his musket at me, and I throw the
knife at his chest. Me arm is weaken'd, and it sticks in his
guts. He falls back and his musket fires. The ball hits me left
arm, and rips off flesh. It stings bad, and for a moment I feel
I be faint'g, but I do not.

The soldier writhes on the ground.

---

violence and vengeance. Given Agent 355's account of her talk with Hall it does not appear that he,
a graduate of Harvard, fit in well with Moody's gang of cutthroats. He certainly showed her some
compassion.

I crawl to his body, and the knife is in his stomach. I takes and pushes it up and back and round, and the soldier is screaming because I is slicing his inner bowels and flesh so he is sure to be dead soon. The other soldier did carry a long rifle which is accurately deadly at distances. I takes it from his body and removes his leather cartridge case. I cuts the dead man's shirt, and puts it on me arm wound, which is bloody, and burns like me flesh is ablaze. Neither dead is with canteen or food pack, but I cannot worry it over because Moody is coming down on me in moments after he hear'd the musket shot.

Into the night I run, the long coat for the cold bedraggled in the dirt behind me. The woods soon ran to swampland. To counter cravings of hunger, I lost count of the many water snakes I kill'd and ate; and I chews beech tree leaves, which is not bitter like others and does not upset stomachs. I trudge through water which smells like dung and I know'd the water is not good, but I drinks it to stay alive. Now I remembers the malaria of Boston, and wonders whether this swamp brings it back. Such thoughts is how the mind works when the body is in dire peril.

I cannot say how many days and nights I walk, and in a meadow I remember falling and me mind thinks "I is dying," and the next time I wake it is in a hospital tent in New Windsor [New York], and a surgeon is telling me I be lucky to be still alive because I lost much blood from the musket hole in me arm, which did not hit the bone so he did not amputate same. He says a Continental Army patrol discovers me and brings me to the hospital, fear'g I be dead or close enough.

For weeks me stomach is sick with dysentery from putrid water and food. I is able to tell officers the farm which Moody's cutthroats hide, and within days I is told Moody his self is capture'd and is to be tried for murder and crimes against rebels and Whigs and even against his own Loyalist followers. I tells officers it is Moody who kill's New Jersey Militia Captain Edward Drake of Governor Livingston's personal guard in raid to kill or kidnap the governor at Parsippany.

Continental Army officers be in wonderment at the information I know'd.

One day a Major appears in the hospital to talk to me and tells me thank you for leading his army to the farm of James Moody. "I do not understand something," says the Major after thanking me. "Why does a very successful Cowboy like James Moody kidnap a mere housemaid?"

I thinks fast, and cannot tell him the truth. "I works in the house of Governor Livingston," I say, "and Moody thinks the governor is to pay ransom for me release." The lie satisfies the Major.

Then he tells me of Moody's cut face. "His face is sliced up terrible," says the Major.

"Uh," I says.

Then the Major says: "I ask'd Moody how he gits this saber wound and he says he fought close combat with a patrol of Lieutenant-Colonel William Knowlton's Rangers." The Major continues: "Fearless steady fighters serve under Colonel Knowlton, some say the best in the Army, as good as Rogers's Rangers in the last war [French and Indian War]."

Me throat goes dry, and I cannot utter a word. Moody will not admit his disfigurement is cause'd by a wench, I thinks. And I know'd if he fights with Robert Rogers his head is what would be cut off. I says: "I would not know of such things as Rogers's Rangers, Sir."

"No, I suspect a housemaid would not," he says. "Thank you Miss Tabitha for leading us to outlaw James Moody."

I recuperates at this hospital for weeks. Me arm feels healed and is no longer stiff to move, and me stomach ill is in submission. In this time the Continental officers take by express rider me secret message to Colonel Tallmadge; these same officers is in total astonishment I know'd Tallmadge!

In a month I hear'd back from Tallmadge to git to Colonel Robinson's Hudson River Country for spy'g, "if yer able." Tallmadge sends a new French pistol, short dagger and short-handle tomahawk with the express rider, and I cannot describe the looks on faces of the Continental officers in New Windsor when they see'd these armaments put over to me.

"If she's a housemaid, I'm a pigeon [weak fellow]," I hear'd a Lieutenant say.

♦ ♦ ♦

Hudson River Country must wait, as I go to Long Island to git money from Rogers's gold box. There I gits the terrible word: Yer Uncle Ebenezer be kidnap'd by rebel skinners.

What is happen'g much in Long Island is marauders, Loyalist Cowboys like Moody's and rebel skinners from Connecticut. They do what the Redcoats call "grabs," which is stealing goods and people from homesteads. Cowboys take cattle and sell it to the Redcoats and skinners take people and ransom for silver or exchange for rebels which be already kidnap'd by Loyalists. This state of it is so bad the people of Long Island live lives in fear.

Abraham Woodhull tells me he is scared to be kidnap'd or kill'd by rebels who raid us from Connecticut, and they do not know this, if they take Woodhull who masquerades his self as a Tory, they be taking their own kind in the rebellion. I tells Woodhull this and he is not humor'd by it. Then I tells Woodhull this Loyalist bandit James Moody is capture'd, and Woodhull says he hear'd of it, and it is the clever Continental Army which capture'd the lawless brigand, and he hopes he is shot. He says he hear'd His Excellency's army set a trap for Moody, how clever is it?

"Very," I says, say'g nothing more.

But now I be thinking about me Uncle. This is what happen'd to Uncle Ebenezer, a Tory, when he is taken by Whig skinners to Simsbury Mine.[88]

---

[88] It is tantalizing to think Agent 355 has finally slipped up and revealed information that could lead historians to her true identity – in this case the name "Uncle Ebenezer," who she writes was taken to infamous "Simsbury Mine" prison in Connecticut. I immediately researched inmate records, as they were, at the old underground prison, later called Newgate Prison, which is a tourist attraction today. There is record of an "Ebenezer Hathaway" being a prisoner about the time her uncle was kidnapped. However the circumstances of Hathaway's case – he was captured aboard a Loyalist privateer boat – is completely different from her uncle's. Of course I do not discount Agent 355 masking her uncle's identity by also relating a false narrative about his kidnapping. But keep in mind, she will tell this same story, or so she claims, to John Simcoe of the Queen's Rangers, in seeking his aid. Simcoe had the power and resources to investigate whether she was lying. I conclude that "Uncle Ebenezer" is not her uncle's real name, but yet another clever device used by Agent 355 to deny us clues to her true identity. In Revolutionary War Simsbury Mine prison was a place to flee. Here is how a contemporary, Loyalist Reverend Samuel Peters, author of *General History of Connecticut*, described it: "In working one (copper mine) many years ago, the miners

Uncle Ebenezer is home at night and a band of a dozen skinners kick'd out his door in Setauket, and he is sleeping in his bed and they beat his body with clubs. They carries off his possessions, and me Uncle, too, and leaves his wife, who cries and cowers from the raiders. Ebenezer, I learn'd, makes many enemies in 1777 when he leads a band of Loyalists to protect Setauket when General Parsons attacks the Caroline Church. When the Loyalist populace is ordered by British to remove headstones from the cemetery and pile for a redoubt around the church, Uncle Ebenezer tells his Loyalists to take "only grave marks of Whig families" and leave headstones of Loyalist dead and buried untouched, and this is what they done. Ebenezer is hated by Whig families since this day.

Now he is taken, and me Aunt tells me to go to Major Simcoe of the Queen's Rangers to effect his return. At Oyster Bay and the house called Raynham Hall of Samuel Townsend, which is taken by Major Simcoe, I is stop'd by three Queen's Rangers who be tossing knives in a contest at a painted circle on the wood of a hut. They says I must go away. I protest, I must see Major Simcoe, and they says he sees none but soldiers and certainly not a wench.

"I be no wench, brother of the blade [fellow soldier]," I says. "Major John André his self is a friend and he gives me a draw'd picture for Major Simcoe to express his best friendship. I is here to deliver same." I takes out the ink drawing André draws of his friend Simcoe in Lancaster from me pocket, and shows it to the tallest, vociferous fellow. "Major André asks me to present this to his friend Major Simcoe." The Queen Rangers peer at the picture, and agree it is their beloved Major, and all eyes is in surprise. The three looks at the other confuse'd, as if to speak, "what is it we do?"

---

bored half a mile through the mountain, making large cells forty yards below the surface, which now serve as a prison, by order of the General Assembly, for such offenders as they choose not to hang. The prisoners are let down on a windlass into this dismal cavern, through a hole, which answers the triple purpose of conveying them food, air, and – I was going to say light, but it scarcely reaches them. In a few months the prisoners are released by death and the colony rejoices in her great 'humanity' and the 'mildness' of her laws. This conclave of spirits imprisoned may be called, with great propriety, the Catacomb of Connecticut." A prisoner who later escaped recalled the smell down below the surface: "A ventilator shaft was intended to provide fresh air but charcoal pots burned constantly in an effort to clear the foul odors."

I takes the situation in hand. "Yer throw'g the blade at the circle, and I see yer pretty fair at it. Yet, I be better."

They begins the mirth and laughs at me which is what happens when this female provokes a grow'd male. "A dumb wench?" says the tallest and boldest. "Go back home and cook potatoes."

"If I best yer knife-throwing will you let me see the Major for Major André's wish?" I says to the tall one, "We will throw at the center of the circle, and if ye best me I be on me way to cook potatoes. If I best yer throwing, I be on me way to see Major Simcoe."

The tall one gives the affirmative gesture with his head.

"I do not carry a knife," I says.

The tall one tells another to surrender his weapon to me, and the soldier does same, with much mirthfulness in his voice. I walks to the circle, scratch a 'X' mark in the middle, and strolls back fifty paces. I see'd all these Queen's Rangers is astonish'd at how far I is from the circle.

"This be too far for ye?" I says.

The tall one says nay in a boastful way.

I turns and throws the knife as I does a thousand times at Robert Rogers's camp, and it hits the X, dead in the center.

"Next, Sir," I says, and gives the knife back. "Or do ye yield?"

I see'd the tall Ranger is hot-temper'd at me, a lowly woman and a wench, and his two friends is laugh'g at him, and it is clear he does not want to throw and prove by evidence me is his better. He takes his hat which rests on a wagon and says, "Come." At the door of Townsend's house the tall Ranger speaks to a sentinel who gits a Lieutenant who asks me why I want to see the Major and I says John André asks me to tell his friend Major John Simcoe of his friendship and to give this drawing to same.

I show'd the ink picture of Simcoe.

Now the tall Ranger whispers to the Lieutenant, and he orders the sentinel to search me for knives, and he finds none. In minutes I is standing before Major Simcoe who sits in a chair in a great room of the house. His face is of a crapulous look, his eyes be set nicely into his high forehead and it is with a small mouth and nose he looks up at me. "How is it, Madame, you know Major André?"

I tell Simcoe of being in Lancaster, Pennsylvania when his friend is a prisoner with liberty at the Quaker house of Caleb Cope, and Major Simcoe says, "Yes, John tells me of Cope's. He came here many times, did André." It is this moment in time I earn his trust, and me and Major Simcoe talk of John André. Simcoe tells me when he first met his friend and of happy times together, and takes the drawing and says I thank you. I see'd it is time for me to leave because the Major is ready to meet with two staff officers who wait outside. "Where did you learn to toss the knife?" says Major Simcoe, surprise'g me. "They do not teach this in London schools." He smirks at his remark.

This is a question I do not expect, and just as every lie hath some truth in it, I say, "Me Uncle once had a friend who is once a member of Robert Rogers's Rangers and he show'd me Uncle and me Uncle show'd me."

"Robert Rogers?" says Major Simcoe. "Unfortunate case is Rogers."

"I do not understand this," I says.

"He be a drunkard and Sir Henry ask'd Rogers to raise King's Rangers in Nova Scotia and he cannot because of rum and is cashiered from the King's service, and is in prison," says Simcoe.

"Prison?" The word staggers me, and then sanguines me. For the first time in years I be at ease over Rogers kill'g me for not assassinating his enemy General Thomas Gage for which he pays me in gold. In prison Rogers cannot look for me. "Major," I says, "one thing I need to know." Simcoe's face looks back and asks so what is it, and I says, "Me Uncle Ebenezer is hostage'd by skinners and be languishing in Simsbury Mine, and I come to ask if yer Queen's Rangers can git his self out from it?"

"Dear, dear, dear," says Major Simcoe. "I cannot. Fort Franklin is in danger of another raid by Colonel Tallmadge and his rebels, and this requires all regiments to be vigilant. I cannot give succor to any body's Uncle, Madame."

"If I raise a group of able bodied Loyalists to rescue me Uncle, will you provide same with weapons?"

"What man is to lead this Troy troop?"

"Me, Sir."

A vicious smile captures Major Simcoe's pudding face and he does not say a word. To this day I believe he is thinking he wants to see if a band of Loyalists lead by a female defeats rebel men at Simsbury Mine, and this is the reason he says yea to me. If I beat rebel men Simcoe will tell his friends of it, if not, I will be on me own and forgotten. Major Simcoe tells me he will not give me British weapons. He will tell his Lieutenant to give me rebel muskets and pistols which Simcoe his self seized in his night-time raid in 1778 on the house of Judge William Hancock, in which Simcoe's men used bayonets to kill ten rebel militia asleep in bedclothes. In many quarters Simcoe is condemned for it.[89]

◆ ◆ ◆

I raise fourteen Loyalist men of fine stock to help in the raid on Simsbury Mine, all of which is a brother, father, son or uncle of a prisoner in this infamous prison after being taken by rebel skinners or renegade Continental soldiers who desert and pillage for their own greediness. Prisoners at Simsbury is British soldiers and Loyalists and Continental Army soldiers under court martial, and I decide which ever Simsbury Mine prisoner desires freedom he gits it; and I do not care if he his Loyalist or Whig or like me, somewhere betwixt. Planning by me is thus: I gives Caleb Brewster three pounds for use of two whaleboats and two helmsmen, and on the day before this raid, I gives Simsbury prisoner John Young's wife, Abigail, fifty-two silver dollars to bribe corrupt

---

[89] It is unknown where Agent 355 got her information about Simcoe's 1778 raid on Judge William Hancock's home. In his own memoir, Simcoe, who was a major at the time of the raid and was later promoted to lieutenant-colonel and ultimately general, wrote that his Queen's Rangers raided the house of "twenty or thirty men" and "all of whom were killed." He also lamented that "Some very unfortunate circumstances happened here. Among the killed was a friend of Government, then a prisoner with the rebels, old Hancock, the owner of the house, and his brother." Historians say Judge Hancock was not home during the raid. In his memoir Simcoe attempts to show he tried to limit killing of friendlies. "Major Simcoe," he wrote in the third person, "had made particular enquiry, and was informed that he (Hancock) did not live at home . . . The information was partly true; he was not there in the day-time, but unfortunately returned home at night. Events like these are the real miseries of war."

sergeant of prison guards, a Sergeant Lilly. Abigail Young is let to visit her husband and takes same clothes and food, and on this visit across the Sound to Simsbury she pays Sergeant Lilly the silver dollars to leave the lock to the south jail unlocked the following night. She then alerts her husband to be ready to escape with who and how many wishes to come.

We oar across the Sound in the boats which will have space for all who want to return to Setauket from their misery, and we march unmolested and see'd no Connecticut militia, which surprise'd me. It is a dark night, with a little moon light, and at Simsbury we see'd eight guards sit'g on stones near a fire, and it is one easy thing to round them up under threat of instant death. Eight of us storm the guardhouse, and we kill'd two guards with our knives who tries to git pistols for a fight. We open the pit door in the guardhouse down to the kitchen, which is kept unlocked by Sergeant Lilly, who is outside with our prisoners at the fire. Guards in the kitchen surrender and we force same to open the large trapdoor in the floor. This door has a ladder which descends thirty-eight feet to a place they call the "landing." Here the stench of the humanity still far below the surface is horrific to smell, and men in me group wince and cough at the strong offensive odors. We must climb down another forty feet to the bottom of the mine pit, which is lay over with wood ship planks, and which is home to fifty-nine prisoners, all in soiled, tattered clothes and bearded faces, and some be dead already and others be near to Heaven.

I see'd Uncle Ebenezer right off, and he hugs me. He is in amazement it is me who leads his recue.

Some prisoners jump on guards we force down into the bottom and strike them with fists, and I yells, "This is no time for retribution if yer escaping with us," and this fighting stops instantly. Me men helps many up the ladders to the kitchen but some prisoners on the pit's bottom cannot stand at all, and we, sadly, leave these to die in the stink and defilement. In the guardhouse I give muskets to four regimentals and to four Loyalists from Setauket and tells six prisoners from the Continental Army they cannot git weapons and can go in any direction, and we are head'd into British lines.

This order immediately brings protests from a Loyalist prisoner who shouts at me, saying we must kill them for revenge. (I feel a need for revenge on the skinner who kidnap'd me Uncle, too, but it cannot be.)

I puts the pistol to this Loyalist's ear, and says, "Obey or stay here." On purpose it is ambiguous as to whether me meaning is yer dead body stays on this spot or yer self stays living at Simsbury, and the Loyalist's mouth falls silent.

This sends the six rebel prisoners running away unmolested.

We puts all guards in the second level under the kitchen and locks the main door, and this includes Sergeant of Guards Lilly who be fifty-two silver dollars more prosperous.

Near the Sound it happens, which I fear'd.

Connecticut militia patrol of a dozen men armed with long rifles is on the road, and we hide in a copse of trees. I do not want more bloodshed. This is a militia fighting against the King on the same side as me, and we kill'd two guards at Simsbury Mine, already. In me mind, however, I is not who starts this kidnap'g of Uncle Ebenezer, and if it is not done by the rebels I would not be here kill'g. It is the way yer force'd to think when turn'g against yer own side for higher personal interests.

I thinks of a plan, and calls me Uncle over. Minutes later he is on the road escorting two of our four Redcoats in their dirty regimentals under guard with two young Loyalists with muskets, and he approaches the Connecticut Militia.

The Connecticut militia men yells halt or die. Uncle Ebenezer says he is a farmer over Colebrook way, and these two guards is sons, and we, "Capture'd these deserter Redcoats on our land, foraging. We be taking them to Simsbury Mine for detainment."

"Old man," says the Lieutenant in charge of the patrol, "Simsbury is back that way, ye be turned around."

All eyes of the rebel militia is on the Redcoats and me Uncle, and they do not see us surround them in the darkness.

"Lieutenant," I yells, "We make aim at yer boys who will die unless all weapons hit the ground now!" Me group of Loyalists and prisoners far outnumber the patrol and in war numbers matter, and the Lieutenant orders his men to disarm.

"A woman," I hear'd the Lieutenant say.

This is why I stay in the shadow of a tree and shout instructions. I know'd Colonel Tallmadge would protect me but I did not want this raid know'd by his self. "We is not here for kill'g," I says. "Tie them and come, men." So it is. We leave this militia patrol tied to trees off the road, and gits to the whaleboats. Not all prisoners come with us because some are from New Jersey, Connecticut and one poor man with a bad leg is from Boston, and they go in different directions – all away from Simsbury Mine. The four Redcoats come in the whaleboats back to Setauket. We take them to Raynham Hall in Oyster Bay so they can tell Major John Graves Simcoe the story of a female besting guards at infamous Simsbury Mine prison and a rebel Lieutenant's full patrol – all men – for his amusement.

Uncle Ebenezer never asks me how it is I be leading this raiding party at Simsbury Mine, which meant I never fabricated a lie about it. I suspect it is me Aunt who makes her husband promise to never ask me. She is a wise woman.

In days I git another coded message from Colonel Tallmadge who is say'g Abraham Woodhull reports I is still in Setauket and not on me way to Colonel Robinson's Hudson River Country for spy'g. He orders me to leave immediately, which I do, but not a fore I see'd Abraham and say, "Stop yer own spy'g on me!" I scare this weak man I know'd, but Woodhull needs to understand saving family from Simsbury is me first duty, not revolutions.

1780

It takes much time for me to journey to the Hudson River country and find the camp of Loyal American Regiment, which is in the forests on the east side of the Hudson, across from West Point, in the Cat Rock Road area near the area called Garrison. Colonel Tallmadge asks me to venture into this hostile Loyalist place and find Colonel Beverley Robinson, a Tory of great wealth, lands and influence in the Hudson before his lands is taken by his Whig enemies. Tallmadge tells me Colonel Robinson is leader of his own Loyalist spies on the Hudson, which is important to Colonies commerce and to General Washington. He tells me to keep eyes open, ears to ground, which I do.

I takes the Monmouth name of Mary Fletcher, peddler, and I sells knives I buy'd in the city of New York to the Loyalist soldiers. I gits to know one, because I hear'd talk he is confidante of Colonel Robinson. He is Lieutenant John Howard. He is not what I call a handsome man and I know'd his experience with females is but a courteous doff of his hat in they'r presence, and nothing of carnal intimacy. He talks much, and more when I pour cups of rum in the day's late hours.

I be invite'd in the tent of Colonel Robinson on two occasions. He buy'd a knife from me collection of wares one time. When he learn't I buy'd knives in New York, he calls me again to talk of how people make it after these years of the fire. Me talking of the fire I start'd secretly is more irony, and I be uncomfortable telling the Colonel of the people still in canvas tents in the neighborhood I see'd on me visit.

"Damn Sons of Liberty," Colonel Robinson says, yelling it like, "which ignite'd the conflagration."

"So it is," I says.

I like Colonel Robinson, even if a Tory. A more gentle soul and kind to me there is not, and he is rich, or is at one time. He tells me of his house the Whigs "took in their pilferage" and he says it is large with broad beams overhead in the rooms, and fireplaces with polished tiles warm each one.[90]

One night I comes to Lieutenant Howard's tent with cups of rum and he is happy, so much so he sings a tune I never hear'd a fore.

"Ye, Tories all rejoice and sing, success to George our gracious King.

"The faithful subjects' tribute bring, and execrate the Congress.

"These hardy knaves and stupid fools,

"Some apish and pragmatic mules,

"Some servile acquiescing tools,

"These compose the Congress.

"Then Jove resolve to send a curse,

"And all the woes of life rehearse,

"Not plague, not famine, but much worse,

"He cursed us with a Congress."

I applaud for Lieutenant Howard's singing, and says, "Congress, a curse'd band of knaves is truth!"

We laugh and I gits the rum, and he drinks to the health of the King, and says, "This war is near'd over."

"Lo," I says, "not of it I see'd. Washington fights. We fights. It never ends. It is wishing it, not more."

To which Lieutenant Howard says, "Nay, it is near'd over because a General of the rebels is altering allegiance to our King."

"This never happens, not a General. Privates, yea, Lieutenants, surly; not a General. It be idle talk."

Lieutenant Howard is angry, and says he know'd what he know'd because the Colonel his self says it.

I know'd the Lieutenant and Colonel Beverley Robinson is friends, and talk of the war, and I says, "If this rebel General renounces Washington how is it, it ends this old war?"

---

[90] In his "The History of St. Philip's Church," E. Clowes Chorley describes Beverley Robinson's mansion, which until the 1890s when it burned down, as "a wooden house lined with brick" in the fields below Sugar Loaf Mountain in Garrison. Robinson was the area's most prominent citizen and his land consisted of 60,000 acres covering parts of Garrison, Philipstown, Putnam Valley, Kent and Patterson. He was the first Church Warden and principal benefactor of St. Philip's Chapel. He married Susannah Philipse, daughter of Frederick Philipse who was a nephew and heir to Adolph Philipse, the holder of the original land grant from King William III. When Robinson declared himself a Loyalist and led the attack on Fort Clinton his lands were confiscated. In the months before his defection to the British, American General Benedict Arnold lived in Robinson's mansion.

Lieutenant Howards stops talking and gives me a serious look, and I see'd by his eyes fix'd on me he is thinking I be too curious about this, so I says, pouring more rum, "One rebel will not make a difference."

"If he surrenders the army, too, it does."[91]

"So putrid Washington his self is surrender'g?"

Lieutenant Howard says he is not privy to who is surrendering, but knows British officers will soon sail *H.M.S. Vulture* up river to meet this General in secret."

"If ye do not know who then where and when?"

As soon as these words pass through me lips I know'd I is seeking too much information. "Yer too curious of this matter," says the Lieutenant. "Why so much interest on this?"

"When this war ends is important to me," I says. "That is all. Let us find more pleasurable matters this night." I lies on his blanket, thinking this is the time to show this Lieutenant what his manliness is for.

"Not in the Colonel's camp," he says in a whisper, and he sounds scare'd to me. He is not a youngster, but in his third decade, and it is strange to think he never has one whoring wench.

"The old horse barn," I says, and he agrees.

I know'd the other troops is a distance away from these horses, and they will not hear what it is I must do. Because I know'd once Lieutenant Howard opens his mouth about the deserter General, he closes his grave shut. It cannot be another way. I must leave and report and if he is alive he know'd I is gone to tell of this deserter General meeting Redcoats on the ship *Vulture*. This General will not meet his Redcoats and will change his plans to meet them another day, another time, another place. It must be done.

Poor Lieutenant Howard.

---

[91] If they still teach American history in U.S. schoolhouses, every fifth-grader in American would know that the Continental Army general who was going to defect to the British is Benedict Arnold. His plan called for surrendering troops at West Point to the British. Benedict Arnold was a personal friend of Washington and there is little doubt his defection struck Washington hard, emotionally. For an excellent account of their relationship see Nathaniel Philbrick's *Valiant Ambition: George Washington, Benedict Arnold, and the Fate of the American Revolution*, 2016.

In the barn, Lieutenant Howard show'd me a elegant horse in from Pennsylvania, and it is a fine steed. I walks to a pen and says we can lay in this hay, and I lays on it. The Lieutenant lays and I leapt on top, and pulls the dagger and pushes it into the skin of the poor man's throat. He screams, and I cover his mouth with me hand. "Tell the name of the turncoat General?" He is startle'd and scare'd, and I set free me hand.

"A bloody rebel spy," says he, fear and horror in his wide eyes.

"Ye be a bloody dead body if you do not tell me the name of the turncoat General meeting on the *Vulture*."

"The Colonel did not privilege it to me," he says, and he moves his arm.

I sticks the knife a ways into his skin, and blood squirts out. "Ye want to join yer great grandfather?" says I. "Tell me the British officer who sails on the Vulture."

"God as me witness I do not know this," he swears.

"When does the *Vulture* sail?"

He moves his head side to side, saying nay.

"Where do they meet?"

More movement of his head, in negative motion.

"I be full of sorrow for ye, Lieutenant Howard." With these solemn words I puts me hand over his mouth so he cannot scream out, and I cut his throat deep. Soon he is dead. I must work quickly. I move his body outside the barn, and go inside and loose seven horses from stalls, and scare same into a gallop. I secret the dagger in the barn for later.

Screaming, I run to Colonel Robinson's camp. I gits to the camp and Colonel Robinson's aide is at the Colonel's tent, and asks what happens. "Rebel skinners," I yells, frighten'd; "they kill'd Lieutenant Howard! Pilfer horses!"

"How many skinners?" he asks.

"Four or so!"

He wakes Colonel Robinson and the Colonel, the aide and six Loyalists chase after the skinners, and return with one horse. "Must have slipped off his harness," the aide says of the horse.

This night I tell Colonel Robinson and his aide what happens: Lieutenant Howard and me go to barn to see a horse he likes from Pennsylvania and is ambush'd by rebels. When Lieutenant Howard fights, a skinner stabs him. When Lieutenant is fighting, protecting me, I runs away and yells for help. The skinners run with horses.

"Miss Mary, you are a brave lass," says Colonel Robinson. I see'd tears in his eyes for his friend Lieutenant Howard, and I feel bad for his sake.

I stay for a full week, and with the complement of the Loyal America Regiment, Lieutenant Howard is put in the grave with full bestowment of honors upon a soldier of standing. In this week I keep me ears open for any new information on this turncoat General, and none exists. In me own mind I begin this wondering of the identity of the turncoat General. George Washington his self? Nay. Could it be General William Alexander; or Generals Horatio Gates, Nathanael Greene, Edward Hand, William Heath, Lachlan McIntosh, Alexander McDougall, Philip Schuyler or Anthony Wayne? Me head is dizzy from thinking.

In two weeks I tells Colonel Robinson I must take leave and journey to New York for a supply of wares, knives and such, and asks if he requires something special from the divers merchants of this city.

"Extract of Butternut bark," says he. "They say it is a cathartic and treatment for pox. Me wife requires it for our medical stores."

"It is done," says I, and the Colonel says I should return to his camp the soonest. I bundle me cart, and at the barn I gits the dagger with dried blood of poor Lieutenant Howard.

I troll and trundle on the way south, along the Hudson River.

It is September 21 when in the area of Verplanck's Point on the river I see a rebel camp of artillerists, and show me flag from General Benedict Arnold, which I gits from Colonel Tallmadge, to one Colonel James Livingston, who welcomes me into the encampment.[92] I tells Colonel Livingston that I

---

[92] A "flag" is a document issued by the military to businessmen who crossed military lines to buy and sell wares. These passes were essentially honored by both the Americans and British. Agent

require an express to take a vital, coded message to Colonel Tallmadge, and he makes a rider report, and I writes of a plot of the unnamed General ready to bolt from rebel ranks and his meeting British officers on the ship *H.M.S. Vulture*, a sloop of war. The express rider leaves.[93] In private I tells Colonel Livingston be watchful of the British sloop *Vulture* sailing upstream from New York, as it houses the King's spies. Colonel Livingston promises vigilance.[94]

This same night the Colonel provides a fine horse to take me to Black Rock in Connecticut, and from there to Setauket by whaleboat. This does not happen as by fate I be taken by escort to Tappan, N.Y. instead.

Today, a cold October in 1810, the events which happen the next day, September 22, 1780, is know'd to all, and is fresh in mind to me as yesterday's breakfast, and smolders in a sad heart. Colonel Livingston's artillerists see'd the *H.M.S. Vulture* on the Hudson and fires on it so the sloop cannot retrieve the British officer who confers on the bank with turncoat General Benedict Arnold. The *Vulture* flees, and the British officer, calling his self "John Anderson" is caught and taken to Tappan and General Washington.

Oh, beloved John André, how I betray ye.

Major André is this "John Anderson" who is dressed as a townsfolk and taken as a common British spy.[95]

---

355 got her "flag" or travel pass from General Arnold because at the time New York, where she obtained it, was in his jurisdiction. At this time, she nor virtually anyone else knew of Arnold's planned defection.

[93] Apparently this military express rider never made it to Colonel Tallmadge because there is no mention of this letter in his historical papers or in his memoir. Express riders were used by the military because communication was difficult. For instance, Benedict Arnold wrote a secret message to British General Sir Henry Clinton, saying he would sell out West Point and his country for 20,000 pounds and didn't know his offer had been accepted until a month later.

[94] Colonel James Livingston, commander of Verplanck's Point artillery battery, retired from the Continental Army in January 1781 and in recognition of his service, and certainly in light of his role in foiling Benedict Arnold's plot to hand over West Point and its soldiers to the British, he was granted 3,500 acres of land in New York. In addition, in 1801 he was granted another 1,280 acres of land in Ohio. In other words, Agent 355 made him a relatively rich man for the times. The Hudson River was the main navigation route for the British Navy in the Revolutionary War. It runs 315 miles through eastern New York and originates in the Adirondack Mountains and drains into the Atlantic Ocean between New York City and Jersey City, and is the boundary between New York and New Jersey. The river is named for English explorer Henry Hudson who sailed up the river in 1609.

[95] On September 20, 1780 Major John André and Colonel Beverley Robinson sailed upstream on

In the presidential election which began November 2 and ended December 5, 1792, I talk with Colonel Tallmadge about President Washington, and tells him if I be a member of the Electoral College I could not vote for Washington for a second term as president. I would vote for Vice President John Adams for President.

Tallmadge asks why.

"He shan't never hang'd John André," I says. "He is hate'd for it by me."

---

the Hudson on *H.M.S. Vulture* and, the following night, General Benedict Arnold's accomplice, Joshua Smith, brought André, who was dressed in his uniform to Smith's house in Haverstraw where Arnold and André talked about Arnold's audacious plot to turn the soldiers at the West Point, a key Hudson River garrison and crucial link between the northern and southern colonies, over to the British. The plot called for Arnold to replace links in a 1,000-link iron chain, each link weighing 114 pounds, across the Hudson with rope that could be cut. The chain, across the 1,500-foot width of river between West Point and Constitution Island, stopped British ships from venturing far up the Hudson. West Point existed to guard it. (Similar to a chain across the Bosphorus that protected Constantinople during the Crusades.) Once British troops swarmed into West Point Arnold would surrender and turn West Point over to the British, essentially dividing the Colonies which would, Arnold suggested, lead to the defeat of Washington and the Continental Army. (West Point would become the U.S. Military Academy in 1802.) Arnold sought payment of 20,000 pounds, a paltry amount for such an outcome. Arnold drew pictures of the garrison's defenses for André to take to General Clinton. One showed "Redoubt No. 3, a slight wood work, 3 feet thick, very dry, no bomb proofs, easily set on fire, no cannon." Before the mission, Clinton instructed his personal aide André not to remove his uniform and not to accept papers from Arnold, lest he be caught and treated as a spy. The next morning when the artillery battery fired on the *Vulture* and forced it a dozen miles downstream, André was left on his own to find his way to British lines. He hid Arnold's drawings in his socks and donned civilian clothes and a hat. These two acts later convicted him of spying and lead to his death. He was captured by chance when he came across three rebel "freebooters" playing cards by road at Tarrytown. He mistook them for being part of Oliver De Lancey's Loyalist militia and identified himself as a British officer. Once he realized the mistake he offered them his gold watch and 500 guineas to let him escape. Instead they took his watch. When one of the skinners removed André's boots to steal them, he found the West Point documents, and began calling him a "spy." At this point Major André proclaimed, "All's gone, by God." They turned him over to the American army and General Washington was alerted. However, the same Colonel John Jameson who alerted Washington of the capture of a man who identified himself as "John Anderson" and who was in possession of papers about West Point, also alerted Benedict Arnold. Arnold was Colonel Jameson's immediate superior, and knowing the jig was up, fled downriver and boarded the *Vulture*, escaping. Major André immediately confessed his identity to Washington. Word of Arnold's treachery spread quickly. In Philadelphia an image of him dressed in British uniform was paraded in a cart, showing him with two faces and being followed by the devil with a pitchfork, pushing him to Hell. Wrote the *Pennsylvania Packet* newspaper of October 3, 1780: "The procession was attended with a numerous concourse of people, who after expressing their abhorrence of the Treason and the Traitor, committed him to the flames . . . and oblivion." Continental Army Major Samuel Shaw in a letter to his father in October 1780 summed up what fellow officers thought of him: "I suppose you have all been . . . thunderstruck at Arnold's conduct . . . It can scarcely be matched by any piece of villainy ancient or modern. I have not time at present to detail that most diabolical piece of rascality." (*Life and Journals of Major Samuel Shaw*, 1847.)

Days pass and I gits this letter from Colonel Tallmadge, and it is his account of Major André's capture. I put it in this diary for all readers now, and do so because it shows the man André is. "From the moment," writes Tallmadge, "that André made the disclosure of his name and true character, in his letter to the Commander-In-Chief, which he handed to me as soon as he had written it, down to the moment of his execution, I was almost constantly with him. I walked with him to the place of execution, and parted with him under the gallows, overwhelmed with grief, that so gallant an officer and so accomplished a gentleman should come to such an ignominious end. The ease and affability of his manners, polished by the refinement of good society and a finished education, made him a most delightful companion. It often drew tears from my eyes to find him so agreeable in conversation on different subjects, when I reflected on his future fate, and that too, as I believed, so near at hand. . . . Soon after our first acquaintance, being mutually disposed to indulge in the most unreserved and free conversation, and both being soldiers of equal rank in the two armies, we agreed on a cartel, by the terms of which each one was permitted to put any question to the other, not involving a third person. This opened a wide field for two inquisitive young officers, and we amused ourselves not a little on the march to head-quarters. . . . My principal object was to learn the course of the late plot. On every point that I inquired about, where any other person was concerned, he maintained most rigidly the rule; so that when that most infamous traitor, Arnold, was concerned and he out of our control, so nice was André's sense of honor, that he would disclose nothing. When we left West Point for Tappan, early in the morning, as we passed down the Hudson River to King's Ferry, I placed André by my side, on the after seat of the barge. I soon began to make inquiries about the expected capture of our fortress then in full view, and begged him to inform me whether he was to have taken a part in the military attack, if Arnold's plan had succeeded. He instantly replied in the affirmative, and pointed me to a table of land on the west shore, which he said was the spot where he should have landed, at the head of a select corps. He then traversed in idea the course up the mountain into the rear of Fort Putnam, which overlooks the whole parade of West Point. And this he did with much greater exactness. . . . Major André supposed he should have reached that commanding eminence without difficulty. In such case that important key of our country would have been theirs (the enemy's), and the glory of so splendid an achievement would have been his. The animation with which he gave the account, I recollect, perfectly delighted me, for he seemed as if he was entering the fort sword in hand. To complete the climax, I next inquired what was to have been his reward, if he had succeeded. He replied that military glory was all he sought; and that the thanks of his General, and the approbation of his King, were a rich reward for such an undertaking. . . . After we disembarked at King's Ferry, near Haverstraw, we took up our line of march, with a fine body of horse for Tappan. Before we reached the Clove, Major André became very inquisitive to know my opinion as to the result of his capture. In other words, he wished me to give him candidly my opinion, as to the light in which he would be viewed by General Washington, and a military tribunal, if one should be ordered. This was the most unpleasant question that had been propounded to me, and I endeavored to evade it, unwilling to give him a true answer. When I could no longer evade his importunity, or put off a full reply, I remarked to him as follows. 'I had a much loved class-mate in Yale College, by the name of Nathan Hale, who entered the army in the year 1775. Immediately after the battle of Long Island, General Washington wanted information respecting the strength, position, and probable movements of the enemy. Captain Hale tendered his services, went over to Brooklyn, and was taken just as he was passing the outposts of the enemy on his return.' Said I with emphasis, 'Do you remember the sequel of this story?' 'Yes,' said André, 'he was hanged as a spy. But you surely do not consider his case and mine alike?' I replied, 'Yes, precisely similar, and similar will be your fate.' He endeavored to answer my remarks, but it was manifest he was more troubled in spirit than I had ever seen him before. We stopped at the Clove to dine, and to let the horse-guard refresh. While there, André kept reviewing his shabby dress, and finally remarked to me, that he was positively ashamed to go to the head-quarters of the American army in such a plight. I called my servant, and directed him to bring my dragoon cloak, which I presented to Major André. This he refused to take for some time; but I insisted on it, and he finally put it on, and rode in it to Tappan."

◆◆◆

In Tappan on September 29, 1780, I attend the board of general officers inquest into Major André's case, thanks to a pass by Tallmadge who I tell of Major André's kindness to me at Caleb Cope's in Lancaster and later at Carlisle, and Colonel Tallmadge tells me he is sad André will die like his friend Nathan Hale. "War makes no favorites," Tallmadge says. "Good men and bad men die equally, and must to win."

General Nathanael Greene is President of the commission of six Major-Generals and eight Brigadiers. André gives a brief narrative of what occurred between the time of his coming on shore and that of his capture, which agreed in every point with his confession letter to General Washington. He confesses papers show'g West Point defenses (drawn by General Arnold) are concealed in his boots. He says a pass for "John Anderson" in handwriting of Arnold is same as he exhibited to his captors. Interrogated as to the manner in which he comes on shore, and whether he considers it under a flag of truce, André answers, "It is impossible for him to suppose he came on shore under the sanction of a flag," and adds, if he is on shore under this flag he might have "returned under it."

Here is the findings of the commission I write this day: "First, that he came on shore from the *Vulture* sloop-of-war, in the night, on an interview with General Arnold, in a private and secret manner. Secondly, that he changed his dress within our lines, and, under a feigned name and in a disguised habit, passed our works at Stony and Verplanck's Points; was taken at Tarrytown in a disguised habit [attire], being then on his way to New York; and, when taken, he had in his possession several papers, which contained intelligence for the enemy." The board of Generals say it is their "opinion that Major André ought to be considered as a spy, and, according to the law and usage of nations, to suffer death."

I cry in the room, and hear others sob.

◆◆◆

In his 1792 letter to me about Major André, Colonel Tallmadge says he has in his possession a letter John André writes to British General Sir Henry Clinton on September 29, 1780, minutes after he is informed he will die for being a spy.

I offer this letter for readers now: "Tappan, 29 September, 1780. Sir, Your Excellency is doubtless already apprised of the manner in which I was taken, and possibly of the serious light in which my conduct is considered, and the rigorous determination that is impending. Under these circumstances, I have obtained General Washington's permission to send you this letter; the object of which is, to remove from your breast any suspicion that I could imagine I was bound by your Excellency's orders to expose myself to what has happened. The events of coming within an enemy's posts, and of changing my dress, which led me to my present situation, were contrary to my own intentions, as they were to your orders; and the circuitous route, which I took to return, was imposed (perhaps unavoidably) without alternative upon me. I am perfectly tranquil in mind, and prepared for any fate, to which an honest zeal for my King's service may have devoted me. In addressing myself to your Excellency on this occasion, the force of all my obligations to you, and of the attachment and gratitude I bear you, recurs to me. With all the warmth of my heart, I give you thanks for your Excellency's profuse kindness to me; and I send you the most earnest wishes for your welfare, which a faithful, affectionate, and respectful attendant can frame. I have a mother and two sisters, to whom the value of my commission would be an object . . . . It is needless to be more explicit on this subject; I am persuaded of your Excellency's goodness. I receive the greatest attention from his Excellency General Washington, and from every person under whose charge I happen to be placed. I have the honor to be, with the most respectful attachment, your Excellency's most obedient and most humble servant, John André, Adjutant-General."

♦♦♦

In Tappan on October 2, 1780, in a tent waiting, Colonel Tallmadge walks in and says, "General Washington approves yer request to talk to Major André. I told His Excellency ye know'd André in Pennsylvania and the General insists we search yer self. He is aware André is alluring to the likes of women."

After the danger, killing, spying, sneaking and trusting in me, his words hurt and anger me. I immediately remove me smicket and pantaloons and stands naked before Tallmadge. "Search me," I says, and hold me arms out.

"No need," he says, embarrassed. But I know'd he is unmarried and spies me in a lustful way. "I will escort ye to the Major's quarters."

"Will I see him alone?"

Colonel Tallmadge thinks some time on it, and when he gits to the door of Major André's rooms, he orders two guards to let me in alone. André is filled with astonishment to see me, and kisses me hand profusely, and welcomes Miss Tabitha Baldwin, and I is surprise'd he recalls me name.

"I is not Tabitha Baldwin," I says, telling him me real name and the fact I spy for General Washington when duty calls.

"O, be some other name," says Major André, in citing William Shakespeare's *Romeo and Juliet*, "What's in a name? That which we call a rose by any other word would smell as sweet."

I embrace André tenderly and kiss his cheek, and say, "There shan't be another John André in this world." I begins to cry and he stops me.

"Do not," says he. "I am reconciled to me fate."

I gaze fondly and sadly at me dear friend who I love. It be true: John André is the handsomest man I ever laid me eyes on. His hair is longer and more beautiful than I see'd it in Carlisle, and it is wound with a black ribbon, fashion of the day, and hung down his back. His face is of deadly paleness but its features tranquil and calm. His manner is easy, like he is set for a ballroom rather than the gallows and grave.

We then talks of happier days at Caleb Cope's Quaker House and André asks about Cope's son, John, and how his India ink drawing is, and I say it is masterful thanks to the teaching of John André the last time I see'd it. I say I be in Philadelphia for his party for General Howe, and André's face is alight with joy in this memory and of young beautiful Peggy Chew and his jousting matches. "Did ye see me with the black hair of curls?"

"I did not," he says. Then he says, "Alas! The story of yer hair being cut short at Monmouth is also a fabrication?"

I know'd he speaks of the Battle of Monmouth when I is in disguise of peddler Mary Fletcher and I gives André the watch, and he calls on the rider to remove me from danger of Monmouth Courthouse, and I says, "Yea, it is a lie."

On the table I see'd a ink picture and I asks him what it means, and André says it be a picture of the North River he draw'd last night. He says it is the view he see'd when he look'd out the window of a house [Joshua Smith's] to see where the sloop *Vulture* moved when fired at. The moment is come and I must do what is the reason I come here. I admits that it is I who tells the rebel artillerists at Verplanck's Point to watch for sloop *Vulture* because I learn't it carries British officers meeting a turncoat Continental Army General.

"Ye know'd of the meeting with General Arnold?"

I can tell by his quivering voice he is of utter astonishment of what I say.

"Not names of General Arnold or John André," says I, in a contrite manner of sadness. "Nay, John, if I know'd it is ye on the *Vulture*, I never . . . ."

"We do our duty," says André, stopping me. "Say nothing more of it."

"Can you forgive me?"

"Yea," he says, saying me real name tenderly. It makes me weep.

The door opens and it is one of the guards who stays with André in the guard-room, and he carries the Major's clean regimentals, a new uniform for his demise. The man is crying. "Leave me till you can show yer self more manly," André says. He reaches in his pocket to git his gold watch, which I present'd at Monmouth. It is gone, he is forgotten. "The freebooters," he says, "stole it." He asks the guard the time, and it is ten o'clock.

I know'd it is moving towards twelve set for his death.

I remembers something. "I see'd yer dear friend Captain John Graves Simcoe on Long Island, and will venture to his lodgings and speak again, if it is yer wish. Tell me what to say."

Simcoe's name unleash'd a torrent of fondness from André, who says, finally, "Tell of the deep friendship and respect his servant has," and I promise to tell Captain Simcoe his words. He walks to a table and says, "Take this Miss Tabitha," calling me by the name he knows me best, and it is a pen-ink drawing of his self seated at the small table in the brick guard-house. "I drew this last night," says he. "If you see young John Cope, give it this with John André's most abiding compliments."[96]

The time is come, and I kiss André's cheek. With hopelessness I cry openly and briskly.

"Do not weep," says André. "His Excellency will adapt the mode of death to the feelings of a man of honor," he says, and I ask, what is it he means? "I will not die on the gibbet [exposed to ridicule dangling from the gallows]. I will be shot."

---

[96] During his time as a prisoner in Tappan Major André took solace in his art. As one historian put it: "In the midst of the somber thoughts, which must have thronged upon his mind, he resorted to the art, which had given him so much delight, when all the opening prospects of life were gilded with hope and gladness." While the picture André presented to "Tabitha Baldwin" for Major Simcoe has not been found, a similar picture of André seated at the table in the Tappan guardhouse hangs in the Trumbull Gallery at Yale University. Here is a letter written by Ebenezer Baldwin to the president of Yale on August 8, 1832: "It affords me pleasure, as the agent of Mr. Jabez L. Tomlinson of Stratford, and of Mr. Nathan Beers of this city [New Haven], to request your acceptance of the accompanying miniature of Major John André. It is his likeness seated at a table in his guard-room, and drawn by himself with a pen, on the morning of the day fixed for his execution. Mr. Tomlinson informs me, that a respite was granted until the next day, and that this miniature was in the meantime presented to him (then acting as officer of the guard) by Major André h mself. Mr. Tomlinson was present when the sketch was made, and says it was drawn without the aid of a glass. The sketch subsequently passed into the hands of Mr. Beers, a fellow officer of Mr. Tomlinson on the station, and from thence was transferred to me. It has been in my possession several years." That Ebenezer Baldwin and "Tabitha Baldwin" share the same name is coincidence.

I see'd the hangman's noose outside on the expanse. I do not possess the heart to tell André what waits, the lonely gallows, a black painted coffin and a shallow open grave.

It is this instant, which I learn't hate for The Commander.[97] He gits his public ridicule of this kind and honorable man. Why and for what? For shame. For shame.

I turn at the door and see John André, a tear in his eye for me. I cannot abide it, and runs back into the room and kiss his dry lips. "Thou shall live inside me forever, John André, I love ye." The guard pulls me back and away, and the Major stands upright, a true gentleman in the proud British officer corps, ready to breathe his last breath.

◆◆◆

Thereafter, this is what I see'd and hear'd, and write it down. When the hour of his execution is announced André receives it without emotion, and while all present is affect'd with gloom, he retains a calmness and composure of mind. His breakfast is sent from the table of General Washington and he partakes of it. Shaved and dressed, he places his hat on the table, and cheerfully says to the guard-officers, "I am ready at any moment, Gentlemen, to wait on ye." Outside a large detachment of troops is paraded, and an immense concourse of people assembled. Almost all the general and field officers, excepting Washington and his staff, is present on horseback. Melancholy and gloom pervades all ranks.

The scene is affecting and awful. André walks from the stone house in which he is confined, between two officers, arm-in-arm. His beauty shone in his bright red and green regimentals, fully adorned except with sash, sword and gorget [clothing covering the throat]. Eyes of the immense multitude is fixed on André, who, rising superior to the fear of death, appears as if conscious of the dignified deportment which he displays. He betrays no want of fortitude, but

---

[97] It is interesting that after the execution of Major André, Agent 355 never refers to General Washington as "His Excellency," which was the standard protocol for addressing him at the time. It is obvious that she believed Washington could have either spared the life of her dear friend, or, at the very minimum, allowed him to meet death like a soldier in front of a firing squad, which was André's request. From this point on in the diary she refers to Washington as "The Commander" or "Commander-In-Chief" but not "His Excellency." To put it simply, I do not think she found anything "excellent" in General Washington after André's death.

retains a complacent smile on his countenance, and politely
bows to several gentlemen he know'd, and each is

[98] Being assigned to carry out André's execution had a negative psychological effect on Harvard-educated attorney Alexander Scammell, 1742-1781, who was the Continental Army's adjutant general. Six weeks after hanging John André, Colonel Scammell asked Washington for reassignment to the front lines. He got his wish and fought in at least two battles before being mortally wounded less than a year later. He was buried at Williamsburg, Virginia, where a monument was erected for him. Here is a description of André's execution from the 1871 book, *The Life of Major John André, Adjutant-General of the British Army in America* by Winthrop Sargent: "André walked arm-in-arm between two subalterns; each with a drawn sword in the opposite hand. A captain's command of forty men marched immediately about these, while an outer guard of five hundred infantry environed the whole and formed a hollow square around the gibbet within which no one save the officers on duty and the provost-marshal's men were suffered to enter. An immense multitude was however assembled on all sides to witness the spectacle, and every house along the way was thronged with eager gazers; that only of Washington excepted. Here the shutters were drawn, and no man was visible. Neither the Chief himself nor his staff were present with the troops; a circumstance which was declared by our people and assented to by André as evincing a laudable decorum." Once André saw the gallows, "he beckoned Colonel Benjamin Tallmadge, and inquired anxiously if he was not to be shot: "Must I then die in this manner?" Being told that it was so ordered, "How hard is my fate!" he cried. "But it will soon be over." Ascending the hillside, the prisoner was brought to the gibbet . . . He shook hands with Tallmadge, who withdrew. A baggage wagon with the coffin on it was driven beneath the crosstree, into which he leaped lightly, but with visible loathing. He walked the length of the coffin and turned and walked back . . His last words murmured in an undertone were, "It will be but a momentary pang!" . . .The signal was given; the wagon rolled swiftly away; and almost in the same instant he ceased to exist. The height of the gibbet and sudden shock as he was jerked from the coffin-lid on which he stood produced immediate death. He remained hanging from twenty to thirty minutes and during that time the chambers of death were never stiller than the multitude by which he was surrounded. Orders were given to cut the rope, and take him down, without letting him fall . . . Shortly after, the guard was withdrawn and spectators were permitted to come forward and view the corpse. 'When I was able to do this, his coat, vest, and breeches, were taken off, and his body laid in the coffin, covered by some under-clothes,' recalled a witness. 'The top of the coffin was not put on. I viewed the corpse more carefully than I had ever done that of any human being before. His head was very much on one side, in consequence of the manner in which the halter drew upon his neck. His face appeared to be greatly swollen, and very black, much resembling a high degree of mortification. It was indeed a shocking sight to behold . . . Wishing to see the closing of the whole business, I remained upon the spot until scarce twenty persons were left, but the coffin was still beside the grave . . . I returned to my tent, with my mind deeply imbued with the shocking scene.' Every authentic account that we have, shows how much our officers regretted the necessity of André's death . . . The tears of thousands fell on the spot where he lay; and no one refrained from proclaiming his sympathy. Many wept openly as he died; among whom it is recorded La Fayette . . . It was believed that Washington's soul revolted at the task, and that he could scarcely command the pen when he subscribed the fatal warrant." André entered popular culture with airing of AMC's *TURN*, portrayed as a dashing ladies' man and lover of beautiful Miss Peggy Shippen before she married Benedict Arnold. But he also emerged in the culture in Life Magazine on February 23, 1968, when it published a story on lost letters by George Washington to General Alexander McDougall, which included letters about General Arnold and André. One Life headline proclaimed, "Gallant Death for André."

respectfully returned.

I know'd it is his desire to be shot, and at the moment when suddenly he comes in view of the gallows, he involuntarily starts backwards.

"Why this emotion, Sir?" says the officer by his side.

Recovering composure, he says, "I be reconciled to me death, but I detest the mode."

When I hear'd John André protest being hang'd, I curse'd Washington, and will for as long as I live.

I wait near the gallows and observe trepidation in André. The provost marshal takes two white handkerchiefs from his pockets. André removes his hat and puts one over this eyes with perfect firmness. This self-act melts hearts of the assemblage of spectators. André then puts the noose over his own head and adjusts it tight to the right of his neck without the aid of the dirty executioner.

Head of the execution Colonel Alexander Scammell[98] says it is time for André to speak if he wishes, and me André raises the white handkerchief from his eyes. Says he, "I pray ye to bear me witness, gentlemen, that I meet me fate like a brave man." Sobbing is hear'd in the assemblage. The wagon is moved and John André is hang'd. This day me heart is cut from me breast, and I weeps for a full three days long.

Many months pass and I hear'd from a friend, Major Benjamin Russell, who is among the small inner guard which walk'd André to the gallows. This is what he writes to me:

"Throughout the whole of this scene, from the time he left the house in which he was guarded, till the last fatal moment, his demeanor was such as to excite the respect, sympathy, and sorrow of every beholder. His step was steady, his carriage easy and graceful, his countenance placid, but thoughtful and firm, indicating a solemn sense of his impending fate, and a resolution to meet it in a manner consistent with his character and the previous tenor of his conduct. He was dressed in the uniform of a British officer. When life had departed, the body was taken down and interred within a few yards of the place of execution.[99]

---

[99] Remains of Major André were exhumed from the common burial below the gallows in Tappan in August 1821 by order of the King's Consul in New York, under instructions from the Duke of York,

Whig or Tory? I is not one for government, Congress or Parliament, and it is hard to fight for either of these lobcocks [relaxed penis or dull fellows]. I never accept'd the black or white of rebellion, yer on this side or yer on that side. Not each and everybody is a rebel and not each and everybody is a Loyalist. A great number in the Colonies is of the opinion a little of each side is good, and much of either is bad. Many want to stay out of it. Stay home. I do not know what to call it. Half-bred rebels? Half-heart'd King's men? It should be know'd by all who read this diary, it is what most Americans be. In the middle.

It is why when I be forced to kill the skinners, rebels like me, I be not full of a remorse or a guilt.[100]

---

and interred in the nave of Westminster Abbey three months later. A monument to his memory shows a mourning figure of Britannia with a lion, seated on the top of a sarcophagus. On the front of this is a relief showing George Washington with officers in a tent receiving a petition and flag of truce and Major André being led away to be hanged. The inscription reads: Sacred to the Memory of Major John André, who raised by his merit at an early period of Life to the rank of Adjutant General of the British Forces in America, and employed in an important but hazardous Enterprise fell a Sacrifice to his Zeal for his King and Country on the 2nd of October AD 1780, Aged 29, universally beloved and esteemed by the army in which he served and lamented even by his foes. His gracious Sovereign King George the Third has caused this monument to be erected."

[100] I cannot be sure about this but it seems Agent 355 doesn't consider herself a rabid revolutionary, as say a member of the extreme Sons of Liberty did. But what she says makes me wonder whether she would have become a spy in the first place had it not been her lover Alexander Hamilton who recruited her. Her remark makes me believe that she was content with being part of the British Empire, up to a point. She is certainly no lover of Congress, and in this she shares the view of Loyalists who saw members of Congress as robbers. Take this item from "Clift's Diary" in the Troy newspaper, *Pennsylvania Evening Post*, February 25, 1777, which highlights how Loyalists viewed Congress. "Two or three members of Congress, one or two of them worse than nothing, and the other involved in debt, have realized great sums, which they have remitted to Holland and some of the European banks; where, it is supposed, they mean to retire when the desperate game they are now playing can be no longer maintained. This is plunder upon their country, under the infamous pretense of patriotism and public virtue. Charity itself cannot wish that men with such ill-gotten goods, acquired at the expense and ruin of a once happy and flourishing country, should ever be able to enjoy them in peace and security." If Agent 355 had split loyalties she wasn't alone. Although, those that choose sides were stridently violent about it. Indeed, the American Civil War between North and South was not the first "civil war" for America. The Revolutionary War pitted neighbor against neighbor, Troy against Whig, Loyalist against rebel in violent combat. William Livingston, the eloquent patriot Governor of New Jersey, in a message to the Legislature in 1777, wrote: "The Royalists (Refugees) have plundered friends as well as rebels: effects capable of division they have divided; such as were not they have destroyed. They have preyed on decrepit old age and upon defenseless youth; they have committed hostilities against the professors of literature and against the ministers of religion; against public records and private monuments, books of improvements and papers of curiosity, and against the arts and sciences. They have butchered the wounded when asking for quarter, mangled the dead while weltering in their blood; refused to the dead their right of sepulture, suffered prisoners to perish for want of sustenance, violated the chastity of women, disfigured private dwellings of taste and elegance, and

It is why I wears the black and white feathers in me hair after André is killed.[101] After this sicken'g execution, I, the spy of three names, takes six months off from the dirty business of spy'g, and works in a field hospital in Fishkill, New York. This, however, is more sicken'g business I is to learn.

---

in their rage of impiety and barbarism, profaned edifices dedicated to Almighty God." This item from "Clift's Diary" in the Troy newspaper, *Pennsylvania Evening Post*, claims to report an incident in which a Loyalist was killed by a mob of rebels. "At Charleston, South Carolina, John Roberts, a dissenting minister, was seized on suspicion of being an enemy to the rights of America, when he was tarred and feathered; after which, the populace, whose fury could not be appeased, erected a gibbet on which they hanged him, and afterwards made a bonfire, in which Roberts, together with the gibbet, was consumed to ashes." Here is what a Loyalist author wrote a few years after the war: "At the breaking out of the Revolution, Galloway, a Pennsylvanian of wealth and standing, sided with the Whigs, but soon turned Tory, and his property to the amount of 40,000 pounds was confiscated. Speaking of Refugee outrages, he said: 'Respecting indiscriminate plunder it is known to thousands. In respect to rapes, a solemn inquiry was made and affidavit taken by which it appears that no less than twenty-three were committed in one neighborhood in New Jersey, some of them on married women, in presence of their helpless husbands, and others on daughters while their unhappy parents with unavailing tears and cries could only deplore their savage brutality.' This was the evidence of as reliable a man as ever sided with the Tories. In corroboration of the foregoing we might instance, among other things, the burning of churches in Essex County, of ravishment of women (one of them nearly seventy years old). And Jersey men have the mortification of knowing that wretches pretending to be natives of this state disgraced the soil that gave them birth by acts of brutality elsewhere, among which may be mentioned the cold blooded murder of the brave Col. Ledyard at Fort Griswold, Conn., by a wretch known as the 'Jersey Refugee, Bromfield.' After the Americans had surrendered the fort, Bromfield asked who commanded it. The heroic Ledyard replied, "I did, but you do now," and he delivered his sword to Bromfield. The cold blooded villain took it and immediately stabbed Ledyard to the heart."

[101] After the death of Major André, his friend Lieutenant Colonel John Graves Simcoe ordered his own regiment of the Queen's Rangers to wear black and white feathers in their headdress as mourning for a soldier "whose superior integrity and uncommon ability did honor to his country and to human nature. The Queen's Rangers will never sully their glory in the field by any undue severity; they will, as they have ever done, consider those to be under their protection who are in their power, and will strike with reluctance at their unhappy fellow-subjects, who, by a series of the basest artifices, have been seduced from their allegiance; but it is the Lt. Colonel's most ardent hope, that on the close of some decisive victory, it will be the regiment's fortune to secure the murderers of Major André, for the vengeance due to an injured nation and an insulted array." André wore black and white feathers in his headdress at the gala for General Howe in Philadelphia, and Agent 355 donned them to mourn her friend as well.

1781

At Tappan I meet with Colonel Tallmadge and tell him I require a break from the spy business, and he, knowing of me being distraught over the death of Major André, says the field hospitals at Fishkill require nurses. He shows me a letter from the Medical Director of the Continental Army at Fishkill which says, "Wanted immediately, a number of women who can be recommended for their honesty, to act in the capacity of nurses."

"I will recommend ye," says Tallmadge, and I accept it.

Fishkill east of the Hudson River is where thousands of The Commander's Continental Army soldiers go with wounds and sicknesses because it is the location of hospitals and barracks. It is where I train as a nurse under surgeons who learn't medicine in Philadelphia, and who train others like me without previous medical knowledge.[102]

Under the name of Virginia Redman, (me third spy name) I count forty physicians at Fishkill, and this is not sufficient.

Here under surgeon Cornelius Osborn I learn't Medicine. Instead of the dagger, pistol, musket and tomahawk, I get train'g in field hospital surgery, and become skill'd with amputating and trepanning instruments, incision knives, pocket instruments, bullet forceps, crooked needles, straight needles, pins, bandages, foliated bandages, ligatures, simple and double rollers, splints, tourniquets, tape, thread, towels and sponges.[103] I help'd Surgeon Osborn on twenty-three

---

[102] A sprawling complex of barracks, stables, blacksmith shops, hospitals, armories and stockades, the Fishkill Depot in Dutchess County was just a couple miles west of the Hudson River. Thousands of soldiers passed through the depot, and it is reported that more than 1,000 died there. Archaeologists says the southern tip of the property alone contains 300 graves. Most of the soldiers at Fishkill hospital facilities died not of rifle or cannon shot but of illness and disease. Hospitals in the Revolutionary War ranged from the smallest in which a surgeon or physician, an assistant and an apprentice served, to the largest facility in which there were six medical officers and forty-eight assistants and additional staff such as an apothecary and nurses. Assistants included stewards, ward masters, dispensers, "surgery man" with "attendants as needed," seamstress, laundresses, barbers, cooks with "laborers as needed," servants, keeper of packs, bathers, and a "man for Itch ward." The largest hospital teams served 400 patients at a time.

[103] The medical case used by surgeons included all of the items "Nurse Virginia Redman" lists in her diary. The medical items correspond closely to a list of instruments and medical necessities carried

limb amputations, mostly legs with bones damaged by musket balls and beyond fix'g with splints, artillery shot and bayonets and sabers; and cutting off of hands and arms; and three times after one battle which British Horse Grenadier Guards throw'd grenades and explode'g soldiers' feet, and we cut same off at the ankle bones. I work'd all day on maladies of soldiers: abscesses, gangrene, incised and puncture wounds in need of drainage, contusions with pus, ugly lacerations, cut tendons, chest and abdomen wounds from bayonets and sabers, with potential inside organ damage, simple and compound fractures, and gunshot, knife, hatchet and club wounds, with hemorrhaging or infection or gangrene. Each day many soldiers die at Fishkill, and it is from diseases like smallpox, typhoid fever and dysentery. Me eyes are open to another ill: venereal disease is rampant in troops in which encamped with a large number of camp following wenches and whores. But the worst killer other than muskets is smallpox, and since 1775 it rages in America. This deadly disease gits so serious in Boston, Commander-In-Chief Washington sends only Continental soldiers with variolation [inoculation] against smallpox into this city. Fishkill Surgeon Cornelius Osborn who teaches me and other nurses about smallpox, which he calls variola major, is a strong advocate of variolation, which is the practice of injecting tiny pieces of variola major into human bodies so it gits a minor case of smallpox and builds what Osborn says is "immunity" to smallpox. After I be school'd in medicine I gits weeks off to travel to the city of New York, and, Osborn lets me take a medical kit to study the instruments used by his surgeons who I assist on battlefields.

---

by regimental surgeons enumerated in a speech by Dr. John Morgan, medical director of the Continental Army in 1776.

In New York I takes rooms and it is only four days past in which I gits a knock on the door by a old woman dressed in dirty rags and gray hair never clean'd and wash'd.

"The doctor's wife, I presume?" she says to me at the door.

"Nay," says I. "A physician does not live here."

"We see'd yer medical bag on the street in yer hand," she says. "What is it, then?"

"It is a medical kit," I says. "I be a nurse, not surgeon."

"Come then, sick children are in need," she says.

"Go to New York Hospital," I says. "It is at Broadway and Pearl Street."

"Never, they be grave robbers," she says.

I never hear'd such a thing.

"These young doctors hire men to dig up those who is buried and they cut them into pieces."[104]

What can I do? "Where is this place of sick children?"

I takes the medical kit and follows this old woman to a shabby house in "Holy Ground," the district of whores and misery which I know'd too well from the Great Fire. It gits its name from Trinity Church which it borders all the way to King's College and is built with gambling halls, gin distillers and hundreds of whores selling their bodies to sailors and soldiers and any other human things which walks the night in lust.

This dwelling inside and out is filthy, and I smell the putrid odor of vomit everywhere. This stench is rich and thick, and I know'd what Surgeon Osborn teaches us of smallpox, which causes vomiting in the diseased people.

---

[104] In his 1873 book, *The Great Riots of New York, 1712 to 1873*, Hoy J.T. Headley wrote about the New York "Doctor's Riot, 1788." It was caused when a doctor hung an amputated arm from the window of the New York Hospital at Broadway and Pearl Street as a practical joke, and people rioted because they thought it was the arm of a recently deceased woman, who, when her husband re-opened her grave to see, her body was gone. Headley wrote that "body snatching" was not as frequent as in early times but did exist in the mid-1700s, mostly by medical students studying anatomy at the New York Hospital who hired "resurrectionists" to steal bodies shortly after burial. So the fear of the woman who came to Agent 355's rooms to seek medical aid wasn't as farfetched as one might think. The doctor's apparent prank caused a mob to rip down the door of the hospital and find dissected bodies. Before the smoke cleared the militia was called and four rioters slain. The following year the city passed a law banning grave-robbing but allowing anatomy students to dissect bodies of criminals who were hanged.

The old woman takes me into a small room where eight children, from a few years to ten or eleven in age be, and three of same suffer smallpox eruptions on their stomachs.

"The children have smallpox," I says.

"The pox!" says the old woman in fear.

The children is hot to the touch of me hand, and two of them say they ache in their bodies. "Where is the mothers?"

"Whoring," says the old woman.

Just then a woman with matted red hair of me same age staggers into the room, and says, "I be mother of two." She is weak and can hardly stand. I sit her on a bed and feel her head. She is feverish and complains of headaches.

"Yer contagious," I says. "Old woman," I says to her. "The five children who is not sick must be moved out of this room now."

Then a fat man in a black suit walks in. "And who is this wench?" he asks, very stern of voice.

"She be a nurse for the children," the old woman peeps in me behalf.

"These children be sick with smallpox," I says. "They must be moved from here."

I figures he is the bull of his stable of prostitutes, and he nods to git the youngsters out. He sits in a chair to relieve his legs of his dreadfully fat body. I turns me gaze to the sick young woman. "She must stay in this room with the sick children for three weeks," I says. "She is ill with pox."

The bull gives out a wail. "She works this very night. If she does not, she gits worse than the pox to kill her."

I feels me whole body swell up with anger. I reach into me medical kit and pulls out me pistol and shoves it hard between this bull's fat legs. His voice rises into a squeak, and I says, "She is contagious and will infect every man she touches with smallpox. Now maybe they deserve it. I do not know. But I know this: if I see her on the street tonight I will put this pistol up yer arse and ye will never sit and shit again."

Before I leaves, I tell the old woman to send someone to New York Hospital to report the cases of smallpox, and she reluctantly agrees. I also tell her to bring the five children who are not sick to me room for a variolation. At first she says nay, say'g this is a way of killing people by putting pox in their bodies. I tell her John Adams his self and his wife Abigail Smith Adams gits this inoculation and so does Commander Washington so it must be good. It quiets her on the subject, and the next morning the five children be at me door.

"Is yer man with ye?" I says.

"Boss Joseph, oh, nay," says the old woman. "He says yer the Devil's wife."

"Aha, maybe he be right." Then I asks, "Did he send the sick whore out last night?"

"Miss Phoebe?"

"Yea, Miss Phoebe."

"Nay," says the old woman. "Says tonight she must go whoring."

"Tell yer Boss, if he does this, he is a dead Boss. I be out looking for her tonight, and for his fat arse."

Before dark I puts the pistol in me sling under me cape, which is warm from the cold. The dagger is in a belt about me middle. For two hours I walks among the whores and the men in dirty "Holy Ground," resting on the steps of Trinity Church, and in all this time I do not see "Miss Phoebe." I pass a alley and see a man standing with his whore's pipe in the mouth of a whore. Later two British sailors say they will pay me ten shillings for intimacy, and I tell these Bloody Backs to go bugger each other, which they curse me for.

I see'd a girl who is looking for her mother and I tell her to leave this place and go home.

But, the night is without Miss Phoebe.

It is near morning by the time I walk to me rooms, and I keep the pistol in a tight grip in me hand under me cape in case Boss Joseph decides to molest me. I be a distance from me rooms when I hear'd the faint sound of steps, and I be unsure from whence it comes. I be alone on the street, and as I turns I see'd a human in a hooded-cape. It be startled and runs behind a building. I be angry to be follow'd again. I yells, "Boss Joseph, ye Jack Weight [fat man]!" Me voice bounces off buildings in the dire cold. I do not care if this being is the Gorgon Medusa her self, I shout, "Come from the dark shadows and face me, ye blackguard."

Nothing.

I pulls the pistol from me cape and runs towards the building where the hooded creature disappears. I takes the dagger from me belt, and, with it in me left hand and the pistol in me right, I look in the alley seeking hell and death.

It is gone away.

"Coward!" I shouts.

I begins to walk to me rooms and be thinking more on it. Boss Joseph is a fat man and he cannot run away like this hooded thing does. It is not Rogers, he be in prison, and I know'd he does not run from a fight. Is it The Shadow Man again? Who is this being? Big Rudolf who I best with the rifle? British intelligence follow'g me for killing spy Guillory? Moody's man who seeks vengeance for his capture? I be dizzied by all these personages. By this time I be accumulating enemies like professors collect diplomas.

◆◆◆

Days later in this winter 1781, I be told to attach to the army in the south as many medical surgeons and nurses be needed, and, Surgeon Daniel Mason from New York, me and a Nurse named Margaret Ward board a French ship in February and sail to North Carolina.

We set a field hospital for the army of General Nathanael Greene and it is running without trouble, with cases of cough, fever, head itch, bilious [yellow] fever, scorbutus [scurvy], hemoptysis [spitting blood] and rupture, but no wounds from rifle or cannon shot, and no amputations is needed. Then, on a sunny morning, March 15, 1781, it ends.

Two thousand Redcoats commanded by Lord Charles Cornwallis march through and take Georgia and South Carolina and now set sights on North Carolina, where, at Guilford Courthouse, four thousand rebels [1,700 Continental Army and 2,700 militia] of General Greene is set to stop them. The armies meet and claw at the other in three lines in field and in forest, and many British and Americans die, as British push rebels back. In one volley shot I see'd fifteen-hundred rebel muskets fire at once and ravage the 71st Highland Regiment, killing half.

In the third line in a patch of field General Greene's Continentals meet Redcoats in fierce battle, with musket, bayonet and sword. I see'd this happen with me own eyes and will never understand what General Cornwallis is thinking in his mind. His army is pushing rebels back when a line of Continentals which flanked Cornwallis's men attacks them from a rear position. Hand-to-hand fighting is happening and General Cornwallis orders two cannons to fire into the center of the meshed together rebels and Redcoats, blasting them all and killing and maiming soldiers on each side. General Greene see'd this and orders retreat, and the Redcoats retreat and claim victory, and leave wounded on the field.[105]

Later I cannot find Daniel Mason, the surgeon, and one hundred and fifty rebels is wounded.

"He is kill'd," a soldier tells me. He points to where. He takes me to Surgeon Mason's body and I find his surgeon's case. Me and Nurse Margaret Ward attend men by ourselves. Many suffer round ball shots and bayonet wounds and I gouge out the lead and Nurse Ward is bandaging open wounds.

Now a private runs up to me, excited. "General Greene is want of the surgeon."

"Surgeon Mason is dead," I says. "Nurse Ward and me is all."

---

[105] Battle of Guilford Courthouse was one of the last major battles of the war, and preceded the Battle of Yorktown which ended hostilities. General Nathanael Greene had placed his soldiers in three lines along the Great Salisbury Wagon Road which led to the British encampment, and despite his being outnumbers by about two thousand men, Lord Charles Cornwallis was confident of victory – likely because he had marched through Georgia and South Carolina unmolested. He attacked Greene's lines under the noontime sun. The British pummeled the North Carolina militia but not before the Carolinians exacted a heavy toll on the Redcoats. The British then hit the second line in a forest setting. The Virginia militia (mostly farmers) pounded the British with heavy losses but were pushed back. Than Cornwallis attacked the third line, which was made up of Greene's Continental Army. Some fresh-to-fighting Continentals folded immediately while more experienced men fought the British to a standstill. This is when Cornwallis, over the advice of his own officers, fired the cannons into the mob of entangled soldiers, killing many on both sides, as is described by Agent 355. That's when Greene retreated and left the battlefield to the Redcoats, giving Cornwallis a propaganda victory celebrated in London. This even though Cornwallis not only left wounded on the battlefield but retreated two hundred miles after this battle. In all, Britain casualties were 93 dead and 413 wounded, while Greene's ranks suffered 79 killed and 185 wounded.

"Then ye be the surgeon," he says.

"What is need'd?"

"Amputations," says he.

"Nay!" I protest. "I never do this by me self."

The private takes me medical kit and says, "Come, it is ordered." I tell Margaret to bandage, and I be returning soon.

The private is running with the case and I try to keep up but fall behind, and he yells, "We be out of sunlight in a hour."

A mile away a tent is set up and it is worse than it ever could be. He is an officer. Captain George Sherman is a militia officer and lays on a blanket and he is screaming when I comes in the tent. "Where is the surgeon? I do not require a nurse," he yells at me.

"The surgeon is dead," says I, removing a coat which is wound tight around his left arm. He is shot above the elbow and the bone is exposed and in pieces. He screams when I takes off the coat and he blacks out. With me in the tent is a Sergeant. "Is there heat'd water," I asks, and the Sergeant says there is a fire to cook, and I say it is needed to wash the wound. When the Sergeant washes blood off the Captain's wound he wakes and screams at me.

"No woman is cutting me," he says, and tries to git up. I push him back with the strength of a man, and he know'd it.[106]

"Sergeant," says he, "I order you to git her out of this tent!"

"Sir," says the Sergeant, a large man a full head taller than the Captain. "General Greene calls for the Surgeon and she is it. She must stay, Sir."

I see'd the bone is splinter'd and more than half gone and I remember Surgeon Cornelius Osborn teaches me if the bone is more than one third missing it will not repair itself, and the bone must be cut off to avoid gangrene and death.

---

[106] Call this an incidental footnote, but it is interesting that Agent 355 bullies a Captain, even in his wounded condition. Surgeons were referred to as either "Mister" or "Surgeon" in the Continental Army and carried no military rank, and, more to the point, weren't allowed to give members of the military orders, especially a captain. Of course given what we know about her fighting abilities there is little doubt she could have handled him wounded or not.

"Rum and brandy," I says to the Sergeant, and he feeds the Captain a large cup of liquor for the pang.

I select the small bone saw from the case, and tells the Sergeant to hold the Captain's arm firm, and he does this, and I hold me breathing fast, and cut like I see'd good Surgeon Osborn do it in twenty-three limb amputations. In seconds the bone and flesh is severed. The Sergeant lays the dead arm on the dirt floor. Unlike many other amputations, in this one is not bloody, and I fold the skin over the exposed bone and wrap it in bandages. I find the right size leather in the medical case and fit the leather cap over the stump of bone, and push it down in to its place. The Captain is out, and I feel his heart pumping and know'd he is alive. "Keep his body warm and cover'd," I tells the Sergeant.

Now a hand pulls aside the tent flap. "Nurse," says a Lieutenant, "Is the Mister [surgeon] here?"

"He is kill'd, Sir," I says, wiping the saw with part of the blanket.

Now he spies the Captain's dead left arm on the floor, and with excitement and alarm, says, "Who is it who does this?"

The Sergeant speaks. "She does, Sir, a fine Surgeon she is."

"A woman?" he shrieks it, like he is told a lie.

"Sir, she does it, and quickly," the Sergeant says again.

The Lieutenant is looking at me and at the dead arm and again at me, and I see'd he is pondering his trouble. He says, "I have a private whose leg is bad from the field piece fired by Lord Cornwallis, and it looks like it requires amputation."

I takes the Surgeon's case and follows him.

The very young private is near a fire, and lays on the ground, and a group of Continental soldiers sits around him. The wounded man who is barely more than a teen looks at me like I is the devil, and says, "Where is the Surgeon called for?"

I says, "He is kill'd back at the Guilford Courthouse."

An older soldier says, "He needs a Surgeon not a wench."

"This is Nurse Virginia," says the Lieutenant, and he steps up and tells the soldier to stay quiet'd. He says I be experienced in amputations and cut off a Captain's arm. "He's alive, too," he says, in what is a late thought in his head.

I tell the old soldier to git water, and I wash the wound. I see'd the thigh bone is more than half blown away by the cannon, which I know'd is not a common wound in the war, but the young private's leg cannot be splint'd and saved and must be cut.

"You a nurse?" the boy says. He is crying but I cannot understand why he is not screaming from pang, yet he is not doing it.

"Yes," I says. "I is the nurse who can stop gangrene, and the looks of your leg, this is what is well-nigh for ye."

"Ye a mother?" the boy says.

"Yea, four at home in Pennsylvania," I lie.

"I trust mothers," says he. His face is babyish, and pale as the old moon, and his eyes shows me love for his mother.

"Git rum and brandy," I says, and instantly the Lieutenant says nay to it. "Git this man rum," I says again, in a tone like it is an order.

"He is a Private," says the Lieutenant. "Only officers git rum."[107]

I takes the large bone saw from the medical case, stands and pulls the Lieutenant away from the others. "If this young man is not given rum and brandy for pang, then you will do this amputation, Sir." I put the saw out as his to take. Instantly the Lieutenant is in terror. "And if this boy dies General Greene is going to hear why, it is because of a few drops of rum."

"Git the rum and brandy," Lieutenant tells a soldier. "Hurry-scurry!"

The boy drinks two cups full of liquor, and turns mellow.

I tell two soldiers to hold the Private fast and do not let his body move or writhe, and I take the large saw and move

---

[107] It was Continental Army policy that before an amputation only officers were provided with rum mixed with brandy for pain. Privates and others were given a piece of wood to bite down on as the surgeon sawed through bone. Because it was so unusual to have a woman performing an amputation, as her diary clearly shows, it seems the unnamed Lieutenant wasn't sure how to handle Agent 355's demand for pain "medicine" for the young private.

through the bone. The boy screams, and suddenly blood pours in a rush from the leg artery. Blood flies everywhere, and I hear a soldier retch and gag behind me. I reach into the medical case for a crooked needle to suture and tie off the artery, and there is no crooked needles. Blood pours, and I press fingers on it and the blood slows. "Git me a knife," I says to soldiers behind me. Three hands with knives in them cast themselves down at me, and I tell the soldier with the largest knife to stick the blade in the fire. This he does, and when it is red hot I tells him to give it to me. To gasping souls around me, I touch the artery with the red-hot knife blade and it burns it. The boy screams and is insensible. Odor of burning flesh fills noses and soldiers retreat in disgust.

"Ye kills this boy," one shouts at me.

"Wench, stink'g wench," says another.

"Bloody Mary is more likes it," says the first.

I bandage the bloody leg and cap it with leather, and move away from the soldiers who be looking like they be amputating me. The Lieutenant checks the boy's heart, and says he lives and is sleeping, and the leg is amputated and the blood is stopped.

I tells the Lieutenant I must go to other wounded men and to inform me if the boy's leg gits hot when touch'd, and I leave.

Later I be called before General Nathanael Greene.

"Nurse Virginia Redman," says he, "ye saved Captain Sherman."

I says, "The Surgeon is kill'd, Sir, and I do what he would do." Then I tells him of the poor Private.

"Yea, and what is it ye performed with the hot blade?" says the General. "Many speak of it, and I never heard of it."

"I learn't it at Indian camp where men use tomahawks to split wood, and occasionally cut off fingers," says I. "We stop'd bleeding fingers by thrusting them into fire."

The General winces. "Commendable, and fast thinking. Ye saved two men and many more and ye will be commended to His Excellency," says General Greene.

"This is good, Sir, of the Commander." It is this instant which the bold idea comes to me. I says, "And will Colonel Tallmadge be told?"

"Tallmadge?" says the General in surprise. "Ye attached to Colonel Tallmadge?" I see'd the General's countenance in sudden change.

"One time or another," says I, being honestly frank. He is a General.

His eyes open in a wide way and his long cheeks git red, and I know'd what he is thinking: This wench spies on me for Tallmadge!

Remembering this, amuses me today.[108]

♦ ♦ ♦

I be not honest in every detail of Guilford Courthouse. It takes every strengthened nerve I possess in writing this diary to tell what else happen'd when I return'd to this odious battlefield. . . . Bear with this old woman's emotions.

. . .

Spy'g be a fraction of war, and I never possess'd the feeling personally of fighting this war against the King till Guilford Courthouse, when I watch'd the mangle of men in combat. Call it treasonous, but when I travelled back to the battlefield I also gives medical aid to two British soldiers, both left to die by Lord Cornwallis. I runs to the first soldier, and he is barely alive with a shot which gouged his neck. I takes a towel from the medical kit and is bent over this man to stop his bleeding when a Carolina militia man plunges a bayonet past me ear into his Redcoat chest, ending his life instantly. I scream at the rebel militiaman who runs away towards other Redcoats who lie moaning on the field to end them, too. I picks up me medical kit and finds a Loyalist

---

[108] I admit I pondered her conversation with General Nathanael Greene for a long time before making a judgment. Greene was a very competent military leader and a close confidante of General Washington. Obviously he knew Colonel Benjamin Tallmadge was Washington's head of intelligence at the time, although it is certain he did not know the existence of the Culper Spy Ring nor the identities of its members. I believe Agent 355 invoked the name of Colonel Tallmadge in the conversation because she knew the effect it would have on General Greene. I believe she had had enough of playing nurse – and in this case surgeon and limb-cutter – and wanted to be sent back to New York. It worked, and convinced Greene to put her on the next available ship. Also, I checked the ship's manifest and "Virginia Redman, Contl. Nurse" appears.

soldier on the ground. He is breath'g and lies on his stomach in his own blood.

From the side of me, now I see'd the same Carolina rebel who holds his musket and bayonet like a lance run'g towards me. I know'd he is ready to stab this prone Loyalist in his back. I stands, and kicks the rebel in the lobcock [penis], and he keels over in surprised agony, and falls in the dirt, cursing me. I jump on his chest and takes this rebel militiaman by the throat. I yells I will throttle [strangle] him if he tries to give this Loyalist the "Georgia Parole" [kill rather than take prisoner].

"Git!" I screams.

He runs off, bent over like a monkey from a lion.

I hear'd sound coming from the Loyalist soldier and turns his body over. His eyes open and gaze at me through the cloak of blood covering his face. His cheeks tighten in contort'd disbelief, or maybe it is fright, thinking he is being finished by me.

"I be a rebel nurse," I say, ripping buttons off his waistcoat to find the wound in his chest. "I will help ye."

Now he moans me real name in a whisper.

It staggers me, and me chest heaves. I know'd I hear'd his voice a fore. I stare down at this man's blood-cover'd face, but I do not know his look or name.

"It *is* you," he says, swallowing his own blood, and coughing it up again.

I use cloth from the kit and wipe his face.

"Stephen," I whisper. Me mouth hangs open in utter astonishment. It is Stephen Kent of Setauket, who all these years ago takes me in his father's skiff on the Sound when we see'd the big whale. Stephen Kent who kisses me. I hold in a gush of feeling emotion.

"Yer a rebel?" he says, his breath, diminished.

"A nurse for all wounded," I say. I feels me head git weary and weak on me shoulders as I look at his chest. It is largely gaped open by a cannon. I know'd me old friend be dying.

"I come to yer Uncle's to see you," he says, coughing, and I wipe blood from his mouth.

"I hear'd, and wish I be there then," I says, and I can feel me eyes filling with water. "We could be kids again and takes yer father's skiff."

"When ye save'd the big whale."

His voice is faint.

"And, ye kissed me."

"Ye remember."

It is barely whispered. I cannot stop his blood. "How could I ever forget?" I says, close to his face. I put a gentle kiss on his wet lips.

Stephen Kent is dead.

Me head gits numb, me chest turns inside me, and me mind goes awry. I collapse on this retch'd battlefield.

. . .

The next thing I hear'd is me nurse name.

"Virginia, Virginia Redman," the voice says. I open me eyes. "Where I be?" Me voice is raspy, me mouth dry as a desert, and it is hard to speak. "This is the regimental hospital and I be Dr. Samuels," the man standing over me bed says. He says I be unconscious for two days. I recover, and, as I already say, I be called to talk to General Nathanael Greene, who, after I mention working for Colonel Tallmadge, he ships me out.

In 1781 I is pleased to learn Robert Morris, the man who aids me escape in Philadelphia at Christ Church is the new Superintendent of Finance for the United Colonies, and I remembers Mr. Morris with excessive affection.[109] But I cannot git young Stephen Kent from me mind. His death haunts me like a cemetery ghost, this young man so loved by me. O, death! I think of me young John André, and weep much these days.

Yesterday I find a poem by André's friend, Anna Seward, which she writes in 1781. This poem "Monody on Major André" which is sent to me from London by a friend,

---

[109] Robert Morris is one of the signers of the Declaration of Independence and later a member of the Constitutional or Philadelphia Convention which drafted the federal Constitution pushed by Alexander Hamilton and James Madison in 1787.

following the war contains a stanza which I think is written specially of the friendship of me and André. Here it is:
"Dear, lovely Youth whose gentle virtues stole,
"Thro Friendship's soft'ning medium on her soul!
"Ah no! – with every strong resistless plea,
"Rise the recorded days she pass'd with thee,
"While each dim shadow of o'erwhelming years,
"With Eagle-glance reverted, Mem'ry clears."
Into me grave I will not forget this beautiful man.

By this season in 1781 Long Island and little Setauket and Oyster Bay is a far distance from battles such as Guilford Courthouse, and the war is round the city of New York and South in Georgia and Virginia, and is heading to York Town, and, as we know'd later, the surrender of Cornwallis. Weeks before this I writes Colonel Tallmadge a message which calls the end to me spy'g, and I gits this message in return which says to leave me post is to give up rights to compensation from Congress, and I just laugh to me self because I still possess the gold in the wooden box with the tomahawk carved on top which is give'n to me by Robert Roberts, and money is of no concern.[110] I leaves Setauket and enter New York, which I see'd Sir Henry Clinton is leaving on ships, going in defeat to his King in London. Me deep desire is to forget me deeds done for Washington, and to live in a peaceful place till take'n by the cold cook [undertaker].

I let rooms in "Holy Ground" New York which, all who read this diary already know'd it is a dreadful pox'd and whoring place.

I be drawn back here, perhaps, to punish me self for me barrels of ugly sin? Yer free to say it because it is the way I feels. I deserves this miserable scorched ground.

Oh, melancholy. Death, death, death, oh, lo! The many deaths which is in me hands?

At times of kill'g yer not think'g of kill'g really, or what or who yer kill'g. This comes later in reflection like now, or in

---

[110] A search of the correspondence of Colonel Tallmadge did not find this message, nor is it mentioned in his personal memoir.

dreams of regrets of yer life in old age. This is the way I spend the next years, in regret and feeling dirty, and it is then I know'd why I live in "Holy Ground" with the whores, because I is dirty as they be.

I be a kill'g whore.

Me humors be unbalance'd.

In the days after me spy'g ends, with regret deep in me breast, I toss the pistol, dagger and tomahawk I gits from Tallmadge in to North River. I cannot cast off me evil deeds this easy, and I be drinking rum and brandy much for it, and in these days if I be whoring as well, I do not remember it from all the rum.

Yet, in this diary, I must reckon with one more death. Yes, reader, I will tell it in full honesty. Lies is for spies, and this one is no spy but a human woman in pain.

I comes to me rooms in "Holy Ground" and falls on the bed from too much rum. Looking upwards I think I see'd a large presence in the corner of the room, and for a moment, I think it is the rum which it does a bad influence on me eyes. I stare at this presence, and see'd the outline of a head which is covered by a hooded cape, and I see'd a cloth wrapped around its face.

It is real, and I gasp at this ghostly apparition.

The Shadow Man!

I tries to run, and a powerful arm reaches out and pushes me back onto the bed, brutally.

I still cannot see a man's face.

"Is ye British intelligence to kill me?"

The Shadow Man stays quiet, and watching.

"Moody's man? Tell me!" I hears his breathing, and it is hard behind the dark cloth. He turns slightly and moonlight outside slips into the room, and I sees his eyes. Strange! They glow, but more in sympathy than in rage. "What is yer business with me, then?"

"I seek you for years . . . ."

"It is ye who is follow'd me in the city?"

"It is."

"I know'd I hear'd yer voice a fore, who is it, I cannot remember?" I rise from the bed and takes a step towards The Shadow Man, and he tells me to halt or die instantly.

"Ye cannot be Robert Rogers who is in prison."

"He is, yet his reach is broad," says the man.

"How is it ye know'd Rogers looks for me?"

The Shadow Man steps from the darkness into the moonlight, and he pulls the hood off, and removes the cloth. His face is exposed.

"James!" I shriek.

I know'd Robert Rogers who haunts me mind would return and kill me, but not his Indian son, who runs from me at his father's camp where on our spot in the meadow by the stream he reads poetry and we find love in our arms together.

"James, it be ye, after these years."

He puts his hands round me neck and forces me back on the bed. "Tabitha Baldwin," he says.

I tells James this is not me name, tell'g the true name, and I asks why he follows me so, and does his father know this. He says it is his father who sends James to hunt me and kill me for stealing his gold.

"Does yer father say why I possess his gold?"

"Says it is stolen by Tabitha Baldwin."

"Oh, nay," I tells James. "Rogers pays me this gold to kill his enemy, General Gage." When I gits to Philadelphia, I tells James, Mister Gage is in London, and I cannot do it. "Yer father can have his gold back. It is cursed."

James starts to weep.

"It is the truth," I plea. "At the camp ye ran off on me. Why? Tell me of it. Be agreeable and tell me, please?"

"I tell me father I love Miss Tabitha and he becomes angry and strikes me, and sends me away," James says.

I think to tell James of his father's attack on me in the camp because I know'd it will foster hate for his father, and may save me life tonight. Alas! I do not possess the emotional courage to tell this. I hold out me arms for a embrace and James hugs me dearly. Robert Rogers, says he, will kill James if he fails to kill me, he says, and then: "He makes me pledge it." James weeps like a baby. "I never stop'd loving you," he says using me real name.

"And I, too," says I. "We can live this life together, and run away from Robert Rogers."

James kisses me lips and I kiss his with the same passion as years ago on the banks of the stream under the big tree. For the first time in months I do not think of the ones good and bad which I kill'd, nor of poor Stephen Kent; only of this Indian man who it is I love'd in me past.

"I love'd ye," I tell James.

After much kissing and embracing, I can feel he is want'g copulation. I say me mouth is dry from rum, and I require water, and he lets me up from the bed. I drink water from the pitcher on the table, and as he takes off his breeches, I gits the scalpel I takes from the Surgeon's kit at battle of Guilford Courthouse in North Carolina, and slips it unknow'd to James beneath me bed pillow. I takes off me clothing, and shiver because it is cold. I say we should git our nake'd bodies under the coverlet. James is grow'd into a powerful man like his father and he is stout and muscular yet gentle in his intimacy and it takes me back to the camp, when I did not kill but train'd to kill, and intimacy is a pleasure like with Hamilton and Mr. Morris and how I know'd it would be with me friend John André. All these others is enemies to be bed'd and kill'd. But what is James? He tells me his father says kill me. Is he to bed me and then kill me?

He arouses me passion and I cannot think of it! After time I is worn out, and James is still in his work, and I reach beneath the pillow and takes the Surgeon's scalpel in me right hand. It is what I learn't when his father Robert Rogers ravish'd me and is laying on me, which is a man in the throes of life's passionate pleasure is not a man who thinks of danger round, and is vulnerable to the wicked hand which holds the knife. I thinks of what I tell Abraham Woodhull: family is before duty; as it is when I rescue'd Uncle Ebenezer from Simsbury Mine, and I know'd James will carry forth his pledge to his father to kill this woman who steals his gold; a woman this day who James no longer know'd of her past history. I stretch me arm out with the scalpel in me hand and is ready to thrust the tiny knife into his soft neck and artery. But . . .

I cannot.

Me arm disobeys in its own rebellion, and me mind stings and aches with a remorse I cannot describe in words.

James puts his powerful grip on me wrist, and stops his activity. "Do ye want to kill me?"

"I cannot," I says. I begin to cry hard.

I tries to loose me grip of the scalpel but James moves his strong hand over me smaller hand, and he will not allow me to let the cutting instrument fall on the floor. Looking into me face, James is weep'g a torrent and his tears fall cool between me redden'd breasts. He says he is given his pledge to his father to kill me, and says again if he fails Robert Rogers promise'd to take his life. He stares deep into me eyes with love and hate, tears flowing out. With a violent thrust James sends the scalpel which is lock'd in our hands lashing into his own neck.

"Nay, nay," I yell, and his gushing hot blood takes the place of his cool tears, fall'g on me heaving breasts. James collapses on me, and his last word is "Anna."

Thus is cease'd this true and accurate account of me actions and exertions in the Great War of Rebellion against King George III, as far as memory and age'g makes same possible, prepare'd in Two Parts, 1809 and 1810, in New York by spy Agent 355, obedient servant of Alexander Hamilton and Colonel Benjamin Tallmadge of the Continental Army.

Afterword by

Franklin Alfred Kirby Edwards

Whew! Does Agent 355 leave us with a conundrum.

By ending her diary with the word "Anna" on the lips of James, it begs the question: Was her lover James Rogers referring to her real name? It is perfectly logical to conclude, especially because she says she told him her real name just prior to his death, that he is gasping her real name "Anna" in his final breath. This will provide additional evidence to researchers who say Agent 355's real name was Anna, meaning Anna Smith Strong, among them Alexander Rose of *Washington's Spies* fame.

Or was James referring to another Anna?

The Algonquin Indian name for mother is "Anna" and he might well have been calling out to "mother" with his last breath. We do not know "James Rogers's" mother's name as she was certainly among Indians captured or killed by Robert Rogers when he took the town of St. Francis. His official genealogy does not mention a son or foster son named "James," during the Revolutionary period. I do not doubt the accuracy of Agent 355 stating that his last word was "Anna." However, I also do not rule out that our Agent 355 ended her diary with this name to tantalize generations of historians into thinking that she might indeed be Anna Strong. Don't tell me that authors never write private little jokes and secret incidentals into their narratives, because they well do. And folks, I just wouldn't put it past clever Agent 355 in doing the same.

◆◆◆

In 1810, three decades afterwards, her failure to mention George Washington in her final testimonial shows Agent 355 was still unable to forgive him for hanging Major John André in 1780. While Agent 355 had an entirely platonic friendship with André – as far as we know – he remained the one man she truly loved, I believe. Other than perhaps Hamilton and Tallmadge, although they both certainly used her, André showed her affection and respect even after her emotional confession informed him that it was her actions in alerting the Redoubt No. 4 artillery battery at Verplanck's Point of the *H.M.S. Vulture's* mission that led to his capture, and eventual execution. The extreme inner anguish of these two troubled hearts at that very moment in the Tappan, N.Y. guard house can only be imagined. Yet, even today, it is palpable simply in the knowledge of her confession.

The exploits of Agent 355, as stated in her own words, are many, exciting and remarkable. She saved Governor Livingston's life, helped unmask Benedict Arnold's treachery – albeit at her own personal cost – was responsible for the capture of one of the worst cutthroat Loyalist Cowboys, James Moody, and probably saved lives at the Battle of Guilford Courthouse by amputating an arm and a leg, and then acted honorably in trying to treat fallen British soldiers abandoned by their leader to die – one shockingly a childhood friend from Setauket, Stephen Kent.

But for me, the diary's editor, one action by this amazingly strong and resourceful woman stands paramount. What is more, if you are an American, then you owe your present political freedoms as much to this woman warrior-spy as to George Washington, Marquis de Lafayette of France or the Continental Army. Had she not succeeded in this one mission at the beginning of her spy career, England might have won the war. That is say her killing of mercenary spy Guillory in the prostitute-infested "Holy Ground" of New York City in 1777 is of monumental significance. He was on his way to sell the British information about Frenchman Pierre August Caron de Beaumarchais's three arms-ladened ships bound for America. Had Guillory succeeded the British Royal Navy could have intercepted the French ships. By stopping the British from learning that they had sailed, Agent 355 made it possible for the *Le Romain, La Seine and L'Amphitrite* to deliver 200 field pieces, 300,000 muskets, 100 tons of powder and ammunition and 3,000 tents and blankets and shoes for the 30,000-man Continental Army, which was in dire straits, down to little ammo and figuratively bare feet. Without these armaments and supplies "on loan" from the King of France, Washington would have had to surrender, the war being over less than a year after the ink dried on the Declaration of Independence.

I want to end on this note, a soliloquy of sorts by Agent 355, which was not part of the diary. It was written in her handwriting on the reverse of a page of her diary. It is her personal thoughts on why she felt compelled to join the revolt against her King and countrymen who stayed loyal to him. It is telling, eloquent and historically accurate.

"We be calling this a rebellion and it is, yet, for yer understanding of it, this rebellion with muskets which first happen'd at Lexington, Massachusetts Colony in April 1775 is not the begin'g of it," Agent 355 wrote, probably in 1810. "The King and Parliament turn'd us against it long a fore the fighting by making acts and laws which we is not ones to tolerate, like the Stamp Act.[111] Buy a gazette [newspaper] and pay a tax to the King; buy cards for a game, pay the Parliament a tax. This act makes yer government walk with people in their tasks of business each day, and when

---

[111] What is amazing here isn't that Agent 355 had these thoughts at the time but that she wrote them down, almost as if she were channeling radical Whigs such as John Wilkes or Algernon Sidney. There is no doubt that many Colonists thought the same way, between 1750 and 1776 – that intellectually they were distinctly "American" and feared tyranny of the Crown and Parliament, which they saw as a "conspiracy" against American liberty. However it would not be for another couple of centuries before historians would write about this phenomenon. The best work on the topic is still Bernard Bailyn's *The Ideological Origins of the American Revolution*, 1967, for which the Harvard history professor won the Pulitzer Prize. Also see Bailyn-student Gordon S. Wood's excellent The Radicalism of the American Revolution, 1991, which also explores social and economic factors in the Thirteen Colonies. For reasons why this "revolutionary thought" didn't translate into action sooner, see John V. Jezierski, "The Context of Union: The Origins, Provenience, and Failure of the Albany Plan of Union of 1754," Ph.D. dissertation, Indiana University, 1971. She might have been writing about America two centuries ago but Agent 355's rhetoric about oppressive government doesn't sound much different than the fiscally conservative Tea Party movement of today. If there is one theme of conservatives it is bashing "big government" which overtaxes and overspends. She sounds like a Jeffersonian conservative rather than a Hamiltonian liberal on government intrusion into the everyday lives of Americans. It is ironic, that Agent 355 mentions the Stamp Act in which government placed a tax on printed papers such as legal documents, and today, state and federal governments also tax printed documents like property deeds, and yes, even newspapers. Today, it might be argued, that government has become more intrusive and oppressive than during the American Revolution. What would signers of the Declaration of Independence say today about how their experiment in government turned out? Hmm. They might sign a new Declaration.

Parliament enacts changes to the Mutiny Act and says if British soldiers cannot find quarters in public inns and taverns in America, then we must open our houses to these Redcoats, and to provide beds and to feed same our staples. It is this act more than others which is most intolerable because the King and Parliament walk'd the roads and businesses with us in the Stamp Act, but now this London government, orders all people, not just in New York where in the last war people quartered British soldiers, to let its soldiers sleep in our beds with us. Is it unjust to rebel against a King and his men when same sleeps in our own beds? Nay! Because we learn't to love liberty, no people will tolerate this e'er present and omnipotent government oppression of authority today or forward in our history. When government is in yer every breath of air, rebellion gits stuck in yer throat, and the same is soon heaved out in words and deeds. Revolution be our fix in 1776."

◆

◆

Made in the USA
Monee, IL
20 December 2024

ef11f6c1-15d9-43ad-b9de-50cb887898d4R01